"Do you want to show me her baby pictures?"

Cara's voice broke. "Let me see where she grew up? Hold the stuffed animals she slept with? Why would you want to torture me like that, Tye?"

"I'm not trying to torture you, Cara…. Please, sweetheart."

"Don't call me sweetheart." She rose, ripping her hands away from him, her hair plastered against her head, her wet clothing outlining every curve he'd once known so well. "I'm not your sweetheart—you don't love me anymore, remember? You stopped loving me fourteen years ago."

Dear Reader,

This month marks the advent of something very special in Intimate Moments. We call it "Intimate Moments Extra," and books bearing this flash will be coming your way on an occasional basis in the future. These are books we think are a bit different from our usual, a bit longer or grittier perhaps. And our lead-off "extra" title is one terrific read. It's called *Into Thin Air,* and it's written by Karen Leabo, making her debut in the line. It's a tough look at a tough subject, but it's also a top-notch romance. Read it and you'll see what I mean.

The rest of the month's books are also terrific. We're bringing you Doreen Owens Malek's newest, *Marriage in Name Only,* as well as Laurey Bright's *A Perfect Marriage,* a very realistic look at how a marriage can go wrong before finally going very, very right. Then there's Kylie Brant's *An Irresistible Man,* a sequel to her first-ever book, *McLain's Law,* as well as Barbara Faith's sensuous and suspenseful *Moonlight Lady.* Finally, welcome Kay David to the line with *Desperate.* Some of you may have seen her earlier titles, written elsewhere as Cay David.

Six wonderful authors and six wonderful books. I hope you enjoy them all.

Yours,

Leslie Wainger
Senior Editor and Editorial Coordinator

Please address questions and book requests to:
Silhouette Reader Service
U.S.: 3010 Walden Ave., P.O. Box 1325, Buffalo, NY 14269
Canadian: P.O. Box 609, Fort Erie, Ont. L2A 5X3

DESPERATE

KAY DAVID

Silhouette

INTIMATE MOMENTS

Published by Silhouette Books

America's Publisher of Contemporary Romance

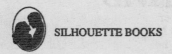

SILHOUETTE BOOKS

ISBN 0-373-07624-X

DESPERATE

KAY DAVID

is a native Texan who currently resides in Argentina with her husband of twenty years. Prior to her writing, her careers included a stint with NASA as a software engineer and five years of designing and building large homes across Texas. In the past, she has also been involved with the diamond jewelry industry, brokering large stones and creating unique pieces for individual clients. Her first love, however, is writing, and she's been doing that since she was old enough to hold a pencil. In addition to her current overseas location, Kay has also lived in the Middle East. Her life in these foreign locations gives her plenty of access to new plots and interesting characters. She has also published under the name Cay David.

To Pieter—

The best of times *is* now. Thanks.

Prologue

"I can't go there."

Richard Lindsey didn't even look up as Cara Howard spoke. Instead, he continued to study the file in front of him, silently, intently. It was Richard's standard technique. Cara had seen other interior designers turn to jelly when he refused to look at them. The silence would grow and grow until they couldn't stand it, then they'd be begging him, in the end, to let them do what they hadn't wanted to in the beginning.

But not Cara.

She could outwait the devil. Especially when it was this important.

Two full minutes passed. She counted them as they ticked off on the pendulum clock behind Richard's desk. She'd waited on Richard even longer before—their record was almost four minutes—but today, he was impatient, and in a really perverse way, she was glad. She wanted to get this over with. At two minutes, thirty-four seconds, he gave in, speaking as though the time had never passed.

"Marshall Montgomery still operates the computer firm even though it divided into a large conglomerate several years ago. I want a shot at the parent company." Richard's gaze zeroed in on her. "This client has big possibilities, and if you play your cards right, this could be a fantastic opportunity. You could be decorating their offices all across the United States."

"I won't go to Angelton."

Richard lifted his eyebrows. Cara stared him down.

His gaze returned to the file on his wooden desk. "Montgomery's wife saw some of our design work several years ago when she was here in New York shopping. She asked who'd done the decorating, and your name was mentioned. When the Marshall Company diversified, they built a new building, but it's never been coordinated inside. They called and asked specifically for you." Richard took up his black Waterman pen and tapped it against the papers. "*You* have to go down there."

"No." She couldn't go to Angelton.

Cara rose from her chair and walked toward Richard's window, her legs shaking, her stomach on fire. He had a perfect view, but as she looked toward the Empire State Building, a sight that normally calmed her, she felt her dread rising. In her career, she'd never said no. It was one of the reasons she was at the top of the firm. The other one was her talent.

She also didn't say no because she needed this job. She needed the stability and the prestige, not to mention the money.

But she couldn't go to Angelton.

Behind her back, Richard spoke again, and this time his voice held a hint of impatience. "Even if I *could* let you stay, I can't send anyone else—there *isn't* anyone else right now. Dick's in London, Pat's in Houston and Bob won't be back from vacation until next week." As though becoming conscious of his tone, he softened his voice slightly. "What's the problem? You don't have to stay there and do the work. Just check it out, then return and supervise from here. You've done that plenty of times, and some of those jobs were even in Europe. You can be in and out in one day—it's just a little hick town in Texas.''

Panic, not from Richard's request but from her past, knotted in the bottom of Cara's stomach. It felt heavy and burdensome and reminded her in a very ironic way of why she couldn't return to Angelton. Two faces accompanied the pain—one she'd never forget and one she'd never known. Both brought a fresh wave of distress...and determination.

She swung around. Richard would have to know part of the story, but only part. Cara herself didn't know all of it, and if there was one sure thing in her life, it was the fact that she didn't *want* to know all of it. She took a deep breath and squared her shoulders, telling the pain that had moved into her heart to go away. "Angelton is where I grew up."

"Good grief, Cara, I didn't know that." His face flushed slightly. "Hell, I didn't mean to insult you—"

She held up one hand. "You didn't, and in fact, you're absolutely on target. Angelton *is* a little hick town." Her jaw tightened with the effort of keeping her voice neutral. "I left there when I was seventeen. . . .''

Chapter 1

"I'm old enough to do what I want to."

"You're seventeen, all right, but that's it. You don't have a brain in your head if you think we're going to stand by and let you continue to see that boy. He's nothing but trouble."

Cara flipped her long auburn hair out of one eye and glared at her mother and father. They were the ones without brains—without hearts, too. Didn't they know she was in love?

"You can't stop me."

"Oh, yes, we can, young lady." Her father started across the marble entryway, his face red with anger. "If I have to lock you in your room, that's what I'll do."

Cara's fingers clutched the doorknob, and she tried not to flinch. She still had a bruise on her right cheek from the last time she'd made her father this angry. It didn't matter, though. "I'll climb out the window," she shot back.

Cara's mother grabbed her husband's shirtsleeve. "Phillip, calm down." Her blue eyes brimmed with frustration as they took in her daughter. "Do you see what you're doing to your father? He's going to have a heart attack, and it'll be your fault.''

Cara's breath caught in her throat, and she shot a worried glance toward him. He hadn't fully recovered from his last heart attack, and he *did* appear ill. Despite everything, she still loved him and wanted his approval. Even more, she wanted to tell him her secret, to confess and have him pat her head and hold her tight and tell her everything would be okay, but if he knew about the baby growing inside of her, it *would* kill him.

So he didn't know. No one did. Not even Tye.

As her confusion grew, she caught the rumble of Tye's car. It was a 1967 Mustang, and she recognized it the minute it turned the corner at Fifth and Elm. She yanked the door open and ran outside.

He watched her fly down the sidewalk, and his heart nearly jumped from his chest. She was the most beautiful girl he'd ever seen in his life, and he couldn't believe she actually loved him.

She was the only person in the world who'd ever even said the words to him.

Behind her, the front door popped open again, and the outline of Cara's parents darkened the opening. Rage contorted Phillip Howard's face, but Tye couldn't hear the words he yelled. Cara's mother, Elizabeth, held down his arm. Tye's chest filled with anger. Her parents had made no effort to hide their opinion of Tye, and he told himself it didn't matter as he watched Cara fly down the sidewalk. They took it out on her, though, and that definitely *did* matter to Tye. Cara didn't look back as she jerked open the car door and jumped inside.

''Hurry,'' she said, her face resolutely turned away from her home and her parents. ''I don't want them coming out here.''

Tye gunned the Mustang, and it leapt forward, gravel and dirt flying up from under the tires. In another second, they were racing down Elm. When they got to the corner, he never even slowed, and the car took the sharp turn with the red needle leaping over the fifty-five mark. Once the Mustang straightened out, he risked a quick glance toward Cara. When they'd first dated, she'd hated it if he went over forty.

Things had changed. A lot.

A frown froze her expression into anger and frustration, and he felt a quick tug of regret. She'd been the perfect teenager until he'd come along. He knew because her parents had told him that very fact several times.

He'd ruined her. They said that, too.

He downshifted once, and they skidded through a traffic light more red than yellow. The rearview mirror was clear though, and Tye stomped the pedal beneath his boot. They were on the edge of town, anyway—the rich edge—and this side of Angelton was rarely patrolled for speeders. The city had only one policeman, and the county constables were usually busy busting heads on the west side—the side where Tye lived.

The trees flashed by in a dusky blur of yellow and red, but to Tye the fall foliage meant nothing. All he could think about was the girl sitting beside him. He lifted his hand from the gearshift and put it on her knee. Her skin was warm and soft, and even this simple touch brought an ease to the aching loneliness that had always plagued him. She represented everything he didn't have—hearth, home, love—and the longer he knew her, the more he loved her and wanted to protect her. "You okay?" he asked.

She nodded once but turned to face the window because she never wanted him to see her cry. Tye's anger grew as he realized Phillip Howard had managed to make her feel guilty and miserable again.

Forcing those thoughts away, Tye concentrated on his driving, pushing the little Mustang more and more. The tires flew over the black pavement, and for an instant, despite their problems, Tye knew pure contentment. He was nineteen years old with a fast car and a good girl—what else did he need?

He pretended for a few minutes that the answer to that question was "nothing," but as they reached the cutoff to Johnson's Ridge, reality hit him again. He was nineteen years old with no diploma and no future. He had to take care of Cara. She was his life—what else could he do?

Cara remained silent until he slid the car into the gas station. She turned in her seat to stare at him. Her question was more statement than query, and they both knew it. "What are you doing?"

"I need gas."

Her eyes went to the instrument panel, then back to his face. "The tank is full."

He ignored her words. "Are you with me, Cara?"

Her eyes filled with tears, and for the first time, she didn't bother to wipe at them. "Please, Tye . . ."

"If we're leaving, I've got to get some money. There's no other way."

She clutched his arm. "There's got to be another way. I . . . I could ask my dad or—"

"Are you nuts?" He ran a finger over the shadow on her cheek, a desperate urgency building inside of him. "He's already hit you once. Do you think I can stand by and let him do that again?"

"He was mad," she said faintly.

"Well, so am I," Tye replied, his gut twisting. "I should have gotten you out of here before it got to that point."

Her face crumpled, and Tye fought the urge to let his own do the same. Reaching out, he pulled her toward him. She fell into his arms, a fragrant warm body, soft with curves and shaking with fear. He ran his hand over her hair and resisted the temptation to bury his face in it. If he did, he'd never do what he had to do.

"There's no other way, baby," he said softly. "If we're going to get out of here—away from your parents—then we've got to have money. Apartments cost, cars cost." His voice turned husky. "Nothing's free, Cara, and until I can find a job wherever we end up, we've got to eat. I've been hungry, but by God, you won't be."

She raised her head and looked at him, her eyes shining in the growing twilight. "It doesn't matter, Tye. If we're together—"

"It does matter. Love *doesn't* feed you." His jaw clenched, and his arms tightened around her. "Nothing but money will do that, and right now, there's no other way to get enough of it to get us out of here."

Her voice slipped into panic as he took his arms away and turned. "Tye, please. Don't do this. I've got to tell you something—"

"Nothing you say is going to change my mind, Cara, so keep it to yourself." He popped open the door of the small car, and cold air swept into the interior. "I'll be right back," he said grimly.

She watched through the window of the car.

Garish painted signs across the glass front obscured the inside of the store. Free Car Wash With Fill-up. Bread— Two Loaves For .99 Cents. Beer and Wine—ID's Required.

Her breath came in quick gulps, and she gripped the car door with white-knuckled fingers. The engine of the car rumbled beneath her, and a Rolling Stones song blared from the radio. She could barely hear Mick's nasal tones as her blood rushed through her veins.

Until she'd met Tye, Cara's idea of being bad was staying out past her curfew. Now here she was, waiting in a running car while he held up a convenience store.

Her parents *would* die—both of them—her father of a heart attack, her mother of shame.

Cara released the door handle long enough to swipe at the frosted window. The long Texas dusk had fallen into darkness while she waited. What was he doing? He'd been in there for at least three minutes.

Her parents hadn't wanted her to date Tye. "From the wrong side of town," her mother had said. "Bad family," her father had added. But Cara hadn't listened. Tye Benedict had literally swept her off her feet. They'd met last year at the car wash where he'd been working a second job. She'd stepped out of her car and slipped on the soapy floor. He'd caught her in his arms, and she'd never wanted to leave them since.

Cara had anticipated her parents' reaction to Tye. But all she could think about was the way he filled out that black T-shirt and how his torn jeans outlined the mysteries she'd only wondered about before.

They weren't mysteries anymore.

She put her hand over her stomach. It was as flat as it'd always been, and the only thing she felt was the clench of fear. Her eyes searched the windows of the store, then jerked toward the clock. It felt like an hour had passed since Tye had jumped from the car, but in reality, he'd been gone less than five minutes.

She'd wanted to tell him about the baby before, but she couldn't. As young and naive as Cara was, she knew Tye wasn't ready to be a father. God, she wasn't ready to be a mother, either. Her mind hopped over the events she'd miss—the prom, graduation, a wedding in white.

A small voice in the back of her mind told her she'd do it all over again, given the choice. The stolen minutes were as precious as pearls to her, and even the remembrance of them shook her to her toes. She didn't have anyone to compare Tye to, but his touch had made her forget everything—including protection. He wasn't at all like the other boys she'd dated, with fumbling hands and wet lips.

He was a man.

She didn't care that he hadn't finished school. He hadn't been able to—who could while supporting himself and a mother who drank? Last year, before his mother had died, he'd driven Cara by his house, and she'd had to hide her instinctive flash of embarrassment. The place was nothing but a shack, and in the blue light of a flickering television screen, she'd seen the outline of a woman slumped over in a chair. Tye had taken off fast.

He had a side that no one else saw, however, and that was the side that drew Cara like a lure. He was gentle and kind and wrote poetry that no one had read but her. He was ambitious, too. He liked to talk about the stock market and companies and things he wanted to do that she didn't understand but listened to, anyway, because she loved the sound of his voice and the strength of his arms around her.

And now she was waiting in a running car while he held up a convenience store.

He didn't have a gun, but Tye kept his hand in his coat pocket and pointed his shaking finger at the clerk. He was an old guy, and for a minute, Tye thought he'd just tell him to go to hell. Finally, his rheumy eyes focused on Tye's pocket, then grew large with fear.

"Put the money in a sack," Tye ordered, "and hurry up. I don't have all day."

It took the fumbling clerk three tries to open the cash register, but the drawer finally banged out, hitting him in the stomach as the lock released. He grunted once, then grabbed a handful of dollar bills and began to stuff them into a small paper bag.

Tye glanced nervously toward the door. He was scared. Through the glass, he could see his idling car and the vague outline of Cara in the front seat. The parking lot remained empty, and he issued a small prayer that it would stay that way. The irony didn't escape him.

His mother had taught him to pray. Considering what she was, it seemed only right that he end up praying while he robbed a two-bit grocery store.

His eyes jerked back to the old man behind the cash register. "Hurry up." Tye kept his voice level and cool, trying to sound calm even though he was quaking inside. Appearances were everything, he thought to himself, because if they weren't, he wouldn't be doing this right now. He'd be sitting in Cara's parents' living room and talking with her dad about football or cars or fishing.

But they'd already decided he was trash—so he was simply proving them right.

The thought burned all the way down to his quivering stomach, but Tye forced himself to ignore it. He wasn't robbing this store for them—he was robbing it for their daughter.

There was nothing else he could do. He had to get Cara away, and leaving took money. Just like dying did. He'd spent his last dime putting his mother in the ground not six months ago, and *desperate* had become his middle name. There was no one else to turn to, and even though he knew what he was doing was wrong, Tye didn't know what else *to* do. At nineteen, he didn't have answers—he only had questions.

With a start, he realized the old man had finished and was holding the bag out to him. Tye grabbed it and ran, his legs threatening to give way before he even made it out the door.

She had the car door open by the time he got there. He jumped inside, threw the bag in the back, then grabbed the gearshift, his heart thumping against his rib cage as if he'd just run a mile instead of the twenty yards from the door of the store.

"Get down," he yelled belatedly. "I don't want him to know you're with me."

Cara immediately stuck her head between her legs. Her voice was muffled. "Who?"

"The clerk—he's an old guy—if he doesn't see you, he'll think I'm alone."

Tye punched the accelerator, and the steering wheel slipped wildly in his nervous hands. For a second, he fought the little car, the powerful engine pulling it one way, Tye's fright pulling it another. The oversize tires fishtailed against the gravel, the dual mufflers rumbling like tornadoes. Cara screamed as she fell against the car door.

Her wail had a hint of panic in it that tore his eyes from the road. She had her arms across her stomach in a curiously protective way, but Tye had no time to think about it. The car careened across the highway, and his attention jerked back to the task at hand. His pulse racing with fear and adrenaline, he popped the clutch, then flicked his eyes to the mirror and cursed.

Behind them, a red-and-blue light broke the darkness.

Cara knew the little car was reaching its limit. The engine screamed beneath the hood, and beside her, Tye shouted a curse. He shifted again, but there was no more power.

Then she saw the lights.

Her stomach plummeted to the floor.

Cara didn't have to look back to know who was driving the black-and-white car. Angelton's only policeman was her mother's brother.

She reached out and seized Tye's arm, her fright spilling over her like burning coffee. "Pull over," she pleaded. "You've got to stop."

He tore his arm from her grasp. "I can outrun him."

"No, you can't." She grabbed the dash and held on as he wheeled the car into a country lane. The wheels hit a pothole. They went down, then up, Cara's head bouncing against the roof of the car. On the radio, a ZZ Top song blared.

"This is crazy," she cried. "He's right behind us, Tye. You'll never outrun him."

The car continued to careen at top speed, but Tye turned and looked at her. The expression on his face seared past her eyes and burned straight into her heart. It was nothing but desperation, pure and simple. "If I stop now, we'll never get out of here, Cara. Never. Is that what you want?"

"No," she said, despair raising her voice. "But we have nowhere else to go. Uncle Jack will *not* give up, believe me."

Tye threw a glance toward his rearview mirror, and in his eyes, Cara saw confirmation. His fingers gripped the gearshift until they gleamed white in the rising moon. When he faced her once again, his face matched their paleness. "Then you have to jump," he said grimly. "I'll stop. You open the car and roll out." He nodded toward a rise in the road. "We'll do it just past there."

Cara was already shaking her head. "No, no. If he catches you, he gets us both. We're in this together."

"Don't be stupid, Cara." Tye's voice cut through her sentiment with ruthlessness. "You weren't even doing anything but sitting in the car. I'm not going to let you go down with me." He threw a glance toward her. "As soon as I stop, you jump."

His voice was hard and cold—a voice she didn't recognize—and for the first time, she began to wonder about the choices she'd recently made. Her hands went over her stomach. "I . . . I can't."

"Sure you can. I'll slam on the brakes, then take off. Just tuck your head down and roll."

"No, Tye." Her voice was frantic, but he'd already reached across her.

"You have to, baby. It's the only way." He shot her another look. "I can't let you go to jail because of me, Cara. I love you too much."

She clutched his arm, but it was too late. The door opened, and she was flung from the car.

Chapter 2

At the last minute, she remembered his advice, and Cara tucked her head down as the ground came up to meet her. The winter rains had softened the shoulder of the road, and the mud cushioned her impact. Still, it jarred her, and she couldn't hold back a scream of fear as she tumbled head over heels down into the ditch.

Dazed, covered with mud, shaking with fright and pain, she raised her head in time to see two sets of taillights disappear into the night.

A wash of relief hit her. Uncle Jack obviously hadn't seen her fall from the car or he would have stopped. In the next minute, though, she realized that the delay gave him what he needed. He'd be able to catch Tye now, regardless. All Cara could do was drop her head back into the dirt and begin to sob.

God, how had this all gotten started?

Robbing the store was such a stupid idea. She could have gotten a job, he could have gotten two. How had they ever thought they'd do it and not get caught? Without thinking about her actions, she curled into a ball and wept, her arms crossed over her stomach. They'd never be together now, and what about the baby? What would she do?

She cried herself numb, lying in the ditch, covered with dirt, eight weeks pregnant.

"That's him, all right. I'd recognize that face from a mile away." The aging store clerk nodded his head vigorously and pointed a gnarled finger in Tye's direction. He was the only one in the cell, so there was no confusion. Jack Glasser, Cara's uncle and Angelton's finest, nodded wearily, catching Tye's eyes in the process. This wasn't the first time they'd crossed paths, but it was by far the worst. Glasser led the old man away.

Tye glared at their disappearing backs, but it was a sham, and he knew it. Inside he was trembling with fear and dread—not for himself, but for Cara. The sight of her pale oval face as she'd jumped from the car haunted him. He'd hated the risky move, but it'd seemed like their only option at the time.

Just like holding up the store.

Cursing his stupidity, he flung himself down on the mattress, the bed creaking against the strain. Where was she? What had happened? Was she hurt? He'd only wanted to protect her, to get her away from what looked like an impossible situation, but instead he'd made it worse. A helluva lot worse.

He thought briefly of telling Glasser, of begging him to stop and see about her, but that would have defeated the purpose. Tye couldn't bear the thought of Cara being arrested, going through the shame of being fingerprinted, locked up, all that kind of stuff. She was too good for that.

And she was too good for him.

The thought rattled in his head for the rest of the night, and when he woke up the next morning, it was still there. He loved Cara more than he loved life, and he'd do anything for her. Anything.

Including turning her away.

By the time Jack Glasser came for him in the middle of the afternoon, Tye had made up his mind. No matter how badly it hurt, he'd have to make Cara think he didn't love her anymore. It was the only way. Besides, he reasoned, once he was out of the picture, her parents would go back to treating her like they always had before he'd come along—as if she were a princess. He had to make sure she was okay first, though.

Jack approached the cell with the keys in his hand. "Get up, Benedict. We're going to see the judge."

Tye stood and tried to straighten his shirt, but it was hopeless. He knew he looked like a bum—he'd slept in his clothes and hadn't shaved. Somehow it didn't matter, though. Only Cara mattered. In his mind, he searched for a way to ask about her and not give away the fact that she'd been with him. In the next second, his problem was solved.

Jack stuck the keys into the lock, but didn't turn them. "I don't guess you'd know anything about Cara's whereabouts last night, would you?"

Tye never flinched. "Why should I?"

"Dave Herrington picked her up about eight o'clock, out at the rest stop on the highway. She was bleeding."

Stone-cold fear settled in Tye's stomach, and he had the feeling it wasn't going to leave anytime soon. "Wh-what happened to her? Is she okay?"

"She's a little sore, but she's okay. Said she'd fallen. Said you two had a fight, and that you'd dumped her out at the park, then roared off." He switched his cigar from one side of his mouth to the other. Jack Glasser was no fool, and Tye knew it. He also knew that Jack occasionally gave his whole paycheck to down-on-their-luck families passing through Angelton. More than once he'd bought Tye a hot meal, too. Jack eyed him warily. "That true?"

Tye stuffed his hands into the pockets of his jeans and lifted his chin. "Yeah. We broke up. What business is it of yours?"

Jack pulled a deep puff on the cigar, held it, then blew it out directly into Tye's face. "I'm a cop," he drawled. "Everything's my business."

Tye waited for him to push, but Jack said nothing more. With slow deliberation, he turned the keys in the lock and held the bars back so Tye could pass through. Tye stepped out, then waited for the older man to pass ahead of him. Tye knew the drill. Jack had picked him up for speeding, had picked him up for disturbing the peace, had picked him up for several other minor offenses. Each time the husky cop had dealt out his own kind of punishment, which usually consisted of several days of forced labor at the jail, as well as a long lecture.

This time Tye knew it was going to be different.

They reached the end of the hall, and Jack unlocked another door. He paused and looked back at Tye. His expression was a mixture of regret and misunderstanding. "Why'd you do it, son? You got your whole life ahead of you, and now you're gonna go through it with a real millstone around your neck." He sucked on the cigar, his bright blue eyes even brighter in the haze of smoke. "Life is hard enough without being labeled a con."

No one had ever looked at Tye with so much compassion, and he didn't know what to do with it. His mother had stared at him with hatred, when she even recognized him at all. His teachers, when he'd still been in school, had looked at him with frustration. And Cara's parents—they were disgusted by him. He wasn't good enough for their daughter, and every line in their tight faces told him so.

Jack Glasser was Elizabeth Howard's brother. How had he turned out so kind, so understanding? One day, Tye vowed to himself, he'd try to understand if *his* kid went wrong.

If he ever got out of jail to have one.

For now, all he could do was thrust out his chin and nod toward the door. "Open it up, Glasser," he said with false bravado. "Let's get this crap over with."

* * *

Cara sat outside the judge's chambers and tried not to let her fright show. For three weeks, she'd been trying to see Tye at the jail, but he'd refused to talk to her. Discouraged, scared and depressed, she'd tried to telephone, too, but to no avail. With every attempt, another piece of her heart had broken off. Something was wrong. Bad wrong.

Today she was determined to find out what was going on. She'd skipped school just to see Tye, despite the fact that there was no stupider place to be than the county courthouse. If Sue Rocher, the truant officer, happened to pass by, Cara would be in deep trouble.

But she was already in trouble so deep she was about to drown.

She glanced toward the heavy wooden door for about the twentieth time in five minutes. How much longer could they be? From her hiding place around the corner, she'd seen Uncle Jack, Tye and some dark-suited man whom she assumed to be Tye's attorney go in there over half an hour ago. She had no idea what they were doing, but she was sure it wasn't good. Since she'd fallen out of Tye's Mustang, her entire life had spun out of control, and she knew nothing good was ever going to happen to her—or to Tye—ever again.

Her fingers nervously found the small scar that crossed her left eyebrow and went upward into her hair. The mark had almost healed completely, but a thin line would always be there to remind her. Her parents had been livid when their neighbor, Mr. Herrington, had dropped her off. Livid and horrified. They'd immediately rushed her to the Angelton Community Hospital, and Cara had vomited in the car. Not because she'd been hurt, but because she was scared to death the doctors would find out she was pregnant and tell her parents.

Her secret had stayed a secret, though. Dr. MacAllister had simply bandaged her, then kept her overnight at the clinic. And he'd only done that because she'd thrown up.

So she hadn't even been there when Uncle Jack had called and told her parents Tye had been arrested for holding up a convenience store. She'd been lying in the hospital bed, trying not to cry and looking out at the fog that had rolled in. Her mother had bounded in the next morning and told Cara the news, wearing that fake little frown that was supposed to make her think she was sympathetic.

Cara hadn't been fooled. And neither had her father. His eyes told her that he'd known she was with Tye when he'd robbed the store. But Phillip Howard couldn't prove it, and even if he did, Cara knew he'd do nothing about it. Beneath his anger, under his rage, he loved her too much.

Just like Tye.

She gripped her hands together under her pink wool coat and willed the door to open, desperate to talk to him, desperate to see him. Even though she was scared, she had to find out what was happening, why he refused to talk to her. He'd be going to the state facility soon, and this was her last chance—Uncle Jack had told her. Just as he'd let it slip at dinner last night that Tye would be at the courthouse today. At least, Uncle Jack had acted like it was a slip.

Suddenly the door sprang open, and Cara jumped to her feet. Her uncle came out first, then the man she didn't know, and then Tye. Their eyes locked, and she read an instant's love before he shuttered their dark blue depths and looked down at his feet. His actions confused her. In his glance, he said one thing, but his refusal to meet her eyes said something else.

"Tye?" She stepped toward him, her voice tentative, her hand held out.

He raised his face, his long eyelashes brushing up toward his eyebrows. His expression was closed—that of a stranger. He wore a dark blue suit she didn't recognize and a red tie that matched its narrow stripe. The white shirt underneath the jacket emphasized his handsome Texas tan. His blond hair hung just a little over the collar in the back.

He looked remote, somehow more mature, and she felt a rush of apprehension. He was only two years older than her, but she realized at that moment what a big two years it was. He looked like a man, even if he really wasn't. And she was still a girl, even if she was pregnant.

Jack stopped, looked at Cara, and then at Tye. "Do you want to talk to her?"

Tye cut his eyes toward her, a foreboding glance that made her already weak knees threaten to collapse. He didn't look right—he didn't look at all like the Tye she knew.

It wasn't just the strange clothes. It was his attitude. And it scared her.

The lips she'd kissed so often and so long curled up in mock derision. "Naw," he drawled slowly. "I don't have nothing to say to her."

Cara's heart went into a free-fall, and it didn't stop until it hit the linoleum floor. She thought she might follow it down.

He spoke again, still directing his words to her uncle Jack. "We broke up already. Remember?"

For a moment, Cara thought he was simply trying to protect her, but a slow, painful hole was developing where her heart had been. She thought of the times she'd waited outside the city jail, of the times she'd called and he wouldn't come.

"Tye?" She stepped even closer. "I...I think we need to talk."

He looked at her then, but it didn't help. His glance was completely empty of love, even of recognition. She was obviously invisible to him. "Go away, Cara," he said harshly. "I don't have anything to say to you."

The words cut into her with surgical precision, but she couldn't stop. "What's wrong?" Her voice was a paralyzed whisper. "Why are you doing this to us? Don't...don't you love me anymore?"

"No." He looked her up and down with undisguised contempt. "You're still a baby. I've only been playing with you." He paused, and she watched his throat move as he swallowed hard. "And playtime's over."

* * *

"Impossible." Cara's mother's eyes were the size of the turnips Uncle Jack grew every year in his backyard. Her face was just as white, too. "You must be mistaken."

Cara shook her head and stubbornly held her mother's gaze. "No, I'm not mistaken," she answered in tones more mature than her years. "I'm pregnant. Three months, to be exact."

Collapsing onto the flowered sofa, Elizabeth Howard looked at her daughter with total disbelief. "How could you do this to me?"

Cara turned and walked to the window that overlooked their backyard. In the cold February wind, the swing she'd played on as a child swayed back and forth, hitting the mulberry tree with desolate thuds. Overblown clouds, dark with depressing rain, scudded across the sky. She spoke toward the glass. "Believe me, Mother. I wasn't thinking of you when this happened."

"Don't get smart with me."

Cara blinked rapidly at her reflection. She was going through hell, and all her mother could say was "Don't get smart with me"? Cara licked her lips, then pulled her bottom one between her teeth. She wished she could have told her dad first, but it was too late now. Some misbegotten sense of sisterhood had brought her to her mother, some hope that maybe she might understand how Cara felt and would offer some help. What a joke.

Cara straightened her shoulders and turned around. "It's Tye's."

Her mother had taken out one of the stale cigarettes in the malachite box on the coffee table and lit it. She was puffing like crazy. Since Phillip Howard's two heart attacks he was under strict orders not to smoke, and Elizabeth had told Cara she felt disloyal to him whenever she did. But she'd lit one now. Blue smoke rose between them like a curtain.

"He's trash."

Cara's heart tumbled.

"Your father and I both told you to stay away from him, and you wouldn't listen. Now look where it's gotten you."

She pointed the cigarette at Cara. "Three months pregnant and the father in the pen." Her short bark of almost hysterical laughter ripped through the room like a knife through silk. "My God, it sounds like a country-western song."

Crossing her arms protectively, Cara stood behind one tapestry-covered chair. "It may sound like a song to you, Mother, but it's real." She stuck her chin out. "I've been to the doctor, and he confirmed it. This baby's *very* real."

"Oh, I don't doubt you, Cara Ann." Her mother angrily stubbed the cigarette out, then instantly lit another. She drew on it deeply, then lifted her chin, two thin streams of smoke streaking from her nostrils. "Why do you think I told you to stay away from him? All I had to do was look at Tye Benedict, and I could have told you this was how it was going to end up. Even at nineteen he's the kind of man who—"

"Who what, Mother?" Cara gripped the back of the chair. She wanted to strike back, to hurt her mother, just like she was hurting her. Tye still wouldn't talk to her, she didn't know what to do, and she was scared—scared spitless. "Who what, Mother? Who would never be interested in your country club or your stupid tennis games or your silly parties? Is that why you hate him so?"

"I hate him because he's nothing." Elizabeth rose from the couch with an angry rustling of silk. "You're better than he is, Cara. He's poor and uneducated and now he's got a record. What on earth would possess you to sleep with a boy like that?" She held both her hands up to the ceiling, the manicured nails gleaming, her voice almost hysterical. "What on earth could you possibly see in him?"

Cara turned away. "You wouldn't understand if I told you."

Her mother groaned, a useless sound of disapproval and displeasure. "Have you told your father?"

Tears instantly filled Cara's eyes, and she had to tilt her head and blink to keep them from tracking down her cheeks. "No."

"Then I suggest you do so. Immediately." Elizabeth ground out her cigarette and picked up the phone. "I'll call him home from work. *You* can tell him when he gets here."

Fifteen minutes later, Cara heard her father's station wagon pull into their drive. With a squeak, the car door opened, then shut. They had a joke about his slamming the car door—she said she could always tell what kind of day he'd had by how hard he closed the door.

When he slammed it this time, it rattled the windows.

Elizabeth moved toward him when he entered the living room. She put her arm around his waist as if to support him and lead him to his favorite chair. "Cara has something to tell you, Phillip."

He sat down, then looked up at his wife. "This damn well better be important. I'm trying to run a business, you know. I can't come home whenever one of you breaks a fingernail."

Elizabeth looked at Cara with an accusing expression. "It's important, all right. Tell him," she demanded.

Cara took a deep breath and repeated the words she'd just spoken to her mother. "I'm pregnant."

Her father's mouth fell open, and his face drained completely of color. Even his knuckles, as they clenched the arm of his recliner, turned white. "You're what?"

"Pregnant," she repeated. "Three months. Tye's the father."

For a moment, she watched him struggle to regain his composure, to let the words sink in, but the sight was too painful. Guilt came over her. In spite of their problems, she loved her father and had always felt closer to him than to her mother. She turned away.

"Tye doesn't know," she said stiffly. "And I want it to stay that way."

"*You* want it to stay that way?" Her mother's voice rose slightly. "The whole damn county is going to know. You gain weight, Cara. Your body changes and nine months later, a baby comes. Pregnancy is not something you can keep secret."

Cara swirled around. "I'll leave. We were going to leave, anyway. That's why Tye ro—"

Her father spoke, interrupting her. It was obvious from the look on his face that he didn't want to know what she was going to say. Mentally, Cara corrected herself—he *knew* already. He just didn't want to *acknowledge* that he knew. "You *can* keep it a secret," he said in a brutal voice. "You will go to Austin and have it taken care of."

Cara's sharp intake of breath sounded like a scream in the suddenly silent room. Outside, a nesting squirrel chattered at a blue jay, warning him away. "Have it 'taken care of'?" she repeated. "Do you mean get an abortion?"

"Yes. It's the only way."

"No." She shook her head violently. "No. No. No."

"What else can you do?" he demanded. "*He* won't even talk to you, will he?"

"*He* has a name!" she screamed, suddenly fed up with their relentless condemnation. Her breath came in short, quick gasps, her breasts rising and falling. "It's Tye. Can you say that, Daddy? His name is Tye, and I'm going to *have* his baby—not get rid of it."

Her mother's eyes became round with fright and disbelief as they turned back toward Phillip. She obviously couldn't believe this was happening in their family. Daughters like hers didn't yell at their parents, didn't refuse to mind, and most of all they didn't get pregnant. Her father looked equally flabbergasted, then he seemed to recover, and he rose from his chair. "You *will* do as we say, young lady."

"No."

"There is no other option."

Cara drew her lips into a line of resistance. "I will not have an abortion."

"Then what are you going to do? Wait till that no-good boyfriend of yours gets out of jail and shack up with him in that dump he called a home?"

"I...I don't want him to know about the baby." Her legs quivering from the fear of it all, she stopped speaking for a moment, then finished in a rush. "I'll give the baby up for adoption."

"Oh, God." Elizabeth spat the words out as if the very idea made her ill. "What in heaven's name do you think this is, Cara? Some kind of soap opera? Wake up. This is reality. Just get rid of it, for pity's sake."

Elizabeth's hurtful words slashed their way into Cara's heart, piercing her soul with a hatefulness for which she'd never forgive her mother. Phillip nodded his head. "Your mother's right, Cara. It's the only possible way out of this mess."

"No abortion." Cara lifted her chin. "I *will* have this baby."

Her father's face flushed this time, and Cara's heart pounded with fear—fear for herself, fear for her father, fear for her unborn child. "No," he said, shaking his head with absolute conviction. "Not in this house, you won't." His eyes turned flat and cold. "You either have the abortion or leave. The choice is yours."

Chapter 3

The rented Cadillac ate the miles without complaint, but Cara hardly noticed. She tried to think ahead, to marshall her thoughts into some semblance of order.

For God's sake—she was a grown woman, wasn't she? What could possibly happen in Angelton that she couldn't handle? Hadn't the worst already occurred—over fourteen years ago? She glanced in the rearview mirror and shook her head as if to admonish herself. She needed to get a good grip on her feelings.

If she didn't, the temptation to turn around and go home to New York would overwhelm her, and Richard would never understand.

Just like he hadn't understood her refusal to come to Angelton in the first place. In the end, if she'd wanted to keep her job, she had to come. That was that. He hadn't cared about her brief explanation. To Richard, only the bottom line counted.

Cara's fingers gripped the leather-wrapped steering wheel. Telling herself she needed to recover from the flight before going into Angelton, she'd flown into Austin and rented the car last night. She knew that wasn't the real reason she'd come in early, though. She'd wanted one more night to reconsider. To weigh her career and its responsibilities against her fears and her past.

She loved working at Lindsey and Sons. It was the only job she'd ever had that didn't seem like work, and Richard Lindsey had been good to her, despite his lack of understanding of this situation. She'd done well at the interior design firm, and the idea of leaving it, especially now when things had been going so well, was more than she could face.

But so was going back to Angelton.

In fourteen years it had to have changed, she told herself. Nothing could stay static that long.

Nothing but memories, she thought in bitter silence.

The outskirts of Austin took longer to reach than she recalled, and by the time she'd reached the city limit, the car had warmed. She steadied the steering wheel with one hand and adjusted the heat with the other. Texas in the fall was nothing like New York, she thought. Instead of bright reds and golds, the western countryside looked burned, used-up. There was no invigorating chill, but a sluggish warmth instead—something that seemed to be left over from summer.

She glanced down toward the folded map on the seat beside her. The fresh-faced college student behind the rental-car counter had carefully drawn a circle around Austin, then used a yellow highlighter to show her the way out of the airport. She didn't need a map, but she hadn't had the heart to tell him so.

She could find Angelton blindfolded. On her hands and knees. In the pouring rain. In her dreams. She did it every night.

Cara shook her head to dislodge the nightmarish thoughts and reached for the digital button of the radio. With a quick push of her finger, she tuned in a local radio station. The song was country, the rhythm slow, the lyrics sad.

They fit the day.

* * *

Three hours later, the edge of Angelton shimmered in the fall sunshine, and Cara felt the fear that she'd been battling all day rush in and take control of her. In desperation, she told herself there was no one left who could possibly remember her. Even this Marshall Montgomery, whoever he was, must have moved there since she'd left, because she didn't recognize the name at all. He wouldn't know her past, probably wouldn't even care if he did. After all, there were only two people now who really mattered, and both of them were nowhere near Angelton.

Just ahead, a roadside park waited, and without another thought, Cara pulled the Cadillac into the shade beneath a huge oak tree. With shaking fingers, she jerked the car to a stop, switched off the keys and threw open the door. Her legs trembled as she stepped out into the torpid air.

Stumbling toward a battered picnic table, her feet crushed dried leaves and dusty white rock. Overhead the oak tree whispered secrets, secrets Cara had hidden for far too long.

She'd come home, she realized as her fingers bit into the scarred wooden table. Home where her pain had started, where her love had died, where nothing but memories remained. Her gaze fell to the picnic table, then her heart stopped. It hadn't *really* hit her until now...until now when the words carved so many heartless years ago leapt off the marked-up wood and landed on her soul.

Tye loves Cara.

Her knees crumbled, and she fell more than sat on the wooden bench beside the table. Of all the places to stop! Why in the world had she come here?

Bleakly she raised her eyes and took in the curved bank of the river. The gently sloping ground had once been tended and green with flowers and grass. Now it was covered with weeds and empty cans, a well-worn path leading down to the swiftly rushing water. This had been a favorite hangout for the kids in her class, and she hadn't even recognized it when she'd pulled the big car over.

The strident call of a mockingbird shattered the silence, and horrified, she glanced down at her watch. She'd been running just on time already, but if she hadn't stopped, she could have gotten to Marshall Montgomery's office, might have even been able to see him. Now it was too late.

Exasperated with herself but halfway relieved, too, Cara sighed and rose. Procrastinating was something she detested—in herself and in others. Now it had cost her a whole day. She hadn't really thought she could get in and out of town in twenty-four hours, but she'd hoped she could at least meet Montgomery today and leave tomorrow. She could scrap that plan now.

Poking her hands into the pockets of her ivory silk slacks, Cara started toward her Cadillac then stopped. She'd already blown the day—why not indulge herself some more? She turned around and headed for the path that led to the river.

Trailing fingers of lavender and gold, the sun dipped westward as Cara took the path toward the water. Twenty years ago, there had been a gazebo here and flower beds tended by the local chapter of the Daughters of the Texas Republic. When they'd misbehaved at school, Cara and her classmates had had to report to the DTR for weed-pulling duty. They hadn't really minded, though. Even as teenagers, they'd appreciated the sound of the moving currents, the whistle of the blue jays, the warm sun on the slanted bank. And when they got bored, they could always watch the boats float by on their way to the lake.

As if on cue, just as Cara reached the edge of the river, a sleek, white cabin cruiser came into view under the bridge. She knew nothing of boats, but the smooth, clean lines of this one told her it had to be expensive. Across the water, the rumble of the engines reached out and touched her, their powerful motors throbbing as if impatient to get on with the task. On top, underneath a small white canopy, a solitary man stood, his face bathed by the dying light.

From this distance, she couldn't discern his features, but she could see he held his body with an easy kind of grace, a poise that immediately caught her eye. He seemed to match the boat. Elegant. Polished. Forceful.

She shook her head to dislodge the fanciful thought, but as she did, he turned and looked at her, his hand grabbing the polished brass rail that bordered the small area where he stood. At least a hundred yards separated them, but she felt his stare with an almost physical intensity.

Although he was still under the awning, he lifted his hand to shield his eyes in an obvious effort to see her better.

Within thirty seconds, the powerful engines had swept the boat down the river, and the man with it. Cara rose and returned to her car, her melancholy complete. She had no idea who he was, but she wished she was with him and going anywhere but here.

The following day, as Cara reached for the door of the Marshall Company's office, she glanced at her dim reflection in the glass of the starkly modern building. Usually she studied the exteriors of buildings and took her design cue from that, but at the moment all she saw was herself. In the darkening Texas dusk, she looked older than her thirty-one years, and she had Marshall Montgomery to thank for that. Montgomery's office had called and canceled her 8:00 a.m. appointment, rescheduling it for seven o'clock that evening. No explanation had been given. Working on the proposal and fretting over being stuck in Angelton, Cara had spent all day holed up in the hotel room.

Jerking open the door, she threw a quick glance at her watch. She'd had hours to prepare, and she was still late. Good God, she was never late. What was happening? Had simply driving past the city-limits sign of Angelton done this to her? Had it somehow unhinged everything she'd worked so hard to achieve?

That thought didn't bear examination, and she let it fall through the holes like everything else had in the past twenty-four hours—including her presentation. She'd believed it was acceptable when she'd left the coast, but this morning it had suddenly taken on the dimensions of a child's crayon drawing. Nothing about it seemed right or even profes-sional. Starting all over and working until a few minutes ago hadn't made it any better, either.

As she neared the receptionist's desk of glass blocks in the center of the waiting area, Cara's fingers tightened on the leather briefcase at her side. What's done was done. If Marshall Montgomery didn't like her ideas, it was too bad. She'd *told* Richard not to send her here—if she didn't get the contract, she'd almost feel vindicated. A small voice in the back of her mind knew that wasn't really true, though. She'd feel awful if she went home without the business. Failure, even if it proved a point, was not something Cara Howard handled well.

She reached the desk. "I'm with Lindsey's—the interior design firm," she said, handing the well-dressed reception-ist her card. "Cara Howard. I believe Mr. Montgomery is expecting me."

"I'll call him," the receptionist said immediately, her perfectly manicured nail already punching the phone be-side her. "Why don't you take a seat?" She nodded toward one corner of the minimally decorated waiting room, her red hair gleaming in the low spotlight over her desk. "There's coffee if you like."

Without a second invitation, Cara headed toward the black built-in drink bar. White china mugs lined a glass shelf above the coffee service, but before she could reach up and get one, a stunning young woman with long blond hair ap-peared at her side. Her eyes were sea-green and oval. "Ms. Howard?" she asked in a soft, lilting voice. "I'm Mr. Montgomery's assistant, Peggy Nassar. If you'll come with me, Mr. Montgomery can see you now."

"That was quick," Cara said with a smile.

"I was passing down the hall, and I heard you introduce yourself to Jessica." She smiled, then nodded toward the coffee. "I'll get you some when we get to his office." She winked once. "We keep the good stuff back there. I grind it every day so it's fresh. Everyone drinks pots of it, espe-cially when we work this late."

"Does he always work like this?"

The assistant hesitated before answering, as though judging Cara. "No," she said, "but he's had some personal demands lately. I hope it didn't inconvenience you too much to postpone your appointment to this evening."

"It's fine," Cara lied.

She followed the tall, willowy blonde out of the reception area, then left, down what looked like the main hallway of the building. The lights had already been dimmed, and only a few employees remained at their desks. From what Cara could see, the building was new, but that was all. No wallpaper, no art on the walls, nothing but a plain Berber carpet on the floor—a standard commercial building that held absolutely no interest for the eye.

Richard had been unable to tell her much about the reclusive Mr. Montgomery, other than that he'd sold the small software firm quite some time ago, but still ran the day-to-day operations. Apparently, he'd decided the time had come to upgrade the company's image, and he wanted to start by decorating their office space in a more pleasing way.

As they rounded a corner, Peggy opened a tall wooden door and stepped inside what looked like a conference room. Her eyebrows knit together. "That's funny. I didn't see him in his office when we walked by. He must have gone to get coffee." She held her hand toward the room. "Let me go find him. If you like, you can wait in here or go on into his office—it's through that door."

Cara smiled and nodded her head, then entered the door, stopping with a start in the murky light. One giant, curved window made up the entire back wall of the room, and the view literally took her breath away. He might not have done anything else right, but Marshall had placed his building perfectly.

Lying below her in the fall sunset was Bear Lake. The deep blue water gleamed like a perfect sapphire, the silver lights of several small boats complementing it with diamond brightness. Above the water, rays of gold streaked across the sky.

Cara dropped her briefcase on a massive marble table and walked toward the window, ignoring the rest of the deeply shadowed office. Both hands came up and palmed the window. The lake seemed so close, so beautiful, that she almost felt disappointed when her fingers touched glass instead of water. For the first time in her career, she didn't think about the design possibilities the view presented. All she could think of was how many hours of her high school days had been spent on Bear Lake. Swimming, boating, just lazing around in the hot Texas sun. She hadn't realized how splendid it really was.

Without warning, her throat closed against itself, forcing her to swallow quickly. Together, she and Tye had gone there only once. Under a full harvest moon, they'd sneaked her father's fishing boat out of the marina and paddled it to the center of the lake. Tye had said he didn't want to start the engines because someone might catch them, but she'd known better. It was more romantic with the silence wrapping around them, more poetic. When they reached the middle of the water, he'd pulled her to him, and with the stars their only witness, they'd conceived a child.

Abruptly she stepped back from the window. This was exactly what she'd thought would happen, exactly why she'd hated to return. The sights, the sounds, the smells of Angelton were dredging up all the old memories she'd managed to bury fourteen years ago. They were rising like ghosts, but they were much more real.

Turning around, she forced herself to concentrate on the task at hand. There was nothing left of her here—she didn't need to be afraid of those ghosts. In college, she'd lost her father, her mother had remarried and moved to Florida, and Uncle Jack had been gone a long time. Nothing—absolutely nothing—waited for Cara but bad memories in Angelton.

And a job. She picked up her briefcase and headed for Marshall's office. Time was wasting; she might as well get on with the show. Any minute now Peggy would return with

Montgomery in tow, and it'd look better if Cara was already prepared.

Moving to her right, she opened the door and stepped silently into a room that matched the one she'd left. If anything, the view was even better in here, the expanse of glass wide, the scene panoramic, even though the sunset was fading fast, and the light with it. Cara allowed herself another glance, then resolutely turned away.

That's when she saw him. A lonely figure standing in the shadows staring out the window as she had only a second before.

"Oh, I'm sorry," she said instantly. "I thought..."

She had no idea who he might be, but for some reason she remembered the man on the boat she'd seen last night. This man had the same air of melancholy, the same stance of power. He turned slowly, but the gloom hid his face.

"It's all right," he said in a slow, measured voice. "Were you looking for someone?"

Cara placed her briefcase on the desk and stood near the chair behind it. "Yes, as a matter of fact, I'm looking for—"

The outer door to the office opened, and Peggy Nassar entered, her quick glance taking them both in. "Oh—there you are." Peggy turned toward Cara, and she started forward, holding her hand out. "This is Cara Howard. She's here to see—"

He'd started forward, but as soon as Peggy spoke, he abruptly halted, a tapestry of light and dark enveloping the three of them. He said nothing, but his posture, his demeanor, the very way he held his body, had frozen into an attitude of tense rejection. To Cara it seemed as if they were woven together, spun into a surreal fabric, and it wrapped her with a chilling fright.

"Are you—" Peggy broke in, then paused as if she couldn't find the right words in English "—all right?" Her accent thickened, the Scandinavian lilt as beautiful as she was.

He looked straight at Cara. "Leave us," he said in a strangled voice. "Just leave us."

Something was drastically wrong, and for just a second, Cara thought the man might be physically ill, might even be having a heart attack. Her father had spoken in that same kind of agonized voice once when his chest pain had started.

"I... I'll be right outside," Cara said instantly. "I'm sor—"

"Not you," he barked, his head turning to the blonde. "You, Peggy. Leave us alone."

Peggy glanced toward Cara, then looked back at her boss. "But I—"

"Now."

"Of course." Once more Peggy looked at Cara with puzzled eyes, but all Cara could do was raise her shoulders in a small sign of confusion. She had no idea what was wrong.

Without another glance, Peggy swept by Cara, then stopped at the man's side, putting her hand briefly on his arm. He didn't speak. He just shook his head, and Peggy left, heading toward the conference room and closing the door behind her.

He didn't move, and Cara's concern increased. The dim spot beside the windows showed nothing but shadows, and as they'd spoken, the darkness had grown. She hated not being able to see his face, but the thought of moving closer suddenly seemed worse. The air vibrated with tension, an almost throbbing pressure that Cara felt in every pore of her skin.

"Is... is there something wrong?" she asked in a hesitant voice, tilting her head slightly. "Are you Marshall Montgomery?" She couldn't see him, except as a silhouette. He was a tall man with shoulders that filled the glass behind him, and a presence to match. Power, she thought instantly. This is a man who has power. Power over people. Power over events. Power over himself.

And he definitely had power over her.

"Cara Ann," he finally said, ignoring her question. "I can't believe you're actually here."

He came out of the shadows.
Her heart tumbled, then stopped.
It was impossible.
But it was reality.
The stranger was no stranger. He was Tye Benedict.

Chapter 4

Cara's knees buckled, and she found herself reaching for the desk chair at her right. "Tye?" Coming from her lips, his name sounded rusty, as though she hadn't spoken in years. "Is that you?"

He moved closer to her, and she saw for real what had been seducing her dreams for the past fourteen years—dark blue eyes, thick blond hair, sensuous full lips she knew better than her own.

"I...I can't believe it," she stuttered. "I had no idea you worked here."

He looked as stunned as she felt, but when he spoke, his tone was slightly amused. "I guess you could say that. I'm the CEO of the parent corporation that owns Montgomery's."

His voice was deeper than she remembered and so was the navy of his eyes. The color warmed even more as they slowly took her in. She cursed her tumbled hair and slightly rumpled suit. Why hadn't she changed into something more dramatic, something more stunning?

Why did she even care?

His words registered slowly, and her voice revealed her disbelief as they finally sank in. "*You* are the CEO of this company?"

He didn't smile. "Yes. Is it so hard for you to believe?"

"Well, of course not, but I just..." Half-numb, she lifted one hand and gestured weakly toward the desk. "I...I thought this office belonged to Marshall Montgomery."

"This is Monty's," Tye said, moving closer, then stopping. He crossed his arms. "We were talking but he had to leave. I stayed to watch the sunset." He nodded toward the window. "My office is a mirror of his—on the other side of the conference room—but he's got a better view of the lake."

"You always did like the water," she said faintly, automatically. *Tye Benedict? CEO of the Marshall Companies?*

"That's right." His eyes pulled hers with a steady gaze. "There were a lot of things I liked back then. Some I still do. Some I don't."

His words stole the breath from Cara's throat, and for a second, she didn't think she'd ever breathe again. Nature took over, though, and air rushed into her lungs despite her paralysis. "How...how long have you lived here?"

"In Angelton?"

"Yes."

"Twelve, thirteen years."

She sat down abruptly, the desk chair moving under her. "How in the world did you manage—"

"A position like this?" He moved toward her, his long legs covering the short space quickly. Her heart began to pound as he neared, then settled into an uneasy rhythm when he kept going. A second later, the lamp resting behind her came on, and soft light puddled around them.

The situation seemed so bizarre to Cara that she blinked, almost dizzy in her confusion.

Circling the desk, he faced her, and Cara caught a glimpse of something she couldn't quite define. "It's a long story, but let's just say Marshall Montgomery helped me, and I helped him." He picked up a black pen and moved it rest-lessly between his fingers. "What about—"

"I work for Lindsey's," she answered before he could finish. For some reason, she needed some control over the situation, and jumping in seemed like one way of getting it. "Mr. Montgomery expressed interest in our firm. We're designers—interior decorators. His wife saw some of my work a few years ago, and they decided to call us when the new building was completed." Her hands rested limply in her lap. She turned them up, the palms facing out. "M-my boss sent me here," she explained needlessly.

One corner of his mouth lifted, and her heart flipped over. How many times had she seen that very lopsided smile? How many times had she wished she could see it again? "You make it sound like a jail sentence," he said.

Her eyes jerked to his, and the silence that followed was awkward until he raised one eyebrow and shrugged. "Bad comparison, huh?"

She answered with a tentative smile of her own. "I don't know," she said with a curious lilt. "You tell me. How bad was it?"

The amusement disappeared from his expression, and his eyes turned almost black. When he spoke, she didn't rec-ognize his voice. "Bad." Leaving the desk, he walked to the window, clearly uncomfortable with the topic.

Silent and still stunned, Cara stared at his broad shoul-ders and trim back. Under the pressed shirt he wore, she could tell he obviously exercised and took care of himself. Without meaning to—without *wanting* to—she recalled a younger, slimmer back, a back that she had clutched in youthful ignorance and boundless love.

She closed her eyes and shook her head. She'd spent the past fourteen years trying to forget this man and his incred-ible magnetism, and in one short second, her efforts had been totally destroyed.

He still affected her.

He still attracted her.

He still *meant* something to her.

With his back to her, he spoke once more. "Where do you live now?"

"New York City."

"And your parents?"

"My father's dead. My mother's in Florida."

"And Jack's been gone . . ."

She opened her eyes. He'd turned to face her, had been watching her as they'd spoken. "Fourteen years. How did you know?"

Tye's gaze fell to his hands. They were gripping the back of his desk chair. "They told me while I was in prison. I'm really sorry, Cara. Jack was a fine man."

"Yes. He was."

"Did they ever catch the man who murdered him?"

"Yes." She looked down at her own hands and was surprised to see how steady they appeared, resting in her lap. "A few months after he killed Jack, he tried to rob another bank. A security guard shot him."

Tye moved back toward her, and this time he didn't swerve. As he rested one lean hip against the edge of the desk, their knees almost touched. His voice was low and sympathetic. "It must have been tough to lose him like that. I know how much you loved him."

"It was bad, but I survived."

His measured stare sent shivers up her back, but Cara refused to acknowledge them. *Bad* hardly described it, but he had no idea. No earthly idea . . .

The thought gave strength to her legs, and she found herself rising from the chair and pushing around him. "That's the past, though, and we have work to do right now." Her voice was false and bright. "Would you like to see my presentation or shall I save it for Mr. Montgomery?"

"What happened, Cara?"

For one heart-stopping moment, Cara froze. He couldn't possibly know about the child, could he? She swallowed past a knot of almost nauseous fear, then took a deep breath, realizing belatedly she must have misinterpreted his question. He wasn't asking about the baby. He couldn't be.

Get a grip, she said to herself sternly, desperately. Rear-ranging her face, she turned back. "What do you mean?"

He studied her, then rose. He wasn't any taller than he had been back then; her head still came to the bottom of his chin. He used to tuck her under that chin and hold her for hours. She would bury her face against his chest and listen to his heart. Right now, all she could hear was her own heart. It had started again, and it was pounding.

"What do you mean?" she repeated, her voice a shade higher.

"What happened to you?" he finally said. "Where did you go after..." He paused, then spoke again. "After I left."

A flood of relief swamped her, relief so strong she had to surreptitiously place her fingers on the edge of the desk and hold on. "That's a long story, too, and I don't think you want all the details." Gathering her thoughts, Cara raised her eyebrows and looked around the room. "I wouldn't say either one of us have done too badly, though. You're a CEO, for heaven's sake. I'm...impressed."

He shook his head, the dark blond hair moving like fluid gold. It was almost as long as it had been in high school, but tamed and trimmed now. The edge curled over his collar, though—it still had a mind of its own. "You're still Cara *Howard?* You aren't married?" he asked abruptly.

"No. Not now."

"What happened?"

"It didn't work out."

"Why not?"

Cara's fingers found her diamond bracelet and moved it restlessly around her wrist. It had been her gift to herself when she'd put her nameplate on her office door. When she'd purchased it, she'd wished her husband had bought it for her—but he was the kind of man who didn't understand a thing about her. It had taken her years to figure out why she'd even married him in the first place, and once she had the answer, she didn't like it. "That's a rather personal question, isn't it?"

"I think we've shared some pretty personal times."

That was more true than he knew, she thought with a start. She took a deep breath and answered. "I think I was too young. I was still in college, and it only lasted a few years." She cleared her throat, desperate to get out from under his questions. "What about you? Are you married?"

"No." He shook his head, his blue eyes steady. "I guess I've never found the perfect woman."

Suddenly the office was too warm, too close, too everything for Cara, and a suffocating wave came over her that she cursed. She wasn't some dippy teenager, for God's sake. Why was she letting this man affect her so? Taking a deep, calming breath, she gathered her control about her like a cape and ignored her rapid heartbeat. "Look, Tye, if you don't mind, I...I need to get back to my hotel room. I have to make some phone calls, that sort of thing." She looked up with a counterfeit smile. "You understand, don't you?"

"Sure," he said easily. "I understand."

His smile didn't reassure her, and Cara realized with a start that somewhere along the line, Tye had changed. The devil-may-care teenager had turned into a self-confident, forceful man. A man she couldn't keep anything from—not even something as simple as her desire to escape him.

He spoke once more. "I understand. Completely."

Cara didn't know whether to have a drink or throw up.

She tossed her briefcase onto the bed and rushed into the bathroom, her jacket, her shoes, her sanity falling wherever they wanted to land.

Tye Benedict.

Tye Benedict.

Tye Benedict.

His name replayed itself over and over in her mind, then finally she heard it out loud. Startled and frightened, she realized it was coming from her own lips, and she angrily clamped them shut. She couldn't believe it. Of all the millions—billions—of people in the world, why in God's name did *he* have to be the CEO of the Marshall Company? And how had he gotten there?

Gripping the edge of the marble counter, Cara stared at her disheveled reflection. She was mad. She was confused. She was terrified.

She should *never* have come here. She'd *told* Richard Lindsey she couldn't come here and now look what had happened. Disaster in the form of Tye Benedict.

She pulled the hotel's plastic ice bucket toward her. Only soft, melted cubes were left, floating around in a sea of water, but Cara didn't care. She reached into the minibar under the counter and removed a tiny bottle of vodka, but when her shaking fingers began to pry off the top, she stopped. She'd never used liquor to solve a problem, and it wasn't the answer now.

In fact, there wasn't an answer.

She replaced the bottle and walked slowly into the bedroom. The maid had left the lights on and the bed turned back, but the inviting scene meant little to Cara. There was even a small fireplace with a sofa and chair waiting cozily in front of it. It was nice, but she'd seen it a hundred times in a hundred different places. Without someone beside you, it meant nothing.

Opening the drapes, Cara stood beside the window and stared out into the blackness. Somewhere out there, Tye was doing what he usually did every evening at this time—eating dinner, reading, watching TV. She'd wondered countless times over the years what he was doing with his life, but she'd never imagined him here, here in Angelton. For some crazy reason, she *had* thought of him as successful. A teenager as determined, as aggressive, as smart as he'd been could be nothing else. But she'd never imagined him to be . . . alone.

In her mind, he'd always been with a family. He would have a faceless woman beside him and at least two children. At Christmas they'd be around a beautifully decorated tree with lots of presents and in the summer around a sparkling turquoise pool.

She'd never, ever thought of him alone.
Just like her.

The black Mercedes glided down the deserted street on
soundless wheels, coming to a stop alongside the curb. The
house before it was dark and unoccupied, the windows
shuttered. Tye had toyed with the idea of buying it and had
even made an appointment with the real estate agent once.
When the time had come, however, he couldn't even bring
himself to walk through the front door. Cara's childhood
home remained empty.

The entire neighborhood looked down-and-out. Since the
new subdivision on the west side of town had sprung up,
none of the young families moving in had wanted to live in
this part of Angelton.

He closed his eyes and leaned his head against the leather
headrest, a wave of almost bone-crushing weariness coming over him. His first reaction had been to go directly to
Monty's, to let the man know exactly what kind of havoc he
was bringing down on Tye's life, but as soon as he'd cooled
off a bit, Tye had known it was better to think it out first.
Seeing Cara had been móre than a shock. It had been a revelation, and his mind and body were still reeling from it.

She was a beautiful woman. Beautiful.

The teenage body he'd caressed had fulfilled its early
promises, and the curves were lush and soft-looking. She
had the kind of shape a man could fit his hands to, couldn't
keep his hands *off* of, as a matter of fact. There was more,
though—a helluva lot more. Underneath that patina of sophisticated businesswoman, Cara Howard defended a core
of dangerous vulnerability.

It completely shattered his mental image of her.

A dog howled down the street, and Tye opened his eyes
to stare at the sidewalk leading to the Howards' front door.
He could still remember how frightened he'd been, frightened and frustrated. He'd loved her so much it had hurt,
and all he'd wanted to do was protect and love her. And her
parents—God, how he'd hated them. Looking back on it,

he decided he'd hated them as much as he'd loved her. He wasn't sorry Phillip Howard was dead, but he couldn't say so to Cara.

A car turned down the street, its headlights throwing long yellow beams toward Tye's Mercedes. Yes, he'd been scared back then—but it was nothing compared to the fright settling over him now. With Cara back in Angelton, it was only a matter of time—a matter of time until she discovered what he'd prayed she'd never know.

A second later, a rattling truck passed Tye on the left. He glimpsed a family in the front seat, four pairs of eyes turned inquisitively toward him before the pickup disappeared and continued down the street, its tailpipe spewing vapor in the cool Texas night. Not too many Mercedes parked on this street anymore.

His entire body tense with almost nauseous panic, he forced himself to release the breath he'd been holding. Leaning back against the seat, consciously commanding his fingers to let go of the steering wheel they still clutched, Tye tried to relax.

He couldn't believe Cara had actually returned, that Monty had actually been able to get her down here. He'd threatened to do it, but Tye hadn't really thought he would. Just like Tye couldn't believe the reaction she'd set off in him now.

When he'd first found out, all those years ago, he'd tortured himself with pointless questions. What kind of woman wouldn't even tell a man that she was going to have his child? What kind of mother would deliver that baby, then turn it over to strangers to raise? What kind of woman would never again inquire about it? He'd been angry—angry and bitter—but through the years, he'd come to realize that she'd had to make those decisions because of one person. Himself.

He was the one who'd gotten her pregnant.

He was the one who'd told her he didn't love her.

He was the one who'd sent her away.

Once he'd matured enough to release the anger and accept the blame, Tye had understood. Cara'd had no other choice. Her parents had kicked her out, Tye himself had pushed her away, and then to top it off, Jack—her only hope—had been killed. She'd done the only thing she could.

But now Tye had to do the same.

If he didn't, he'd lose everything.

And his secret would finally be revealed.

Cara woke up to a sparkling Texas morning totally at odds with the storm still raging inside her mind. The night before, she hadn't bothered to close the drapes, and now the bright sunlight poured through the opening with a clarity she couldn't ignore. Groaning, she fell out of bed and stumbled toward the window.

The hotel was a new one, built on the edge of town and near the Montgomery building. The view wasn't as spectacular as the one from Marshall Montgomery's office, but it was still pretty good. Stretching, Cara craned her neck and stared at Bear Lake. She wished she was there, right beside the water with a fishing rod and nothing more pressing to decide than which bait to use. She loved to fish, but she hadn't cast a line in years. Today wasn't a fishing day, though. It was a working day, and an hour later she was pulling into the office parking lot she'd left the night before. Hopefully, today, she'd see Monty Montgomery, then leave as quickly as possible.

When she entered his office, her eyes automatically went to the corner from which Tye had emerged last night, but it was empty and filled with light. Almost immediately, the conference door opened and an older man walked in, his hand extended.

"Ms. Howard?" he said in a deep, booming voice. "Glad to meet you—I'm Marshall Montgomery, but call me Monty."

As she shook his hand, Cara thought how well his name suited him. Both seemed solid, dependable, conservative. His clothing surprised her, though. Instead of the usual suit and tie, he wore a blue pullover that matched his twinkling eyes, and khaki pants that couldn't hide a well-developed paunch. His silver hair was neatly trimmed, and Cara judged him to be in his late fifties, early sixties. Something about him seemed almost familiar, but she attributed the feeling to anxiety. Nothing in Angelton was as she'd expected it to be.

"Have a seat," he said, lifting one beefy hand toward the chairs in front of his desk. "I'm sorry I missed you last night. I hope it didn't upset your plans too much, but I had a crisis at home. I actually came back to see you, but you'd already left."

Mentally, Cara flinched—that couldn't have made a great first impression—and she had Tye to thank for it. "I'm sorry," she said, taking one of the chairs. "I spoke with Mr. Benedict for a while. Then . . . I decided to return this morning instead."

"Tye told me you two spoke." She wondered what else he'd told Marshall, but she didn't have to wonder long. "I understand you knew each other back in high school," he said.

Cara glanced down at her hands. Again, they were clasped lightly in her lap, and they gave absolutely no indication that her heart was thundering. She hoped her face didn't, either.

"That's correct," she said with a bright smile.

"Quite a coincidence, huh?"

She shrugged her shoulders. "Actually, I think a lot of people return to live and work where they grew up."

"But *you* didn't."

"No." Her eyes met the older man's, and for some reason, she had the feeling he knew a lot more than he was revealing. "I prefer the East Coast—the big city, I guess."

"Don't understand that myself." He swung his chair around and looked out at the lake. "Once I saw Bear Lake I knew I didn't want to ever live anywhere else. 'Course, I'd lived a few other places before then, so I guess I got all that out of my system before I settled down." He rotated back toward her and smiled. "Maybe you'll do that, too. Just seeing the lake this time of year, smelling that good Texas air…seeing old friends—you might just decide to move back here yourself."

"I don't think so," she answered. "I don't really have any family ties here anymore. My father passed away several years ago, and my mother remarried. She lives in Florida now."

Trying to get the meeting back to a less personal note, Cara reached down toward her briefcase. "I've brought a rather extensive presentation to show you, along with photos of some of our previous work." She looked up. "If you're ready—"

"Great. Let's look."

For the next hour, Cara showed Monty exactly what Lindsey and Sons could do for his company. Even though she'd done conferences like this a thousand times, she still got the jitters, and knowing Tye was somewhere in the building didn't make this one any easier. Monty didn't appear to notice, however. He seemed more than satisfied with what she showed him.

"These are great," he said, his eyes indicating the pictures scattered across his desk and her presentation board. "I'm very impressed. Your work is every bit as good as Jerilyn said it was."

"Jerilyn?"

A fleeting shadow crossed his expression, then he spoke. "My wife. She's the one who wanted to bring you down here. She was very impressed with your work in New York."

Cara breathed a silent prayer of thanks. "I'm glad. Lindsey and Sons is a large operation, but we still give our clients a lot of personal attention. I think that shows in our work." She smiled. "Will your wife be helping you make the design decisions?"

Again, his face darkened before he spoke. Then, as if he realized what he was doing, he seemed to deliberately recover and smile. "No, no. She prefers to set things in motion, then let them work out naturally." The smile seemed to waver. "And that's probably best, too."

Before Cara could think about what he'd said, he stood and looked at his watch. "We have just enough time for the ten-cent tour of the office, then we'll have lunch in the conference room with Tye. How's that sound?"

Cara's stomach hit the floor. "Lunch? With Tye?"

Monty had already started toward the door, but he stopped as she spoke. "You do have the time, don't you? I just assumed we were the only reason you were in Angelton. You don't have other clients here, do you?"

By the way his twitching eyebrows met over his eyes, Cara knew instantly what Monty was really asking. He was one of those clients who liked to think their designers had no other clients but themselves. She'd met them before, and they didn't really bother her at all. If Monty gave her the account, he'd be spending enough money that she *should* give him all her attention.

But that wasn't why her face was frozen now.

"No, I don't have any other clients here," she said, finally recovering and heading toward the door where he stood. "We'd be exclusive to you in Angelton." She paused and cleared her throat. "I guess I just wasn't aware that you worked so closely with Tye. Isn't it unusual that a CEO for a conglomeration be based in one of the smaller offices?"

He smiled and held open the door for her. "Yeah, I guess it is, but then Tye Benedict is a pretty unusual guy. He wanted to live here, and he pretty much does what he likes. It was fine with me."

They headed toward the outer hall, Monty's words echoing in Cara's mind. "What do you mean, fine with you? I thought Marshall was owned by an umbrella operation. Wouldn't Tye have to get *them* to agree?"

Marshall stopped and looked at her. "You really like to know the details, don't you?"

Cara laughed lightly. "I guess so. It helps when I think about an account." Her answer sounded lame, even to her ears, but Monty simply nodded his head as though he understood.

"It's simple, really. I started the Marshall companies quite a few years ago. The software world was just beginning to take off, and before I knew it, the company was huge. We were selling canned programs, custom software, anything and everything, including hardware, too. When Tye came to work for me, he suggested we divide it into different companies. The software division was my baby, though, and I stuck with it. I gave everything else to Tye, and he got it organized. He's the CEO of the corporation, even though I started it all."

Monty stopped beside another door, and Cara paused, waiting for him to continue. The blue eyes turned thoughtful. "Tye's a smart one, and I owe him a lot. I thank God every night that we got together, even though it took a few years."

Beside him, Cara paused. "What do you mean, it took a few years?"

Monty looked down at her, but before he could speak, an achingly familiar voice answered from behind them.

"He means we almost never knew each other, but thanks to your Uncle Jack, all we lost were nineteen years."

Confused, Cara turned slowly, her heart racing into her throat as she took in Tye's steady sapphire eyes. "My mother managed to keep it a secret for quite some time, but she couldn't quite match Jack's perseverance." He paused, and when he spoke again, his voice had regained its steady tone. "Marshall is my only family, Cara. He's my uncle."

Chapter 5

Her dark eyes widened in what looked like total disbelief, and she started to speak, but Monty interrupted. "Hell, Cara doesn't care about all that, boy." He grinned and looked down at Cara, his blue eyes flashing. "And if she does, there's plenty of time to explain later. Right, Cara?"

"Of... of course," was all she could answer, and that answer seemed to come out with misgivings. She obviously wanted to know more, but wasn't going to ask.

Monty opened the door leading into the main computer room and indicated Cara and Tye should go in. As they stepped into the chilled room, a high-pitched sound sent Monty's hand to his waist. He lifted the beeper and studied the number. When his head rose, he exchanged a careful look with Tye before turning to Cara.

"I'm sorry to do this to you, but I've got to run." He nodded toward Tye. "You two go ahead and look around, then have lunch. I'll try and return this afternoon, and we can talk some more."

An expression of panic crossed Cara's face, then fled. If Tye hadn't known her fourteen years ago, he wouldn't have recognized it. Did being with him upset her that much?

"Do you think you'll be able to come back?" Her voice was cool, but she couldn't hide her feelings from Tye.

Monty held up one hand, the padded fingers thick and callused. "Maybe—maybe not. I'm real sorry, but I got to go." He turned, then stopped at the door. "You're in good hands, Cara. Tye will take care of you."

The door slammed behind him, and the sudden silence was deafening. The only thing Tye could hear was the rush of blood through his veins. The only thing he could smell was the scent of Cara's perfume. And suddenly, for some totally insane reason, the only thing he wanted to do was crush her into his arms and kiss her.

He actually stepped backward, the thought startled him so much, but Cara didn't appear to notice. "Why didn't you tell me about Monty?"

"I really didn't think you cared." The minute the words were out Tye mentally kicked himself. They sounded harsh and cold and unfeeling, but in a way, that's what he'd become. He'd had to if he'd wanted to survive.

And Tye Benedict didn't want to just survive. He wanted to succeed.

She blushed, the color returning to her face in two bright streaks. "I see."

"No, you don't," he said, taking her arm and ignoring the surprise in her eyes, "but this isn't the place to explain. Let's forget the tour and go have lunch. It should be set up in the conference room by now."

Without another word, she allowed him to lead her out of the computer room and away from the dozen or so eyes that had taken in their conversation. The employees at Montgomery were some of the best in the world, but like any office, it had a grapevine, and Tye didn't want to provide any more gossip to it than he had to.

They made their way back to the main hall, but Tye didn't release Cara's arm. Under his fingers and beneath the silk of her blouse, her skin warmed until it almost burned him. He didn't drop his hold until they were in the conference room, and even then he did it reluctantly. Until yesterday, if asked, he would have said she was the last person in the world he would want to see, but somehow having her next to him, her tantalizing perfume rising up to him, her shiny head of hair tempting his fingers, his mind had changed without him even being aware of how or when it happened.

Or of even wanting it to happen.

A damask cloth covered one end of the marble table, and a service for three stood waiting. A cold salad decorated the gold-rimmed dishes, and several hot plates on the credenza by the window told him the entrées were ready, too. At informal lunches like this, they served themselves, and Tye was grateful. He didn't need the distraction of a waiter popping up every two minutes.

Cara ignored the food and went to the bar at the back of the room, reaching for the bottled water and lemon. After she'd fixed her drink, she turned and studied him.

"I'd like to know more."

"Why?"

Her eyes fell to the crystal tumbler in her hand. One manicured nail thoughtfully circled its thin rim before she looked up at him. "Do I have to have a reason?"

"No, but family secrets aren't often pleasant. Are you sure you want the gory details?"

With a startled glance she jerked her eyes to his, but a second later she'd recovered. She sipped her drink, then lowered the glass. Her lipstick stained the edge. "I'd like to know, Tye, and if you have to have a reason, then try this. We were friends—more than friends—once, and I think that links us somehow. We... share something that other people don't share, something that's..."

He waited for her to finish, held his breath and prayed, but she didn't say anything else. Would she ever acknowledge it? Ever tell him the truth? "Something that's what?" he asked.

She said nothing, but simply shook her head and looked down at her glass, her auburn curls partially hiding her face.

Tye sighed and went to the bar to fix his own drink. The ice plunked into the tumbler, then he splashed tomato juice over it. A twist of lime, and he was done.

She walked over to him and briefly put her hand on his arm. "Please, Tye, tell me." Her dark eyes held more than just memories. "If Jack had something to do with Monty and you coming together, I'd really like to know."

One touch was all it took. Tye had never been able to say no to Cara, and apparently that hadn't changed, either.

"All right." Moving toward the window, he stared out at the lake. He would tell her... but not everything. "About halfway into my sentence, Jack came to me. He... he did that for some of the guys he'd put away. Visited them when no one else would." He turned back around and faced her. He wasn't sure, but she seemed to blanch a little, and the hand that lifted her glass trembled slightly. He pretended not to notice.

"Anyway, one day he started asking me questions about my family. Did I know where my mother's people came from? Did I ever hear her talk about my dad? Would I want to meet any of my family if he could find them for me?" He took a sip of his juice, but didn't taste it. "By this time, I'd had more than a few hours to think about everything I'd done, and the idea of having a family—something I'd never let myself think about before—seemed pretty damned good."

"So he found you an uncle? Just like that?"

Briefly, Tye looked down at her and shook his head. "It wasn't quite that simple, but you know Jack. He was a real bulldog." Tye's fingers tightened around the glass. "He finally tracked down Monty in the Middle East. Believe it or not, Monty had actually been trying to contact my mother for years, but she'd never reply to his letters, never return his calls." He shook his head again, his hair brushing over his collar with a rasping sound. "I never even knew about him till Jack walked into the visitor's room at Huntsville one day and told me he'd found him.''

Tye knew his voice was strained, and all he could do was hope she would attribute his obvious anxiety to the story and nothing more. He'd gained much, much more than an uncle that day.

Cara looked down into the glass she held, as if there were more answers floating on top of the water—answers to questions she couldn't even ask—but when she looked up at him, he saw that her curiosity had apparently been appeased. For a while. He drew a silent breath of relief.

"I—I'm really sorry, Tye. Especially when I think about how tough your life was. I had no idea . . .''

"No one did—except my mother." An old, familiar pull of anger tugged at him, but he ignored it. "I'll never understand why she wanted to make life so miserable for us. If Monty had been around earlier, who knows what would have happened?''

"He helped you, though. That's the important thing. Right?''

"More than you'll ever know." His eyes met hers. "I'll never forget it, either. I got a two-year degree in Huntsville, but that and a quarter would have bought me a cup of coffee. Without Monty and his wife, I'd be nothing but another ex-con.''

"No," she said softly. "You'd never be just that.''

He cut his eyes to her face. Her expression was almost shy, as if she didn't really want him to know she believed him, but had to say something, anyway. It was another side of the vulnerability he'd glimpsed last night, and in a way, he hated to see it. Things would be so much easier if she were heartless and cold.

She spoke again. "In fact, you shouldn't have been there at all. We . . . we were only kids, and we didn't have the slightest concept of what we were doing.''

"You're wrong," he said bluntly. He paused for only a second, then spoke again, emotion forcing his voice into a whiskey-rough resonance. "I knew exactly what it meant, but at the time I thought there was no other way to get you out of there. No other way. And I loved you too much not to try."

Cara thought the lunch would never end. She was too upset to eat and too shaky not to. How much more unsettling news could she take? After nibbling on the salad, she took a bowl of gumbo from one of the dishes on the sideboard and pretended to enjoy it.

Tye's navy eyes watched her every move. "You don't eat much," he finally remarked. "Is that how you keep your figure?"

"Partly. I like to run, too, though. The stress level in this job sometimes takes me over the limit. That seems to help."

He put down his fork and picked up a roll. "You have that much stress in your job?"

"Doesn't everyone?" She nodded toward the empty chair at the head of the table. "Monty seems to have more than his share, also."

Tye's face instantly shuttered. "He's got problems," he said cryptically. "Things he can't quite control."

Cara's curiosity rose, but it was more than clear that Tye would say nothing else. He was obviously very loyal to the man who'd given him his start—the only man he could call his family—and she wasn't about to question him more.

For the rest of the meal, Tye answered Cara's questions about the software the company sold, how many employees there were, what their programs did.

"Did you help develop these programs?" she asked.

"No." Tye picked up his coffee cup and drained it. "I know absolutely nothing about that end of the company. I deal with the growth of the business, handle the stock sales, the retirement plans—that sort of thing."

"You always were interested in those kinds of details." For a moment, the past slipped away, and Cara saw the man Tye had become—so powerful, so handsome, so successful. Any woman would be thrilled to sit beside him, but she could hardly wait to escape.

A second later, in answer to her prayers, the conference door opened, and Monty strode in. "Did I miss lunch?"

Tye looked up at him, and a silent question passed between the two men. Cara didn't know what it was, but she definitely recognized the tension. Monty shook his head slightly as though he could say no more in front of Cara, then headed for the sideboard, speaking again as he generously filled a plate. "I hope Tye was able to tell you more about the Marshall Company while I was gone, Cara."

"Yes, he was." She let her dark eyes turn thoughtfully toward the man who'd been her lover. "He told me a lot."

Sitting at the head of the table, Monty set his plate down and began to eat. "Good, good. I'd like to talk to you this afternoon about the company and some ideas I've got for a few of the offices. I'll even take you into the computer room and let you play with it a little bit."

It sounded like fun, but Cara didn't want to have fun. She wanted to get out of town as quickly as possible. "That won't be necessary, Monty," she answered smoothly. "I don't want to take up too much of your time." She glanced toward Tye, but his face was noncommittal.

"Well, maybe we should skip the computer part. My time is a little short." Monty glanced at his watch, then back at her. "How soon will you get the painters and such in here?"

She smiled. "I'm afraid it's not quite that simple, since we'll be doing this long-distance. I'll most likely hire an assistant for on-site supervision and remain in New York myself."

He slowly put the fork down beside his plate. "You aren't going to stay here?"

Cara pressed her lips together and tried not to panic. She felt as if she were losing before she'd even started, but with Tye there, her usual composure wasn't quite intact. She glared at him, but he simply pushed his chair back, picked up his cup and headed for the sideboard.

Cara looked at Monty. His face had turned stormy. "I generally don't spend the entire time on-site, no. Usually I make an initial visit, like we had this morning, then return to New York and study my samples. Depending on the location, I return a few weeks later with a more formal presentation, or an associate returns for me and shows you what I've done." She tried to soften him, even as she felt it was useless. "We're a big firm, Monty, and we have clients all over the world. I do this kind of thing all the time—it's normal."

"Not for me, it's not. I assumed you'd be here all the time."

Cara turned around and shot Tye a pleading glance. He was leaning against the sideboard, sipping his coffee. Her eyes caught his, but in return she received nothing at all. She licked her lips and tried again. "We have an excellent junior staff of decorators—in fact, that's how I started out. They're very competent and they're trained to—"

"I thought you did the work." His eyes were bright as they pegged her with the question.

She smiled again, but this time it was strained. "I do. But I have too many clients to supervise each job personally."

"But when you *did* do the work, were you good?"

A small tick of worry sounded in the back of her mind, but Cara tried to ignore it. "Well, yes, I was."

"Did your boss think so?"

"Yes." She glanced toward Tye again, but his dark blue eyes were blank as they met hers. Was this something Monty did with everyone he gave work to? Maybe he was trying to decide if she could handle the job or not. She took a deep breath. "I've won several trade awards for my design work and some of them were at the international level. That's always tough competition."

Monty pushed back from the table and pulled an enormous cigar from the pocket of his shirt. The production of trimming it, lighting it and taking the first puff occupied him for several seconds, then when the tip glowed to his apparent satisfaction, he eyed Cara through the haze of blue smoke. "But you're telling me now you don't do the actual work?"

"I no longer stay on-site throughout the job, if that's what you're asking."

Monty took the cigar from his mouth and examined the tip before looking at her. "I like to deal with individuals, Ms. Howard, not a corporation that has a different yahoo for each piddly job."

Cara took a sip from her coffee cup, then carefully replaced it into its waiting saucer. "I can see your concerns, Monty, but you'll get a much better job if I stay in New York. I can be on top of the materials we'll need and any other problems that might arise." She leaned forward and smiled her most winning smile. "Once I get back and find just the right things to complement your offices—colors, accessories, furniture—I'd say we could have you some preliminary sketches in about three weeks, and they'd be sketches that would knock your socks off."

Staring at her, he pulled on the cigar until the ember glowed a deep, dark red. A second later, more blue smoke filled the room. "I don't believe so," he finally answered. "Either you do the work here, or there won't be a contract."

"'Either you do the work here, or there won't be a contract.'" Cara yanked the heavy gold earring off her left ear and pressed the phone closer. "That's exactly what he said, Richard, word for word. Why would I lie about that?"

"Then you'll have to stay."

"Are you crazy?" Cara's voice rose when she got angry, and right now she was sure they could hear her three doors down in the almost empty hotel. "I didn't want to come here in the first place, and I'm sure as hell not going to stay for three months."

"It would probably take longer than three months," Richard Lindsey replied calmly. "I'd say more like four... maybe even five."

Cara collapsed onto her bed. "What about my other clients? The other jobs I've got going?"

"Stephen can take them. Monty wants you."

Cara closed her eyes. "But I don't want to lose those accounts, Richard."

"You won't lose them. When you get back, they'll be yours again." He paused, and in the background, she could hear him tapping his pen against his desk blotter. "What are you so worried about, Cara? If you land the parent company of Montgomery's, it would be the biggest account Lindsey's has ever gotten. Doesn't that possibility mean anything to you?"

"Of course it does, but..." Cara bit her bottom lip then brought up her right hand to massage her temple. Ever since she'd stepped outside of Monty Montgomery's conference room, she'd thought she was going to explode. Tye had been absolutely no help at all, either. But then why in the world had she even thought he would be? A tiny voice in the back of her mind explained it—she'd assumed he wouldn't want her around any more than she wanted to be there. Obviously, she'd been mistaken.

"But I *do not* want to live in Angelton past the end of tomorrow, much less for four months." She opened her eyes. "I *told* you I didn't even want to come down here."

She heard the pen drop, then an angry thud. "What's happened to you, Cara? You're the one I could always count on to understand the bottom line, and now you're letting me down. I don't understand it. Just because you used to live in Angelton does not explain this kind of behavior."

"I don't have to explain my behavior to you," she answered stiffly.

"Maybe not," he answered, "but when it comes to work, I need a better reason than 'I don't want to, Richard.'"

An empty buzzing filled the phone line, and Cara didn't know what to say to replace it. She *couldn't* tell Richard Lindsey the truth, but she *couldn't* stay there for months and see Tye Benedict every day. If just the past few days had been torture, what would a few months be like?

"Can't you trust me on this one, Richard?"

"No." His answer was blunt, and so was his voice. "The potential for this account is too big." He paused for a moment, and Cara's stomach rolled over into a tight, little ball. "I'm sorry, but you have to stay, Cara. There's no negotiating on this one."

By the time the monthly Chamber of Commerce meeting ended, the restaurant was almost completely empty, the windows dark beyond the shadowed pools of lamplight that hung over each table. Tye said goodbye to the last of the cluster of men standing beside the door, then headed toward the coatrack to pick up his jacket and leave. It had been an eighteen-hour day, and he hadn't even had a chance to catch his breath, much less talk to Monty—something he really needed to do. The meeting had seemed to go on forever, and Tye had barely been able to maintain the least semblance of interest in the talk. His mind had repeatedly taken him to shining hair and dark eyes and questions he didn't have the answers to.

At the door, he stopped to slip into his jacket, a deep weariness slowing his usually brisk movements. Shrugging his shoulders into the wool, Tye realized that not only were his movements slow, his reaction time was, too, because it took him almost a full minute to recognize the woman at the other end of the restaurant.

Without thinking, his heart beating an unnatural rhythm inside his chest, he paused and drank in the sight of Cara. She was the only person in the restaurant, and the solitary light over her table highlighted her isolation. A lonely glass of wine sat by her left hand, and to her right, a flattened magazine waited, the pages fluttering briefly when the waitress walked by. Her eyes focusing on the magazine, Cara lifted one hand to the heavy gold necklace at her neck, touched it, then dropped her fingers back to the place setting before her, her buffed nails a dull glimmer against the polished silver.

The action held a hint of resigned endurance, and something inside of Tye twisted sharply. He'd never thought of Cara like this—alone, by herself, no one beside her—and the empty booth opposite her suddenly seemed even more barren and unoccupied. In his mind, he'd always seen her surrounded by family, loved and secure.

He stared at Cara. How had they managed to so completely reverse their fortunes? Before he'd come onto the scene, she'd had what appeared to be the perfect family life. Two loving parents, a beautiful home, excellent grades. Everything he'd wanted but didn't have. And now? Now here she was, sitting by herself in a darkened restaurant, sipping from a comfortless glass of wine and staring at the pages of a magazine, while at home, he had the love of a family and more. It didn't make sense.

And neither did his scrutiny of the situation.

Cara Howard should represent one thing to him—a threat—and if he had any sense at all, he'd turn around right now and leave before she lifted her head and spotted him. Every minute she stayed in Angelton brought her a minute closer to destroying the life he'd built for himself, the life and everything that had come to mean so much to him.

He should leave. Right now. Turn around, go through the door and never look back.

He was still telling himself that a second later as his feet walked slowly away from the entrance and down the line of tables to her booth.

"Hi," was all he said.

She jerked her head up, her nonplussed expression telling him she'd been totally unaware of him.

"Tye! I didn't see you come in."

Her eyes were two pools of darkness, her hair a veil of reddish-brown light. He told himself not to notice the V of creamy skin above the neckline of her blouse or the curve of her breasts beneath it, but the details registered instinctively, and his gut tightened in response. Ignoring his reaction, he forced himself to nod toward the back of the restaurant. "I was probably in the other room. We have our chamber meeting here. Third Tuesday of every month."

"*You* belong to the Chamber of Commerce?"

"The company does, but it's really Monty's thing. He couldn't come tonight, though, and I offered to show up for him. He likes to stay in touch with the local economy, that sort of thing."

"That's very important, I guess. Especially in a small town like this. Everyone needs to be good corporate neighbors, right?"

The conversation seemed awkward, out of place, and Tye knew it was because the words were so normal, so everyday. He and Cara had never had simple discussions. Never talked about the weather, never asked each other the time, never simply talked. They'd had crises, not conversations.

There was no good reason to change that situation now, but his question slipped out, anyway. "Do you mind if I sit down?"

Her dark eyes glittered for a moment, and he thought she might refuse, but she shuttered the expression into something cordial with expert smoothness and waved to the red leather bench across from her. "Please do. I've already ordered, but I can get the waitress—"

As she acquiesced, relief then apprehension cut through him at once. *Leave,* a part of him said. *Leave now while you can.* "I've eaten," he said, "but I'll have a drink." Halfway turning to face the bar, he ordered a beer, then slid into the booth, his leather briefcase and jacket following.

"How was your day?" he asked.

"It was long," she answered. "In fact, I just left the office."

He raised his eyebrows, surprised by her revelation. Working late hours was another issue he'd never associated with Cara, but he couldn't explain why. Another flash of sympathy for her came over him. She had nothing but her work, and he had so much. So very much. "Why so late?" he asked. "Couldn't it wait until tomorrow?"

She shook her head, then rubbed one hand up her arm as if cold, the rustle of silk tantalizing him from across the table. "No, it couldn't. I have accounts back in New York that I had to call and warn."

"Warn?"

A look of pure frustration crossed her face. "Their jobs may take longer if I have to stay here, and that's looking like a reality more and more. I had to let them know in case they wanted to make other arrangements."

"I can't imagine that they couldn't wait for you. I'm sure they'd understand."

"Well, I'm not." She raised her gaze back to his face, and this time he saw a glimmer of guilty defiance. "My job is very important to me, Tye, and a lot of those people depend on me."

"I can certainly understand that feeling," he answered immediately, trying to put her at ease. "I'd feel the same way if I were you."

"You would?"

"Of course. Anyone who works could appreciate that. Being responsible is part of the game."

She looked surprised he actually understood. "It was tough to call them," she said, "and tell them I might be letting them down."

"It's not like that—"

"It doesn't matter." She shook her head. "They don't know the particulars, and they don't care, either. In the past, I've always managed to juggle all my jobs, but this time..."

He leaned closer, his elbows on the table. "I'm sure it will work out, Cara. Things always do."

"Do they?" Her steady gaze locked on his, pulling him across the table with a force he couldn't have resisted had he wanted to. "I'm not so sure about that, Tye."

For two seconds, something crossed between them, something Tye couldn't define but couldn't ignore. She almost seemed to know, he thought to himself, but how could she? His secrets had been secrets a long, long time. One thing was for sure, though. The longer he sat here, the greater the chances were that Cara would uncover them. And that was something he simply couldn't afford to have happen.

She broke his gaze and disconnected the link he'd sensed. Even her voice changed as she spoke again, becoming lighter and seemingly less concerned. "You seem really close to Monty. I guess that's something that definitely worked out right."

Tye eased against the leather bench. "Yes," he said. "We are close. He's done everything he can to help me, and I never even had a chance to say thanks to Jack. He gave me so much."

"I'm sure he knew what it meant to you."

"I hope so."

The waitress appeared and deposited a salad in front of Cara. She raised her fork, then hesitated. "Sure you don't want some? I could share."

He shook his head. "I just finished, really." At that very instant, however, he couldn't have told her what he'd eaten if his life had depended on it. He couldn't even remember his own name, because it suddenly hit him how beautiful a woman Cara Howard had become.

Smooth, sophisticated, beautiful. She was all that and more. With darkly enticing eyes, she stared at him, her mouth slightly open, her throat moving as she spoke. Finally, he came to and realized what she was saying.

"—another beer?"

"Sure," he managed to get out and signal the waitress. Cara looked at him strangely, then refocused on her salad.

He should leave, he kept telling himself, but as he had the thought, he reached toward the magazine she'd been reading and flipped it over. In elaborate script across the full-color cover were the words *The Journal of Antiques*. He nodded toward it as she ate. "Do you collect antiques?"

"Not as many as I'd like to." She sipped her wine. "It can be a very expensive hobby."

"I've never understood the lure myself."

She smiled. "That's because you're a forward thinker. You're too busy thinking about what's going to happen in the future to worry about the past."

Her perception startled him, and he found himself staring at her in surprise. "How do you know that?"

She shrugged, a whiff of perfume making its way across the table. "You always were. I don't imagine anything could change that."

"That was a lot of years ago."

"But the child becomes the man."

Again, they stared at each other across the table, then she picked up her fork and speared a tomato. "I like antiques," she said, her face suddenly relaxing as they reached a neutral topic, "because they represent a simpler time. When families stuck together and talked about their differences and worked things out."

The vulnerable longing in her voice touched him. He tried to tell himself to ignore the feeling, but he couldn't.

She continued. "It's more than furniture. I see an old breakfront or a scarred rocking chair, and I think about the people who used the dishes that would have been stored in it, or the mothers that rocked their babies—"

She stopped abruptly, her words breaking off in midsentence. Putting her fork down, the tomato still on it, she looked up, an expression resembling embarrassed panic suddenly flitting across her face. "You must think I'm a nut."

"Not at all," he said instantly. "I never thought of antiques in that way, but it makes perfect sense to me." Unexpectedly, he found himself reaching across the table and taking her hand. "You *are* a very perceptive woman, Cara. And a very beautiful one, too."

She looked down at their entwined fingers, a startled expression on her face. Tye felt the way she looked—surprised by the connection but caught too short to do anything different. Touching her had seemed so natural, so automatic that he hadn't stopped to even think about it.

The moment seemed frozen, but a second later Cara slid her fingers from under his and put her hand in her lap. She looked cool, calm and collected, but in the hollow of her throat, he could see her pulse pounding.

Her soft voice broke the moment, and by the tone of it he could tell his compliment had made her feel awkward. "I usually don't go on that much about old things, but I've been thinking about my goals a lot lately, and I realized I haven't done much toward them."

"What are they?"

"Do you really want to know?"

"Yes." He realized he was telling the truth. "I would like to know."

"I'd like to own my own antique shop. It's something I've wanted to do for a long time, but my career keeps me on the road so much I haven't had much of a chance to do anything about it."

"You travel a lot with your work, then?"

"Yes. I have clients all over the world."

"Sounds glamorous."

"Try exhausting. My last job was in Rome, where I had three weeks to do an entire villa before the owners returned from a cruise. I had blank walls, ten buckets of midnight blue and three painters who'd never heard of dry-sponging." Rolling her eyes, she smiled and took a sip of wine. "I climbed up on the ladder to demonstrate, but when I turned around, none of them were looking at the wall."

He grinned, his answer automatic. "I can certainly see why. I wouldn't be, either."

Even in the dim light, he could see the blush that crept up her neck. It made her look sixteen again.

"Tell me about your job," she said, obviously anxious to change the subject. "What does a CEO really do?"

He toyed with his glass of beer. "Not a whole lot, actually."

"I don't believe that."

"You should. It's the truth. I go to the office every day, look at what everyone has done, then approve or disapprove. I'm sure I do a helluva lot less work than you do, and I definitely don't have to put up with leering painters."

She pushed away her salad. "But you enjoy it?"

"Yes. I *do* enjoy the business world."

"I always knew you'd be involved with business some-how," she said. "Anyone who understood stocks and bonds the way you did at nineteen had to become a company man. What you knew about it amazed me even then."

"I knew nothing then," he countered, his eyes locking on hers. "Nothing except that I wanted to be with you the rest of my life."

The confession hung in the air between them, and instantly Tye regretted the words, despite their truthfulness. It was too late to take them back, though.

For one long minute, Cara met his stare. *That's all in the past,* her eyes seemed to say. *It's in the past, and I want it to stay there.*

You're right, he silently communicated. *But something tells me it's not going to be ignored.*

He left shortly after that, anxious to put their conversa-tion—the words left unsaid as much as those that had been spoken—behind him. But before he pulled out of the park-ing lot, he looked through the windows of the restaurant one more time. In the halo of light, Cara looked even more alone than ever . . . and for the first time in a very long time, he felt the same way, too.

"Do you think I was too hard on her?"

Tye eyed Monty, then let his glance fall to the fireplace. A norther had blown through that afternoon, dropping the temperatures and bringing with it a flurry of billowing clouds, but he'd hardly noticed. This was the first oppor-tunity Tye had had to talk to the older man about his machinations, and his concentration was focused. He even ignored Monty's question. "You should have told me she was coming."

"I couldn't. You would have stopped me."

"That's right. I would have." Tye stared at the man who had become his surrogate father. He'd done so much for Tye. Since the moment they'd connected, the older man had tried to make up for all the years of abuse and neglect his sister—Tye's mother—had heaped on him. Sometimes though, like now, his help was almost more than Tye could handle. "You're meddling, Mont, big-time meddling, and it's a mistake."

"It'd be a bigger one to refuse." He drank deeply from the glass in his hand. "Jerilyn's insistent."

Tye sipped from his own crystal tumbler. "Well, she's wrong this time. I appreciate what she's trying to do, but I can handle the situation on my own. I don't need Cara." He stared at the fire and thought about their chance meeting the night before. She'd looked so... so alone. His resolve faltered, but he spoke, anyway. "I can do this on my own. I always have."

Monty shook his head, clearly unable to speak. He'd always been a proud man, enormously cheerful, continually upbeat, but the past few years had been too much. Even for him. Tye felt his chest tighten in sympathy.

"I know that, son," Monty answered, his voice breaking. "But I don't think I can." In his own hands, he held a drink so tightly that Tye was afraid the glass would shatter. "Jerilyn wants this for Kit, and I can't refuse her." He raised his face, and Tye saw that his blue eyes were filled with tears. "Could you refuse a dying woman?"

Throughout everything, this was the first time Tye had seen Monty cry, and he'd had plenty of reasons before now to do so. Tye's heart cracked open a little bit wider.

He brought his drink to his lips, but his throat was so tight he could hardly swallow. "I guess she's trying to prepare us, but she's doing it the wrong way."

"There isn't a right way, goddammit." Monty stood up abruptly and went to the bar in the corner of the room. Tye heard ice clink against the glass and then the splash of liquor. When Monty returned to his chair by the fireplace, half the drink was already gone.

"I don't want to let go of her." Monty's voice was softer now, less angry and more sad. "We've been together for forty-five years. Do you have any idea what it's like to sleep with one woman for forty-five years? To see her hairbrushes on the counter every morning, to smell her perfume in the sheets, to warm your feet next to hers every winter?" He shook his head. "I just can't imagine her leaving me like this."

"She's not doing it on purpose."

"I know that."

"She'd stay if she could."

"I know that."

"You still have Kit . . . and me."

Monty raised his eyes to stare bleakly at Tye. "And that's one of the reasons Jerilyn thinks we need Cara here, too." He leaned forward in his chair, his elbows on his knees. "I'm not sure I agree with her, Tye, but she said one thing the other day I simply couldn't argue with—you are the son we never had." He looked down for a second, then raised his eyes again. "And we want to see you happy."

Tye shook his head. "Bringing Cara here isn't going to do that."

"Maybe not, but Jerilyn thinks it will—and she also thinks Kit's going to need a mother. Through the years, Kit's had Jerilyn to come to whenever she had a problem, and soon she won't be able to do that. She's getting to a hard age, Tye."

Tye stood up abruptly. He walked toward the fireplace.

"Cara's haunted you every day of your life, Tye. You're a man with a shadow even when there's no sun." Monty paused. "You always have been."

Tye turned, the flames at his back. "I went back for her once, but she didn't need me in her life, and from then on I knew I had to stay out of it."

"You didn't even talk to her—you just saw her with another man. That doesn't mean anything."

"They were in love."

"Well, they aren't now."

Tye tossed the rest of his drink down his throat, the burning liquid adding an extra edge to his voice when he finally spoke. "Dammit, Monty, I had a good reason for staying away from her for fourteen years."

"I know. It's called fear."

"The only thing I'm afraid of is her taking what I care about."

"Is it?"

"Yes."

Monty shook his head. "I don't think so. You've wanted a family for as long as I've known you. That's one of the things that appealed to me so much about you, son. You know what's important in life—just like I do." He shook his head and took a sip from his drink. "But as much as you wanted a family of your own, you've never been able to find a woman to settle down with. Doesn't that tell you something?"

Tye smiled. "Yeah. There's not too many good women out there."

"That's right." Monty set his drink down with a clang. "And even though I might not agree completely with Jerilyn, that's why I went along with her crazy scheme and brought Cara back here." He stood up. "You're thirty-three years old, Tye. Don't make the mistake Jerilyn and I made and wait too long. As much as I love you and Kit, too, I'd still give my left arm for a child of my own."

At that moment, the front door blew open, and both men turned their faces toward the hall with expectation. Tye could hear the voice that always brought a catch to his throat, a voice so much like the one he'd heard earlier in the office today. A second later, the study doors flew open.

She entered the room the way she did everything—with immeasurable energy, flinging her books into one chair, her coat into another, her purse into a third. Her wild blond hair curled in abandon, and as Tye watched, she flipped it over her shoulder with an achingly familiar movement. He grinned, and she answered with one of her own. She ran to Monty first, and gave the older man a loving kiss, which he bent down to receive. "Hi, Poppy," she said, straightening his sweater and smoothing his gray hair with one slim hand. "How's it hanging?"

"That's not a proper thing for a young lady to say," he answered disapprovingly. His smile weakened the half-hearted attempt at chastisement, though, and she kissed him again, completely ignoring his words. With a graceful swirl she turned and ran toward Tye.

"I don't care," she said gaily. He bent down, and a second later her lips, still cold from the outdoors, brushed Tye's cheek. "I'm not a proper young lady, anyway." She smiled into Tye's eyes. "Am I, Dad?"

Chapter 6

Cara stood in the center of Tye's office and waited for him.

She tried to resist the urge.

But it was too strong.

A second later, she stood beside his bookcase and stared at the covers. Studying their reading material was something she always did with the men she dated.

Of course, dating Tye was absolutely the last thing in the world she planned on doing. In fact, if she'd had any notion of doing something remotely like that, it had been dispelled when he'd sat down in her booth at the restaurant the other night. The casual meeting had been awkward and off-tone, and after he'd left the restaurant she'd quickly left, too. That didn't mean she couldn't look at his books, though, did it? It told her what kind of man she was dealing with, and God knew she needed all the help she could get. Tye had changed, and she no longer knew who he was ... if she ever had.

The young man she'd known—the ambitious, smart, but impulsive young man—had changed. He was a powerful force now, the CEO of a major corporation, and he hadn't gotten there by being impulsive.

Lifting one red-tipped finger, she trailed her hand over the titles. *Hunt for Red October. Winning in the Futures Market. Blood Brothers. Mercy.* She lifted her eyebrows at the final title—so he enjoyed off-beat fiction, too. The case was full of other titles, just as diverse. Apparently her standard test wasn't going to work with Tye—the collection presented too much inconsistency for her to make any sense of it.

But, of course, that said something, too.

Her finger continued over the books, then froze over the last one on the top shelf, its leather cover crushed and worn. She didn't need to read the title to know instantly what it was—*The Angeltonian,* his high school yearbook.

With a will of their own, Cara's fingers started to pull the book from the shelf. It had been wedged in so tightly it wouldn't budge, but finally the bookcase released its hold, and the yearbook tumbled out. She caught it just before it hit the floor. Two small pieces of paper evaded her fingers, however, and they fluttered down to rest on the rug.

Cara bent down to pick up the faded slips, and suddenly her heart tumbled just as they had. The ticket stubs were from a concert in Austin. It took absolutely no effort on her part to remember it, either. She'd lied to her mom and dad, Tye had picked her up at a friend's house, then they'd raced to a blues bar in Austin to see a new band called Triple Threat. The lead guitarist was a guy no one had ever heard of then—Stevie Ray Vaughn—but his music had been magic. Four hours later they'd raced home, and Cara had gotten in before her curfew... but just barely.

Just barely because they'd stopped at the roadside park outside of town and kissed until her lips were bruised and swollen.

Without thinking, Cara's fingers went to her mouth. God, how Tye could kiss! They'd sit in the back seat of that old Mustang, their arms wrapped around each other, and kiss for hours, absolutely hours. He'd start with her ears, nibbling on the lobes, slowly laving them with his tongue, then he'd go down her neck, dropping tiny bites. It would drive her crazy.

The tickets and the yearbook clutched in her hands, her legs unsteady from the memories, Cara rose from the floor. She stumbled to the leather couch against the wall and sat down heavily. As if Tye's hands were on it instead of Cara's, the book fell open to the page he apparently had looked at most frequently.

Still reeling from the idea that he'd even kept the tickets, Cara's hand went to her throat as it closed even tighter. The grainy black-and-white photo on the open page held more than images—it held her entire high school existence. It was a shot of Cara and Tye at a high school dance, with her friends from the staff of the yearbook where she'd worked as the ad manager. She stood directly in the center of the photo, with Tye to her right and her friends to her left.

At that point, Tye had been out of school for two years, and he hadn't wanted to go to any school functions. She'd begged and pleaded, though, and he'd given in, like he always did—for her.

Her eyes focused on Tye. The dark blue suit he wore hadn't fit exactly right, and he'd already loosened the knot of his tie before the photo had been snapped. His expression was slightly bored—very cool—but his eyes gave him away. He was looking at Cara, and even though fourteen years had passed, she could still see the love in their depths. Her frozen expression held a mirror image.

She blinked rapidly. Had they really been that young? That naive? That much in love?

Suddenly, the door to Tye's office opened, and he stepped in. She cursed silently, but there was nothing she could do. He'd caught her red-handed.

She rose from the couch as he crossed the room toward her, his blue eyes dropping from her face to her arms where she held the book protectively against her chest.

He stopped inches from her, his aura of power circling her like a magic ring. "Reviewing old times?"

She swallowed. "You're late."

He ignored her reprimand, choosing instead to reach out for the book she held, his fingers brushing her arm. Cara pretended not to notice, and he made no indication that the touch meant anything to him, either.

The book fell open to the same place. He stared at the photo for five seconds, then shut the book decisively and set it down on the sofa table.

His eyes raked over her blue silk dress, then his gaze turned dark. She hid her shiver.

"What were you looking for, Cara?" His voice was low... and thoughtful. "The key to the past?"

"No." She shook her head. "I was just thumbing through it...."

He lifted his hand to her face, but inches from the smooth plane of her cheek he stopped. If he touched her, he knew that he'd be closing a gap of fourteen years, and he wasn't sure he wanted to think about that breach much less bridge it. He couldn't seem to stop himself, though, and a second later, the silky warmth of his fingers caressed her skin.

There were some things the years never changed.

And this was definitely one of them.

As if it were much, much more, her body instantly responded to the simple touch, responded in a way that it never did to any other man, and she was shocked. The other night in the restaurant, when he'd taken her hand, she'd thought the electricity between them had been an aberration, a miscalculation of jangled nerves and upset plans. Now she knew differently because it was happening again. He cupped her cheek and rubbed his thumb over her bottom lip.

He looked as if he didn't want to stop with just a touch, and Cara's eyes went to his mouth. Suddenly, she didn't want him to stop, either. She wanted him to kiss her, she wanted to taste those lips, to cover that mouth, to bring back all the memories that haunted her and examine them in the light of day.

She stood perfectly still. For several long seconds, their eyes locked, and she let him read her acknowledgment. She knew exactly what she wanted him to do, and for the briefest of moments, she thought she saw a reciprocal need.

In the next moment, she knew she'd imagined it. He moved away and spoke as though the past few seconds had never occurred. "What can I do for you?" he said with a husky growl. "Peggy told me you needed something."

Cara took a deep breath and tried to slow her heart. "Yes," she answered shakily. "I came to ask for your help."

He went behind the desk and sat down, and she took one of the chairs in front of him. They were safe now—they had their barriers up again.

"My help?"

"Yes." She leaned forward and tried to organize her mind. "I want you to talk with Monty."

"About what?"

"About me staying here. I want you to tell him that's not necessary."

The flare of passion she imagined had turned into sober concern. "Why?"

"Why?" Exasperation tinged her voice. "I thought I explained that the other night in the restaurant. I can't stay in Angelton for four months, Tye. I have obligations, accounts, clients back in New York."

He tipped back in his chair and studied her. "Monty wants you to do the work."

"I know that," she said almost desperately. "But I can't abandon those responsibilities, and besides, I can handle his work better from my home office. You have influence with him. You could make him see why I can't stay here."

For a second he rocked back and forth in the leather chair, then slowly he let it come to a stop. "Is that really the reason?" He paused, and Cara felt her face turn tight with tension. "I think you can't stay here because you don't *want* to stay here."

"That's not true."

"Yes, it is," he said slowly. "You don't want to be here because *I'm* here."

She flushed, the heat of the truth rushing to her face. "That makes absolutely no difference to me, Tye. We're both professionals, we're both—"

"No, Cara." he said softly. Their eyes met, and he repeated his statement word for word. "You don't want to be here because *I'm* here."

"What difference does it make *why* I don't want to be here?" Her lips pursed into a thin line of anger, and she hated the brackets of disapproval she knew would be at the corners of her mouth. "I simply can't stay here, Tye, and I think if you talked to Monty you could get him to understand why. I can do the work in New York. I've done it that way a hundred times."

A curious expression crossed his face, and for a second, Cara would have sworn that he was about to agree to help her. But at the last moment, he shook his head, his dark blond hair brushing the collar of his shirt. "Monty wants you here. And if that's what Monty wants...then that's how it's going to be."

The air was clean and sharp, and when a blackbird cawed from all the way across the lake, Cara jumped. It sounded like he was right beside her.

It was a perfect day for fishing.

But she didn't have a rod and reel. All she had were high heels and frustrations.

She carefully stepped, in those high heels, down the almost deserted pier. Bear Lake had seemed like the only place to go when she'd left Tye's office. He wasn't going to help her, and he would do absolutely nothing to change Monty's mind. A second later she'd found herself out in the hall, and she'd stormed from the building.

Stopping at the end of the pier, Cara ignored the few fishermen and sat down on the wooden bench that had been there for twenty years. The dilapidated cover overhead let in as much sunshine as not, and it was easy to see no repairs had been done since she'd last been here. The longer she stayed in Angelton, the more she realized how very little it had changed.

Especially now, after that incident in Tye's office. She'd been able to ignore the brief connection in the restaurant, to tell herself it hadn't mattered, but she couldn't do that now. This second touch, as minor as it had been, had brought with it every yearning, every desire, every passion they'd ever shared. She'd wanted him to kiss her as much as she had fourteen years ago.

Nothing had changed—including her reactions to Tye.

Seeing him every day was painful enough, and her heart couldn't stand much more association with him. It pounded constantly. As much as her reactions to him frightened her, they were nothing compared to the trepidation she'd been unable to even acknowledge until now. If she had to stay in Angelton for months, though, she'd have to deal with this somehow, have some plan of action. And to do that, she had to admit to having feelings about the situation.

Admit to the reality of having a child out there somewhere.

For years, Cara had managed to tamp down any recognition of the child. She didn't look at children and wonder what hers would look like. She didn't pass by the baby clothing and stop to finger the tiny clothes. And she never, ever drove past a school during recess.

As she stared out at the unruffled water, a raw ache developed in the back of her throat. She'd hidden the memories so far down in the back of her mind that she thought they'd been forgotten. But they hadn't. All the hurt, all the agony, all the shame rushed back with an intensity that the years hadn't lessened one drop.

If it hadn't been for Uncle Jack, there was no telling what would have happened to Cara. After her parents had kicked her out, he'd found her a place to stay, made all the arrangements, even shopped for her when she couldn't get out. Even the hours-long drive to Dallas, to the home of his friends who had allowed her to stay in their spare bedroom, had meant nothing to him, and he'd made it once a week without complaint for months.

And what had she done?

Nagged him. From the moment he would appear until the moment he would leave, they would argue, her passionately, him softly. She wanted to keep the baby. He explained why she couldn't.

For months this went on, and now as Cara raised a hand to brush away the tears she thought about those times. She'd been so young, so foolish. She'd thought she could manage on her own, somehow getting a job, somehow finding someone to take care of the child. Jack had known better, of course. He'd realized how impossible it would have been. Even until the very end, though, he'd patiently listened to her teary debates, then explain again—once more—why it just wouldn't work out.

The reality had hit her only after his death. When she was truly alone.

Tye didn't love her, her parents had kicked her out and she was only seventeen. What in the world had made her think she could handle a baby, too?

Jack had told her nothing about the child or the family that had adopted it, and that's how she'd wanted it the day he'd come and taken the baby. She'd signed the papers he'd put before her, relinquishing her parental rights. Then bitter, angry and crushed with guilt and depression, she'd turned away and faced the wall, refusing his kiss of farewell. A part of her had died that day, a part that remained cold and dark and shut away. A few days later, she'd learned of Jack's death, and the little bit of heart—and hope—she'd had left died then, too. Racked with guilt over the way she and Jack had parted, and torn in two by grief over his death, she'd coped the only way possible—by pretending that the pregnancy, the child and her former life had simply not existed.

The lawyers had contacted her shortly after Jack's murder. He had left his meager assets to her, and she'd immediately started college. The years had been extremely lean, but she'd found a part-time job at a hardware store. She'd managed to eat *and* get a degree, although at times she'd thought she was going to have to choose between the two.

Since that time, she'd thought of Tye—in fact, felt haunted by him sometimes. Why had he stopped loving her? What had his life in prison been like? Who was he loving instead of her?

The one thing she'd never, *ever* allowed herself to think about was the baby.

To think about what might have been. To wonder who was holding the child she never would, who was taking it to the doctor, to the playground, to church. Through the years, she made it a point to never attend baby showers, to be out of town when friends were in the hospital with their newborns, to avoid all the toy departments in the shops. In restaurants, she'd sit away from tables with children, and on the subway, she'd avoid their eyes.

She'd managed to build an entire existence without children.

Until now.

Coming back to Angelton had opened a tear in her heart, and all the pain, all the distress, all the denial was beginning to seep through, like water from the cracks of a dam. She knew, without a doubt, that any day the dam would burst, too, and everything she'd worked so hard to hold back would come rushing through—and drown her.

If only she could share the burden with someone. Someone like Tye.

The idea caught Cara's breath and held it. Fourteen years ago secrecy had been the only way. Even if he'd wanted to, Tye couldn't have supported them, and he'd made it more than clear that he didn't love her.

That hadn't changed, so why should she tell him now?

She crossed her arms and stared out over the water. They were more mature, she argued silently, more prepared. It might be incredibly liberating to share that secret with him, to get it out in the open for once and for all.

As soon as she had the thought, however, she shook her head. No way. She had no earthly idea how he would react, and if she had to work with him, that knowledge would only heighten the tension between them. Telling him now would be a big mistake.

He'd start to ask all those questions, too—all those questions she'd managed to bury along with her feelings. Things like *Was it a boy or a girl? What did it look like? What do you think it's doing now? Who adopted it?*

No, telling Tye would only hurt them both, and Cara didn't want to deal with any more hurt. She'd had enough to last her more than a lifetime.

She rose from the bench and stepped to the railing that went around the pier, her eyes going to the calm water beneath her feet. Somehow, somewhere, she'd achieve that same kind of placidity. She'd done it before, and she would do it again.

Turning away, she started down the pier, and for the first time she noticed the small group of people at the other end. They weren't the same people, but they sure reminded her of the regulars who'd always been there, and for a few seconds Cara was instantly thrown back into the past. Even as a teenager she'd come here and fished, and the group of retired people who'd hung around the pier had made her a kind of apprentice, showing her their lures, how best to cast a line, how to net a fish.

Pausing for a second before starting back toward the shoreline, Cara watched as one of the group reeled in a catch. She couldn't see much—there were four older people standing around the successful angler, giving tips and encouragement, just like they had when she was a kid. Finally the line came in, and a fish flopped down on the old cracked boards. It wasn't very big, but then neither was the fisherman.

The group parted at the last minute, and Cara got a quick glimpse of a young girl. The teenager jumped up and down, a bright blue cap bobbing excitedly in the center of the old folks, and as Cara walked past, the successful fisherwoman looked up and smiled.

Cara wanted to die.

For the first time in her life, she gave in to the blindingly painful stab that told her this child could have been hers, and instantly, her heart cracked wide open. Even as she told herself she was being silly, her eyes met the teenager's. They were sapphire blue—just like Tye's.

Blindly Cara ran away, her own dark eyes swimming in unshed tears.

Cara arrived at the office bright and early the next morning, her step determined, her resolve strong. Monty had assigned her a temporary desk, and she went directly to it, not even stopping for coffee. She had made up her mind, and nothing could change it.

She was not staying in Angelton.

An hour later, she wanted to put her head down on her desk and cry.

Richard Lindsey had not only been adamant on the telephone, he'd been unsympathetic. None of her arguments had mattered, and it hadn't helped her case that Monty had already called Richard and hinted about giving Lindseys more work, "if only Cara could do it." Stay or get fired is what it had boiled down to, even though Richard had been too tactful to actually say the words. And for Cara, that wasn't a choice. She had bills, she had responsibilities, she had a mortgage, for God's sake.

She was stuck.

She had to do Monty's work, and she had to do it here.

Taking a deep breath, she removed a mirror from her purse, then checked her makeup and hair. Snapping the compact shut a second later, she moved toward the door, her gracious-defeat smile in place. The best she could hope for now was to do the work as efficiently as possible, avoid Tye at all costs, then get out of Dodge. Intent on what she was going to say to Monty, Cara opened her office door and hurried into the hall—and directly into Tye Benedict's arms.

The collision wasn't a big one, and with anyone else, Cara would have laughingly apologized and moved on.

But with Tye, that wasn't possible.

Instinctively, she reeled backward, and Tye reached out to steady her. Grabbing her arms just above her elbows, he wore an expression of surprise and then something that almost looked like pleasure. That clearly couldn't be the case, so Cara decided she must be wrong—it was probably a grimace from her stepping on his polished wingtips.

"I—I'm sorry," she finally managed to get out. "I was coming out of my office in such a big hurry that I just didn't see you. Are you—"

"I'm fine," he answered before she could finish the question. "But you look a little upset. Is anything wrong?"

For one insane moment, she thought about blurting out everything, but like a spell of dizziness, the urge swiftly passed, leaving her feeling oddly weak and disoriented. Tye was still holding her, his warm fingers pressing into the silk of her blouse, his face inches from hers. She could see the navy rings that surrounded the lighter blue of his eyes. She could see the tiny cut beside his lip where he'd nicked himself shaving. And she could even see his pulse as it throbbed in the veins under his tanned skin.

She blinked and looked lower, at the knot in his tie. That was a safe place for her eyes, right? What could be sexy or appealing about a tie? An alarming jolt of red blazed out at her, and Cara felt her heart leap into her throat. Even his tie somehow seemed to match the energy that always surrounded him. If *he* were a color, she realized with a start, he *would* be red. Fire-engine red. Sexy red. Red-hot.

Cara jumped back as if his touch *had* burned her, and instantly her face flamed. She was acting like a startled schoolgirl, for God's sake. What was wrong with her?

At Cara's movement, Tye's hands immediately dropped, but he didn't move an inch. She had nowhere to go except against the wall. She squeezed against it and tried hard not to look embarrassed.

"Are you okay?" he repeated.

"I'm fine," she answered, smoothing one hand down her skirt.

He looked as if he didn't believe her for a moment.

"I've been on the phone with my boss," she said. "He informed me that I'll be staying here to do the work, or I won't be working at all." She smiled grimly. "How's that kind of news to start off your day?"

He shrugged casually as if it didn't matter to him, but his handsome face tightened slightly, and his eyes cut toward his office. He clearly felt uncomfortable with her pronouncement, yet he'd refused to help her the other day. She didn't understand, but then the realization came to her that he probably felt just as distressed about this entire event as she did.

Finally he smiled, but it seemed forced. "There are worse places to be than Angelton, Cara. Believe me, I know, because I've lived there."

"And not all prisons have walls, Tye." She met his startled gaze. "Believe me, I know, because I've lived in one."

Before Tye could reply, Monty walked up, an uneasy tension stretching between Tye and Cara that even the older man's jovial attitude couldn't dissolve.

Cara realized with a start that he was addressing her. "...and we'd like you to come to dinner Friday evening. It won't be anything special—just a few friends from the office—nothing special..." Monty stopped and looked pointedly at Tye. "Of course, Tye will be there, won't you, Tye?"

Tye nodded with one swift motion, and Monty faced Cara again. "In the meantime, I want to go over your preliminary ideas. Come on into my office now." He took her elbow and started to lead her down the hall, but Cara couldn't resist. She shot one last look over her shoulder at Tye. He'd looked mildly uncomfortable, especially at Monty's invitation to dinner. Now that had changed. Tye didn't know she was looking at him, and in that one unguarded moment, he wore an expression she could describe with only one word.

Desperate.

*   *   *

The day didn't improve.

Late that afternoon, Cara found herself in Tye's office, a conversation taking place that was making her decidedly tense. She tried once more. "I think you'd be pleased with the darker colors if you'd just give them a chance. I know it's not what you're accustomed to, but once you live with them, you'll wonder why anyone would want beige walls again."

Cara spoke as she held up the paint samples in the brilliant light pouring through Tye's window. He was sitting behind her, staring at her, his expression so calm and collected, she wondered if she'd imagined his earlier distress.

His gaze made her nervous *and* ill at ease, and *that* made her angry. Why should he be able to turn her life upside-down like this? It wasn't fair. Hiding her thoughts, she looked over at him.

The bright fall day was reflected in his eyes, their blue color almost dazzling in the confines of the office. He looked like an executive who knew the rules, but didn't care if he broke them. Her mouth went dry.

He was just too damned handsome, she thought. If the years had given him a paunch or stolen some of his hair, or even etched a few wrinkles on his face, she might have been able to resist her growing feelings. As it was, age only became him. His body had become sturdier, more solid. His hair was even thicker. And the only wrinkles he'd gained were those attractive ones in the corners of his eyes that fanned out whenever he smiled. As he was doing right now.

"I don't know, Cara. That blue in your right hand—it looks kind of bright. Are you sure that wouldn't be too strong, too distracting?"

Of course it would be, she thought instantly. *It's the same color as your eyes.*

She mentally shook herself and looked down at the sample in her nervous fingers. "Blues are soothing," she answered automatically. "You'd get a lot of work done with this color on your walls."

He stood up and moved toward her, his long legs covering the short distance in two steps. "I don't know," he murmured, looking down into her eyes. "I find it rather distracting myself."

His voice made it clear that he wasn't discussing paint, but she ignored the implication. "Then maybe something with a touch more gray." She fumbled with the paint chips and finally found the one she was looking for. "What do you think of this? Do you feel more comfortable with it?"

"Is comfortable what I want to feel?"

Their eyes locked in the inches that separated them, Cara's stomach clenching at the expression in his dark blue depths. "I...I think so," she answered slowly. "That's what most people strive for."

"Do *you?*"

In the silence, she was sure he could hear her beating heart. It seemed thunderous to her. "We're not here to discuss me. We're here to select *your* paint color."

"That's true," he said evenly, "but I'm trying to understand the concept here. If you're my designer, and you're telling me blue is a comfortable color, I want to know why. That's the only way I can proceed."

She resisted the urge to step back, to pull away, because that would signal to him exactly what she didn't want him to know—that his very closeness was almost making her dizzy. "Blues are relaxing," she said. "They're supposed to be comforting and calming. That's one of the reasons people like water. The color of it is usually pleasing to the eye."

"I see." He reached down between them and took the small deck of paint chips from her trembling fingers. If he noticed her nervousness, he didn't comment on it. "So you're saying that colors influence our emotions."

"Absolutely."

"Then if I wanted to feel happy and upbeat..."

"You might try yellow."

"Depressed?"

"Brown."

"Sexy?"

Without thinking, her eyes went to his tie. "Red."

His own stare immediately raked over her scarlet suit, and Cara felt the heat rise from her neck and spread over her face. "Red, huh?" He grinned slowly and held up a crimson paint chip, first to his tie, next to her collar. "About *this* shade, do you think?"

Cara reached up and grabbed the samples, her fingers brushing over his. "I think we've done enough work for today," she sputtered. "I'll come back later."

The rest of the week passed in a blur for Cara, and before she knew it, it was Friday evening. She stood before the mirror in her hotel room and ripped off the scarf she'd just tied around her neck.

The knot had been perfect, but it didn't look right, and neither did she. She'd changed clothes three times, and she still wasn't satisfied. The dress had looked too formal, the slacks had seemed too casual, and the jeans had instantly been out of the question. With every outfit, she'd had to think about color, too. Heaven forbid she select anything red. Thirty minutes ago, she'd finally settled on a pink raw silk jumpsuit, but now it was beginning to seem too... too... too something that she couldn't put her finger on.

She snapped the belt up off the bed and whipped it around her waist, her fingernails clicking against the brass buckle. She looked fine. Why was she so worried? It was a simple dinner, that's what Monty had said, with just a few people from the office. They'd eat a little, drink a little, talk a little, then she'd be back at the hotel before the ten o'clock news came on.

The fact that Tye was picking her up had absolutely *nothing* to do with her nervousness. Nothing at all. Nothing.

The phone beside her bed jangled to life, and Cara dashed to answer it, her pulse jumping. Tye's deep voice echoed down the line. "I'm in the lobby. Are you ready?"

She felt her eyes widen. "You're half an hour early."

"I know." He paused. "I thought we'd have a drink in the bar first...if you'd like."

Cara opened her mouth to lie—to say no, that she wasn't dressed yet, to say anything so she wouldn't have to go down there and sit across a small table in a smoky room and look into those eyes. But something completely different came out of her mouth.

"Yes, I'd like that. I'll be right there."

Horrified with herself, Cara banged the phone down and put her hand over her mouth. What had she done? Had she lost her mind? For an instant, she thought about calling him back, but it was too late, and without giving herself more time to think, she grabbed her purse and left. Besides, she didn't want Tye Benedict to think she was a coward.

Even if she was.

He was sitting in a dark corner of the lobby bar, a bowl of peanuts in front of him, a frosted mug beside the bowl. He stood when she walked up.

His dark blue eyes swept over her like an ocean's wave, and when they came back to her face, Cara read the obvious approval. It sent a strange tingle of anticipation down her back, a strangely *familiar* tingle.

"I couldn't decide what to wear," she said awkwardly. "Is this okay?"

"It's more than okay. It's perfect." He smiled then and reached over to brush a kiss across her cheek.

It wasn't much of a kiss, but it wasn't the handshake she'd been expecting, either. When he pulled back, his cologne lingered. She smiled in return without thinking—he still wore the same scent after all those years. Someone besides her was nostalgic, too, it seemed.

By the time she'd slid into the small chair opposite the banquette where he'd been sitting and given the waitress her order, Cara's pulse had almost returned to normal. Almost.

It jumped again when Tye spoke. "You need to do that more often," he said.

"Do what?"

"Smile like you just did. It makes you look like you're about sixteen."

"Sixteen?" she said, reaching for the peanuts with fingers that wanted to tremble. "I don't really think I'd want to be sixteen again."

He met her eyes for just a moment, then stretched toward his beer, the short sleeves of his knit shirt moving up to reveal a very prominent tan line. She'd been right—he *had* been spending some time in the sun—and whatever he'd been doing in it required muscles, too. His biceps looked as hard as the marble-topped table between them.

She must have been too obvious. He glanced down at his arm, then grimaced. "Went out on the boat a few weeks ago and made the mistake of wearing a shirt. Gave me a weird tan, huh?"

She realized immediately that Tye *had* been the man she'd seen that first day back in Angelton. For some reason, though, she kept that knowledge to herself. "What kind of boat do you have?"

"She's not mine, really. She's Monty's, but he hasn't been able to go out lately, and I've been using her. She's a sixty-foot cruiser—almost a yacht, actually." He took a sip of his beer. "I've been looking at buying one of my own, though. Something a little less station-wagonish and more Porsche, if you know what I mean."

"Like a cigarette boat?"

He laughed then, a deep, very male laugh that made the cocktail waitresses turn around and smile in appreciation. She then looked at Cara as if to see who could be amusing such a devastatingly handsome man so much. Cara sat up a little taller.

"No," he finally answered. "That's a little too much power, even for me. I was thinking more about something in between the two—something with a cabin that you'd be comfortable in over a long trip but still a little smaller than Monty's. I just don't need that much room.'' He took another sip of beer. ''Kit, of course, wants something fast....''

For some unknown reason, his words and smile slowly faded, and Cara got the distinct impression that for a moment, Tye had relaxed and forgotten who he was with. She wondered if that was the kind of man he was around women he dated—a man who laughed easily, who enjoyed unbending with a beer, who relished his time away from work—and then it hit her.

Who was Kit?

Was she the woman who made him laugh like that?

Chapter 7

"**W**ho's Kit?"

For years, Tye had dreading hearing those words from those lips. A thousand times he'd thought about Cara asking that very question, and a thousand times he'd come up with different answers.

The time had come to tell her the truth.

But as he opened his mouth to explain, Tye realized he couldn't tell her—not yet. He was too scared. "Kit's not the reason I came by this evening," he said smoothly. "I wanted to prepare you for someone else."

For a minute, Cara looked like she wanted to challenge him, to ask why he'd so pointedly ignored her question, but she didn't. Instead, she said, "Prepare me? Prepare me for what?"

"For Jerilyn—Monty's wife. She's in and out of the hospital a lot and, well, to be brutally honest, Jerilyn is dying. I thought you should know before you went to their house."

"Oh, no." Cara set her drink down on the small table between them. "I'm so sorry."

"Yes. It's tragic. She's been ill for about two years."

Cara's hand came up to her throat. "How horrible."

"It's one of the reasons I think Monty wants you here." *Tell a little truth, tell a little lie.* "Jerilyn loved your work so much in New York that she'd been bugging him for months to send for you. I think he finally called your company because he knew she didn't have much longer."

"I see." The words were spoken so softly they were more of a whisper than anything else.

"They don't have any children," Tye continued, "and they've always been extremely close. When Jerilyn goes, Monty's going to be lost."

Cara looked down into her drink. "How long have they been married?"

"Over forty years."

"My God, that's remarkable. I can't imagine anyone living with one person for that long." She sipped her wine, then met his gaze. "Can you?"

"Sure. If the right person came along."

"Do you really think there's anyone that right?"

Yes, he thought instantly, *there was—and I pushed her away.* He glanced out the window beside Cara's chair. "I read a myth once," he said. "Greek—Roman—I don't remember. The details are fuzzy, but it basically said that everyone is really one-half of a whole, and when you find your other half—your *real* other half—then you fall in love, and it's forever." He let his eyes return to Cara's face. "I hope my other half is out there somewhere."

Her face paled slightly, then she smiled. "For your sake, then, I hope so, too."

Cara wasn't ready.

She glanced across the leather seat to stare at Tye's profile, and her heart automatically accelerated. She simply wasn't prepared for the maelstrom of emotions now raging through her. She wanted, simultaneously, to be in Tye's arms and as far away from him as possible. She wanted answers to all her questions but she didn't want to ask. And most of all, she wanted to know his real feelings toward her, but she was terrified of the possibilities. Was she his "other half"?

One question reached above all those desires, though.

Who was Kit?

Kit—the woman he didn't want to discuss.

He swung the big Mercedes up to a set of motorized gates, and they opened silently as the car apparently triggered an automatic switch somewhere.

Cara put aside the question of the other woman when Monty's house came into view. It was enormous, and it reminded Cara instantly of the older man. It looked solid and dependable and sturdy, and Cara couldn't help but acknowledge that she liked Monty even though he was keeping her in a place where she didn't want to be.

Tye stopped the car, threw the gearshift into park, then turned and looked at her. "This is it." He switched off the engine, and sudden silence enveloped them. "I don't know what Monty's going to do here after Jerilyn's gone. He'll roam around in that huge old house like a ghost." He shook his head. "He ought to move in with me."

Cara turned to look at Tye. "You wouldn't mind?"

"I'd love it. He acts like my father already, so living with me would be the next logical step. In fact, he could do anything he wanted—he's given so much to me that I could never repay him."

"I doubt that he would want you to."

He shrugged his broad shoulders, and his shirt whispered against the leather upholstery. "You're probably right. When Jack found him and brought us together, though, I bet he never thought it'd end up this way." He looked over at her in the darkness. "I was grateful just to have someone on my side for a change, but for Monty, that wasn't enough."

"He made you the CEO?"

Tye laughed. "It wasn't exactly that easy. I worked my way up, believe me. When he got ready to split the company, I was in a position where I could help him and he could help me. It just worked out."

"But you really hit it off together."

"Yes." Tye hesitated for a moment, as if trying to make up his mind about something, then he spoke. "He *is* the father I never had."

"It must be nice to have someone care that much for you."

He shrugged his shoulders again. "It's like any family... it's good until they interfere, and then..."

Something about his tone alerted her, and she couldn't help but stare at him. "And then you wish they wouldn't?"

His eyes met hers. "No—then you deal with whatever they've done." He turned and draped his arm over the back of her seat. It was a strangely intimate gesture, and it evoked way too many memories. Suddenly anxious to escape the confines of the car, Cara moved to put her hand on the door handle, but Tye's voice stopped her.

"Cara, I think we need to talk about something before we go in."

His voice was strong and forceful, without a bit of hesitancy. She swallowed, the thudding beat of her heart taking a sudden jump. "What is it?"

His hand dropped to her shoulder. "I know you didn't want to come to Angelton, and I know you don't want to stay. Despite our conversation in the office the other day, I feel responsible for that."

"It *is* awkward," she answered. "There's... a lot between us."

He nodded solemnly. "Yes, there is, but it's in the past, and I want you to know that I understand that."

A frisson of disappointment, a feeling she couldn't explain and didn't want to understand, skittered down her back. "That's right," she said calmly. "It's history."

He lifted his hand from her shoulder and eased the back of one finger along her cheek. A very soft rain had begun to fall, and the silence it brought with it seemed to wrap around the car and insulate them from the rest of the world. "It was a very long time ago," he said.

She didn't move. The heat of his touch radiated through her jawline, then straight into her heart. "A long time ago," she echoed.

His knuckle caressed the line of her jaw. "We were just teenagers."

"I was seventeen, you were nineteen."

He finally reached her chin and, taking it between his finger and his thumb, he gently grasped it and turned her until their eyes met. "We're adults now and there's absolutely nothing between us. We can face that. Right?"

She nodded without a word.

In the dim shadows, his eyes lost their sapphire color and turned black, black with desire. They were mirrors, she knew, of her own. His hand left her chin and cupped her jaw. A second later, his right hand warmed the other side of her face, cradling it like a fragile vase. She closed her eyes.

Then her world exploded.

A shockwave of desire raced outward from the point where their lips met and reverberated all the way down to her toes, leaving ripples of heat in its path. She felt nothing, heard nothing, tasted nothing—but Tye, and in one single instant, her entire existence narrowed to that one point of contact.

If anyone had ever told Cara that a mere kiss could produce such sensations, she would have laughed at them.

But this was no laughing matter.

This was serious. Real serious.

Under his pressing lips, Cara's mouth parted, and she couldn't hold back the moan that automatically came from deep within her chest. His hands tightened momentarily on either side of her face, then he slid his right one beneath her hair on the nape of her neck. She moved closer and, without thinking, let her arms come out from between them and twist around his neck.

His lips were harder now than they'd been years ago, harder and more demanding, but as she absorbed their insistence, she realized that it wasn't a physical change—it was mental, and all on her part. Years ago, when they'd made love, the experience had been a riot of sensations, all of them new and amazing. Now she understood what was behind the kiss, understood it in a way she'd been unable to at seventeen.

Understood *exactly* what it meant.

For a few seconds longer, the kiss connected them, then slowly, gently, Tye pulled away, his hands still wrapped in her hair. In the spotted light, his eyes met hers, and they looked almost as dazed as she felt.

Her lipstick had left a red smudge across his mouth, and she knew there was no way she could repair the damage to her hair before they went inside. These were trivial points, but they ran through her mind so she wouldn't have to think about what had really happened. They reminded her of the things she'd always had to watch for when she'd returned home after a date with Tye.

She put her hands against his chest, and under her trembling fingers, she could feel his warmth. "Tye...this doesn't mean anything exists between us now. It was...was just an echo from the past, that's all."

"It was a mighty powerful echo."

"Maybe so," she answered, "but all in all, I think we'd better forget it. We're adults, like you said, and it's time we put our teenage infatuation behind us."

His fingers tightened on the nape of her neck. "Right," he said in a husky voice. "You're absolutely right. So why do I have this unbelievably strong urge to kiss you again?"

Monty closed the door behind them and clucked over the weather as Cara and Tye stepped into the marble entry. Taking their coats, he led them into the study. "We'll have drinks in here first. Jerilyn said she might join us for a nip."

Tye watched Cara as she entered the comfortable room. When he'd first seen it, it'd reminded him of Phillip Howard's study. Tye wondered if Cara would make the connection, too.

If the room reminded her of her father's, Cara didn't show it. As Monty took their drink orders and fixed their cocktails, she moved toward the fireplace and its graceful mantel. She ran her fingers over the wood. "This is gorgeous," she said, smiling at Monty. "Is it original to the house?"

Monty shrugged as he brought her the wine she'd requested. "Have absolutely no idea, darling. Don't know a thing about it." He handed Tye a bottle of beer and spoke again. "That's why I hired you. I don't know a damned thing about decorating."

"That's not true, and you know it, Marshall Montgomery."

Monty and Cara turned at the voice from the doorway, but Tye stood still. He wanted to watch Cara's reaction to Jerilyn.

He was amply rewarded. Cara's eyes widened into ovals of surprise, then recognition. They darted to Tye's face as if to ask why he hadn't told her, but he merely smiled and stayed quiet.

"You're Jerilyn Montgomery?"

"The one and only, darling." Jerilyn didn't just enter the room—she *made* an entrance. Monty met her halfway, and only Tye noticed the way she gratefully leaned on his arm. "Don't tell me you actually recognize me?"

"Well, of course I do," Cara said. "I saw you on Broadway." She turned back to Tye. "I had no idea.... You should have told me."

"He couldn't," Jerilyn said, sinking into the couch. She touched Monty's hand in a subtle acknowledgement of thankfulness, then faced Cara. "I've absolutely forbidden anyone to discuss my ancient acting career, and that's why I gave up my stage name when we moved to Angelton." She waved Monty toward the bar. "Bring me a white wine, darling."

Monty turned to do exactly what she told him to, but not before giving Tye a significant look that said *See? I told you this would be good for her.* Cara didn't know it, of course, but this was the first time Jerilyn had been out of bed for almost a month. She was truly determined, Tye realized at that point, to see this thing through.

And after that kiss in the car, he might be ready, too—if it weren't for Kit.

Cara sat down beside Jerilyn on the sofa, and Tye wandered over to the window. Everyone who met Jerilyn was fascinated by her, and he wanted to give Cara the time to get to know the older woman before some of the other guests arrived. Most likely, she'd go up to her room at that point, anyway. She'd confessed to him a few months ago that she was still vain enough not to want to be seen when she wasn't at her best.

But even Jerilyn's worst was better than most people's best, Tye thought as he turned around and watched the two women visit. She was a vibrant, generous person, and when he'd first come to Angelton and met her and Monty, Tye had been bowled over by her kindness and loving concern toward him. At first, he'd thought it was an act, but later he'd realized she truly was a gentle woman. He'd loved her ever since.

And she loved him. As she spoke to Cara, Jerilyn looked over and caught his eye. Her nod was imperceptible, but her expression was more than clear. *I did the right thing by bringing her here,* she silently told him. *Now you do the right thing by her.*

With a quick lift of his mouth, Tye turned away.

A minute later, the doorbell rang, and Monty sent him out into the entryway. For half an hour after that, Tye was kept busy, answering the door, helping with coats and getting everyone drinks along with Monty. By the time Tye was able to get back into the room, Jerilyn had already gone upstairs. And in a way, he was relieved. He didn't want to hear what he knew she'd have to say about Cara.

He knew all her good points already and was fast becoming more and more familiar with them all.

From across the room, she caught his eye and he interpreted her slightly desperate look. Almost fifty people now crowded the room—all Marshall executives—and Tye realized that she hadn't been prepared for Monty's "little" dinner. Monty had invited everyone in the company, and they, in turn, had already begun to tell Cara exactly how they wanted their offices done.

She needed a break.

Tye appeared beside her. "If you'll come to the bar with me, I'll frown and start talking fast."

Her lashes curled up as she raised her eyes. "And what will that do for me?"

"It'll keep everyone away—they'll think I'm telling you how I want *my* office decorated . . . and after all, I am the CEO. I *do* get first pick."

"Sounds reasonable to me," Cara said in a grateful voice.

Seconds later, they stood by themselves in a circle of quiet, Cara sipping a fresh glass of wine and Tye practicing his frown. He'd been teasing, but it was actually working. No one had come near them.

Cara pushed her bangs away from her face in a motion so well-known it made Tye's heart stop. "I thought Monty said just a few executives. This must be half the company."

"I figured it'd be this way," Tye said with sympathy. "Monty gets carried away sometimes. I don't know if he was always like that or if part of it's Jerilyn's influence."

Cara turned. "I was so surprised when she walked into the room. I couldn't believe it. You really should have told me."

Tye shrugged and eyed the crowded room. "Actually, I forget it half the time. I never saw her act, so it seems removed for me."

"Well, it wasn't for me. She was absolutely stunning on stage. So beautiful, so poised. She dropped out of sight for a while, didn't she? Then returned a bit later?"

"Yes, she did, but she finally got tired of traveling and quit for good about nine years ago." Kit had been five years old when Jerilyn retired for good. The girl had needed a real mother, or at least a damned good substitute, Jerilyn had said, then had automatically reinstalled herself in the position she'd had when Kit was just a baby. He'd realized later

Jerilyn had been searching for an excuse to end her career. She loved Angelton and loved Monty. The time they'd spent apart had been torture for her, she'd told Tye many years later.

Cara nodded at his answer, then stared off, obviously lost in remembrances of Jerilyn on stage. "It's too bad you never saw her," Cara said in a dreamy voice. "I'll never forget her in *Macbeth*."

Tye reacted automatically—a small jerk backward—then recovered quickly, brushing at the drink that had sloshed on his arm. *Macbeth* was the one play he *had* seen Jerilyn do, but he couldn't tell Cara that.

Because he'd been in New York specifically to see Cara.

Knowing where she'd worked, he'd actually followed her home one snowy evening in December. He'd told himself for years that he hadn't been sure why he'd gone to New York and had absolutely no idea what he'd been going to say to her when he did finally connect with her, but now he had to admit the truth to himself. He couldn't ignore it with her standing beside him, her perfume rising in the warmth of Monty's fireplace, her hair curling so close it brushed Tye's shoulder.

He'd wanted her—and nothing more.

But when her cab had let her out in front of a multi-storied, obviously expensive apartment building, a well-dressed man, tall and blond, had hungrily gathered her into his arms and kissed her.

And she'd kissed him back.

So Tye had turned away and walked off into the snow.

Now he wondered what would have happened if he'd stayed. A second later, however, he had something else entirely on his mind.

A commotion by the door heralded a new arrival, and Tye needed only a glimpse of blue hat to send his heart tumbling wildly to Monty's Persian rug. *Oh, God—what in the world was she doing here? She was supposed to be at a friend's house all weekend long.*

The copper taste of fear turned heavy on his tongue as he looked quickly toward Cara. There had to be some way to get her out of Monty's living room, some excuse he could think of to remove her before the inevitable happened. He wasn't ready. He didn't know what to say. He couldn't yet explain it all.

Panic gripped him like a strangler's hands, and he found himself stuttering, unable to speak. Like everyone else in the room, Cara had turned to see what the noise was all about, then the room parted and Kit flew toward him.

As she ran across the room, Tye willed her to keep quiet, knowing it was hopeless even as he prayed. She always said whatever was on her mind, regardless of who could hear. And she did just that right now as she skidded to a stop in front of him and Cara, her inquisitive gaze going back and forth between them before she smiled broadly. "Wow!" Her grin spread even more. "For once you're with the best-looking woman in the room! Way to go, Dad."

Chapter 8

Cara heard the word *Dad*, she saw the teenager, and she looked at Tye.

But she didn't understand. It was as if the young girl were speaking a foreign language, and Cara had absolutely no idea what she was saying.

Cara watched as Tye turned, almost in slow motion, and stared at the girl. "Kit! What are you doing here? I thought you were staying with Brittany." His voice was tight with anger, tight and thick. It reminded Cara of the time he'd told her he didn't love her anymore, and she jerked her eyes to his face.

For a moment, all she could do was study him. He was angry, yes, but there was another emotion building behind those midnight-blue eyes, and Cara's brain almost refused to accept it.

Tye was scared.

He shifted his eyes from the teenager to Cara, then quickly back to the girl again. "What happened, Kit?" he repeated.

Cara let her own gaze return to the girl, and she had to admit that her first reaction was relief. This was Kit. She wasn't some mysterious, beautiful woman who loved Tye as Cara once had—she was just a teenager. In the next instant, though, like a ship going down at sea, Cara felt her world slowly sinking into deep waters. A teenager who had called Tye "Dad."

She didn't understand.

"Brittany... got sick. Her mom said it might be best if I came back a different night." Obviously sensing disapproval, Kit flashed Tye an uncertain look. "I stopped by here first just to let you know what was going on. I'm going to stay at Mindy's instead of Brittany's. Is that okay?"

Tye's face cleared as though he realized how he'd sounded. "Sure, sweetheart, that's fine. But maybe it'd be better for you to go now. This is a business event."

The young girl nodded once, then turned toward Cara. "Sorry I interrupted," the girl said with a sweet smile. She stuck out her hand in a very grown-up fashion. "I'm Kit Benedict. Who are you?"

"Cara Howard," Cara answered automatically. "It's nice to meet you." Her heart pounded inside her chest as she took Kit's hand in hers. *This really was Tye's daughter. Now she could see the resemblance—the blue eyes, the slightly long nose, the high cheekbones.* There was something else familiar about her, something Cara couldn't quite put her finger on, then she realized what it was. This was the young girl Cara had seen fishing down at the pier.

"Why don't you go out to the kitchen and ask one of Maria's daughters to run you over to Mindy's?" Tye said, his voice like a coiled spring. "They wouldn't mind."

"Oh, Dad, can't I walk? It's stopped raining and it's not that far, and..."

Tye looked as if he wanted to refuse but couldn't. In fact, Cara thought suddenly, he looked as if he *rarely* refused Kit.

"Come on, Dad." Kit wrinkled her nose, then looked at Cara and blinked in a conspiratorial gesture. "I'm old enough to walk three blocks in the dark, but he still thinks I'm five instead of fourteen.''

"All right," Tye finally conceded, "but call me when you get there."

Kit whooped, then reached up and kissed Tye's cheek. After telling Cara goodbye, she skipped from the room.

Cara watched, but nothing registered. Nothing except that one important word. *Fourteen. Kit was fourteen years old.*

All Cara could think about was the time Tye had made her jump from his car when she was pregnant. She'd looked out the open door for two seconds before she'd leapt, and in that instant she'd seen more than she wanted. The speeding blacktop streaking beneath the tires, the white line blurring into oblivion, the sharp pebbles cutting her before she even jumped.

Cara felt like that right now.

She was teetering on the edge. Peering into the blackness. Seeing but not believing.

For a moment, she thought she was reliving that nightmare as the sound of breaking glass reached her ears. Only when Tye exclaimed did she realize she'd snapped the stem of her wineglass. With a disconnected gaze, she looked down at her hand. A thin jagged line of red welled up along her thumb.

Tye was there instantly, holding her hand and dabbing at it with a snowy white handkerchief. "Are you okay?" Worry darkened his eyes and lines of anxiety creased his forehead.

Cara was so numb she didn't even feel the cut. All of her pain was internal. With each word she spoke, a piece of her heart broke away. "Kit is fourteen years old? Fourteen?"

Tye pulled his eyes away from her hand and looked at her. Again, Cara had the feeling of total disorder—chaos but in slow motion. "Yes," he said slowly. "Kit is fourteen years old."

Cara had never fainted in her entire life, but suddenly she thought she might. She closed her eyes against the spinning room, against Tye's revelation, against the incredible pain that was building to a crescendo inside her chest. But none of it would go away. In fact, it got even worse.

A rush of hot, searing agony came over her that had nothing to do with the minor cut on her hand, and automatically, she clutched at Tye's hand to try and steady herself. He took a deep breath, and unconsciously Cara mimicked him. Something told her she'd need extra oxygen, extra adrenaline, extra something to hear the words she knew were coming next.

His fingers tightened painfully on hers. Vaguely Cara realized her blood had now stained through the handkerchief and onto Tye's hand. She couldn't move, couldn't think, couldn't control anything—including the agony cutting through her. Agony so painful she could only remember feeling that way once before—when a nurse had walked out of an anonymous hospital room carrying a piece of Cara's heart with her.

A piece that Tye had now.

Cara spoke, but she didn't even recognize her own voice. It seemed to come from someone other than her, from a person who couldn't feel, couldn't touch, couldn't hear. "And is she your daughter?" she said.

His face seemed to crumple with emotion, and his eyes blinked rapidly. When he spoke, the words were crystalline, each one of them breaking against Cara's wall of denial, shattering it one single point at a time. The clarity was painfully sharp.

"Yes," Tye answered. "She's my daughter. And yours."

Through the years Tye had often wished for the little Mustang he'd had when he and Cara had dated. He'd never owned a car since that could take the corners like that one.

And he wished for it right now—wished desperately.

Monty's Cadillac hugged the road, but Tye was pushing it too hard, and he knew it. Another five miles per hour and the car would be out of control on the slick pavement.

Out of control—just like he was.

He couldn't get the image of Cara's face out of his mind. She'd looked at him numbly, her eyes almost blank with shock. Then, very slowly, very deliberately, she'd dropped his hand and walked away. Walked into the entryway of Monty's home, picked up the car keys that Tye had left with his coat on the couch, and gone outside. A second later, he'd heard the smooth purr of his Mercedes start up. And drive away.

Tye hadn't meant to follow her. He'd been numb, too, numb with dread and fear, and he hadn't known what to do. Was it best to let her go? She'd obviously wanted to be by herself. Or should he have instantly run outside and jumped into the car with her? She'd been so incredibly shocked it probably wasn't a good idea for her to be driving.

That last thought had sent him straight to Monty. "Is she okay?" the older man had asked. "Should I—"

"I'll handle it," Tye had shot back. "This is *my* responsibility. Just give me the keys to your car."

A second later Tye had jumped in Monty's car and flown out the driveway.

He'd raced to the hotel, but she wasn't there.

He'd sped to her old house, but she wasn't there, either.

He'd even gone to the park outside of town, but it had been empty, too.

There was only one other place Cara might flee to, and if she wasn't there, Tye had no idea where she might be. And not knowing where she was scared him more than anything, because he realized suddenly that if he couldn't find her, if she'd left for good, he wouldn't be able to live.

Monty's Cadillac left the pavement and bounced along the rutted road, the steep incline giving less traction to the tires. The rain had started again, the gentle fall drizzle turning the lake road into more of a hazard than usual. Tye felt his stomach knot—his car was powerful and big, and if Cara wasn't accustomed to driving something like it and she *had* come here, it could be dangerous.

A second later, his headlights picked up the ghostly white of the dock.

She wasn't there.

Tye cursed soundly and hit the heel of his hand against the steering wheel. *Where in God's name could she be?*

The road was too narrow to allow a turn, so all he could do was keep going toward the pier then swing the car around in the area where the boats docked. Easing up on the brake, Tye allowed the Cadillac to continue down the steep incline. The back tires skittered once, then twice, in the rain-slicked mud. His hands tight with anxiety, Tye turned into the parking lot.

And his headlights picked out the outline of the Mercedes. She'd parked the car close to the road, and he hadn't been able to see it from above.

His eyes swept the blacktopped area, but he saw nothing, and his misgivings increased. *She had to be around here somewhere, but where?* With his heart in his throat, he guided the car right up to the pier and switched the lights to high, the windshield wipers swishing the rain away, but not his concern.

That's when he saw her.

She was at the very end of the pier, sitting down on one of the covered benches. She didn't turn around as the lights hit her.

A sweet rush of relief hit him, and Tye threw the car into park. A second later he was bounding down the pier, but when he reached her side, she didn't bother to look up. Even when he spoke. "Cara?"

She didn't answer. She didn't move. She just sat there.

The rain was coming down in sheets now, and the pitiful overhead covering did little to keep the water out. Tye took off the coat he'd thrown on when he'd dashed out Monty's door, and put it over Cara's shoulders. She didn't acknowledge him.

He sat down beside her and stared at her profile. He wanted to tell her what was in his heart, but he didn't know what was there himself anymore—and he hadn't for years. It was a stranger's heart and a stranger's soul—his own had died the day he'd told her he didn't love her anymore.

Until Kit had come into his life.

She'd revived a part of him that he'd thought had died, and now all he could think about was losing *her* again, too.

The rain continued to pour. "Cara," he started again. "I...I'm sorry you had to learn about Kit this way. It wasn't how I'd planned on telling you."

She never looked away from the steel-gray water of the lake. It was dimpled from the pounding rain, and it looked cold and deep to Tye—as deep, in fact, as the hole that was beginning to form within his heart. He reached out and put his hand over hers. She still had his handkerchief wrapped around her thumb, but that wasn't what bothered him— what scared him was how cold she was. Touching her skin was like touching an iceberg. She must have been sitting here since she'd left Monty's, over an hour ago. The partial roof had protected her somewhat, but not enough.

"Let's go back to my house," he said gently. "You can get out of those wet clothes, and I'll...explain everything to you." He paused, then pressed on, almost desperate. "Please, Cara. You're going to catch a cold."

She turned around and looked at him then, her eyes two dark coals against the whiteness of her face. He felt the color leave his own face as her gaze seared him. "You care about me getting a cold when you've been living a lie for fourteen years?" She laughed hollowly, her voice tinged with hysteria. "That's rich, Tye. Really rich."

"I can explain."

"I'm sure you can," she said almost pleasantly. "I'm sure you have a perfectly reasonable explanation for everything. You always did when you were a teenager." Her eyes were hollow when they met his. "You could talk me into any-thing, remember?"

Her gaze left his face and went back to the lake. It was almost as if she were mesmerized by the water—pulled to it, in fact—and a sudden awful question popped into Tye's mind. *What would she have done if he hadn't gotten there?* He refused to let himself consider the possibilities. Instead, he took her cold, cold hands into his and tried to rub some warmth into them. "Then let me talk you into coming home with me right now. We can talk."

"Talk? At your home?" She blinked and turned her head to face him. Water trailed down her cheeks, and Tye couldn't tell if it was rain or tears. "Why would I want to go there?" Her voice broke. "Do you want to show me her baby pictures? Let me see where she grew up? Hold the stuffed animals that she slept with? Why would you want to torture me like that, Tye?"

Her pain was a savage animal, and it had obviously ripped her wide open. Tye didn't know what to do—he only knew he had to get her out of the rain. He seemed to concentrate on that so he wouldn't have to think about the real issue. "I'm not trying to torture you, Cara. I only want to get you somewhere dry and warm. I don't want you sick." He looked up at the sky. The wind had picked up and now it was howling around the pine trees and whipping them into a frenzy—just like the one inside his heart. He stood and tried to pull her up with him. "Please, sweetheart. Please. Just come with me."

"Don't call me sweetheart." She rose, ripping her hands away from him, her hair plastered against her head, her wet clothing outlining every curve he'd once known so well. "I'm not your sweetheart—you don't love me anymore, remember? You stopped loving me—fourteen years ago."

He jumped to his feet. "I was lying," he said desperately. "I *did* love you, but I didn't want you to wait for me, to waste your time while I was in jail." He took two steps toward her. "I was lying."

She took two steps backward. "You're pretty good at that, aren't you?" He hadn't thought it possible, but her face turned even whiter. "In fact, I bet you're so good at it now that you don't even know the difference between a lie and the truth."

"I *am* telling you the truth."

"Are you sure?" she said mockingly, her hands going into fists at her side. "You said you were telling me the truth back then, too. Do you remember? I *begged* you to talk to me, and you told me to go away. Told me that I was a child." Her eyes narrowed dangerously. "I *wasn't* a child, though. I was a woman—and I was carrying *your* child."

Lightning struck across the lake, and the thunder that rolled afterward set Tye's guilt loose. "I didn't know, dammit. If you'd only told me, things might have been different." He raised his hands and ran his fingers through his hair, combing the wet strands away from his face. Water clung to his eyelashes, making it difficult to see. It didn't matter, though. Suddenly nothing mattered. Nothing but Cara. "If you'd just given me a chance, I would have taken care of you, Cara—somehow. We could have been a family," he cried. "A real, live, honest-to-God family."

She raised her own hands, but they didn't go to her hair, they went to her ears. She covered them as if she didn't want to hear what he was saying, couldn't *bear* to hear it. Shaking her head, she stepped backward. "No," she sobbed, "don't tell me that. Don't say we could have been a family. Don't tell me everything I went through was for nothing."

He grabbed her hands and tried to pull her toward him. "It wasn't for nothing. We have a wonderful, gorgeous child, and she's the most precious thing in my life. She *saved* my life, Cara. When I had nothing else to live for, I had Kit. If I hadn't, I would have gone crazy—or worse."

She struggled against his grip, but he refused to turn loose of her wrists. "And what do you think I did?" she screamed. "For fourteen years, every time I saw a child, I turned my head. Every time I heard a baby's cry, I'd leave the room." She pummeled his chest, and Tye took the blows stoically, the pain an almost welcome sensation. It was physical, and a welcome relief from the searing, gripping, killing agony that was exploding inside his heart. "You stole from me, dammit. You stole my life when you told me you didn't love me, and now I find out you've had our child all these years." She delivered one last vicious kick, then stumbled out of his arms as he was forced to release her. "How could you do that to me, Tye Benedict? How?"

He reached out, rain streaming through his fingers. "I can explain it all, Cara. Really—I can—"

"No," she cried. "Nothing you can say could explain it." She lurched backward and into the rickety railing surrounding the pier, the sound of splintering wood joining her hopeless words. Tye's heart stopped, but somehow he rushed forward. His fingers caught only air, and a second later a boom of lightning split the sky. In the blinding strobelike flash, he watched helplessly as Cara tumbled head over heels into the blackened water.

Chapter 9

Reluctantly, Cara swam up through layers of sleep, her legs kicking against the restraint of the cool sheets. She didn't want to come to the surface of awareness. The dark depths had let her momentarily put aside her pain. The minute she regained her awareness however, anguish rushed in. There was nothing that would ever let her forget this. Nothing.

She opened her eyes. She was in a bedroom, obviously a man's bedroom and most probably Tye's. Turning her head, she got the impression of dark wallpaper, plaid fabrics and masculine furniture. A massive desk at the other end of the room held a low lamp whose light supplemented the glow of a fireplace. There was no one in the room.

She felt tired—bone-weary tired—but as Cara eased up from the pillows surrounding her, she saw no casts, no dressings, no obvious signs of injury. The only outward indication that anything had even happened was a tiny, plastic bandage on her thumb. Someone had wrapped it over the cut from the wineglass, but they'd put it on crooked. She looked closer. The bandage had pictures of Minnie Mouse on it.

Without thinking, Cara lifted her mouth into something that was close to a smile. Minnie Mouse had always been her favorite, but instantly the realization hit her of who had probably picked out these bandages, and her amusement faded. Shock replaced it.

She had a daughter. A daughter who was old enough to shake hands but still liked Minnie Mouse, too.

Cara closed her eyes and leaned back against the pillows, trying with every ounce of her brain to remember those quick few seconds she'd had with Kit. Blue eyes, dark blond hair, short. She'd worn something oversize, like all the kids did now. What had it been? A bulky sweater of some sort and leggings? Cara couldn't remember exactly. One thing she could recall was the impression that there was something vaguely familiar about the teenager—something more than just the obvious aspects of appearance she'd inherited from Tye.

Cara pulled the image into her mind and examined it, like a jeweler studying a flawless diamond. *What had it been? What was so familiar yet so elusive?* The answer was there, just out of reach. Then suddenly it hit her. Her eyes flew open and one hand came up to her throat, her gasp overly loud in the silence of the plush room.

Kit had Cara's face. She had Tye's cheeks, and his nose, and those midnight-blue eyes, but she had the shape of Cara's face. That's why she'd looked familiar to Cara— she'd been looking at herself.

The realization was so incredible that Cara could do nothing but lie against the pillows and listen to the thunder of her heart. She *really* did have a child.

She turned her head against the pillow and stared blindly at the window beside the bed. The draperies had been drawn, but a crack showed her only darkness. For what seemed like a very long time, Cara lay there, one silent tear after another running unchecked down her cheek and to the already moistened pillowcase. Her mind danced from one thing to another, to all the forbidden subjects she'd kept at arm's length through the years.

School photos. New shoes. Baby blankets. First words. Refrigerator art. Yellow buses. Picture books.

She'd missed so very, very much, and suddenly the decision she'd made—albeit reluctantly—at seventeen seemed horribly wrong now. She should have tried harder, she suddenly thought. She should have refused to let Jack take the baby. She should have gotten three jobs. She should have done whatever it took. Even now Cara realized, she was looking at the situation through thirty-one-year-old eyes, but somehow that didn't seem to matter. All she could think of was the fact that she hadn't been there.

And Tye had.

The door of the bedroom eased open, and Cara automatically felt grateful for the interruption. She didn't want to think about him, to sort out her feelings. There wasn't a way to successfully do that right now because anger was all she could feel.

Tye walked in. Quickly Cara brushed at her cheeks and tried to sit up, but her arms didn't want to work. Tye was at her side in an instant, his hands on her elbows, steadying her. When she was finally up, he dropped his hands awkwardly as if he knew she didn't want his touch.

The peculiar thing was—she did. Even after everything that had happened, even with everything that she knew, Cara felt a tremor down her back at the warmth of his fingers against her skin. It made absolutely no sense whatsoever, but this was something else she couldn't deny, and at once she felt exposed and confused. All her defenses were gone, collapsed as surely as the railing that had allowed her to tumble into the lake.

"How are you feeling?" Tye's voice was serious, and he stared into her eyes as though trying to read the truth in them before she spoke.

"Okay," she lied. She was far from okay. *In agony* would have been a better answer, but it was agony in her heart, not her body.

He nodded and tucked the blanket closer. For the first time, she realized she wore a silky nightgown, pale apricot with tiny spaghetti straps over her shoulders, delicate lace cupping her breasts. *Had Tye undressed her?*

Her question must have shown on her face. "It's Jerilyn's," he said by way of explanation. "The doctor put it on you."

"Doctor? This is a hospital? I . . . I thought I was at your house."

"You are," he said quickly. "Dr. Hamilton came over here, and she helped me get you out of your wet things and into that. Monty brought it over—Jerilyn sent it. She thinks of everything." His eyes stayed on her face. "I hope you didn't mind. I guess I could have gone to the hotel and retrieved your things, but it seemed pretty unimportant at the time. I was more worried about you than your clothes."

She looked down at the ivory blanket and twined her fingers into its soothing warmth. "I remember falling into the water, but nothing after that. What happened?"

"I managed to haul you out. You must have hit your head going into the water, because you were already out. Dr. Hamilton wanted to keep you in the hospital overnight, but I convinced her to let you stay here. She left just a little while ago. Said she'd be back later to check on you."

Cara reached up and gingerly touched the back of her head. "I did hit it," she confirmed. "How stupid of me! I shouldn't have—"

Tye interrupted her. "It was all my fault, Cara. If I hadn't stepped toward you, you would never have backed up. You had nothing to do with it."

"Don't be ridiculous," she said, more sharply than she'd intended. "I should have realized the railing was weak. I was at the lake just the other day. In fact, I saw...Kit there, but of course, I didn't know who she was...."

Silence stretched between them like a taut wire, ready to snap and flail them both at any minute. It was obviously too much for Tye, too. He rose and stepped away from the bed, stopping at the window. Pulling the curtains back, he stared into the darkness.

The tension grew until Cara felt compelled to break the silence. "I can't believe you still have doctors who make house calls."

"Mercy Hamilton is a special doctor," he replied, his voice just as mechanical as her words. "She cares more about people than making money."

He let the drape fall and turned back to face Cara. His eyes looked almost black in the flickering light of the fireplace. "Do you hate me?"

The directness of his question threw her off, and she answered without thinking. "No. I don't hate you. I'd like to kill you, but I don't hate you."

He looked startled for just a moment, then a reluctant expression of amusement came across his face. "Thank God for small favors."

"It's a very small one," she said, her eyes meeting his, "and it's probably going to be the only one you get. You *should* be grateful."

"I am." All expression of pleasure fled. "Every day of my life, I thank God for what I have."

She turned her head against the padded headboard and stared into the fireplace. "That's good," she said bitterly. "I wish I could have done the same."

She heard him come back to the bedside, then his tall frame blocked the light. He sat down, the mattress tilting under his weight. "I did what I had to do, Cara. I don't expect you to understand, but I would like to tell you what happened."

"I'd like to tell you, too," she shot back, her anger flaring like the sparks coming up from the fire. "Kit was mine before she was yours, if you recall. I carried her for nine months. Would you like to hear about that?"

He blinked at the venom in her voice, but Cara didn't regret it. It was time to face the truth, to lay bare all the pain and agony they'd forced upon each other—some of it the result of being irresponsible teenagers, some of it deliberate. "Go ahead," he said softly. "You first."

Instantly, Cara regretted her hasty words. She didn't really want to tell him what she hadn't faced herself in fourteen years, but it was like lancing a wound. She *had* to do it.

"I knew I was pregnant when I went to see you that day in jail," she began, her voice husky as if it hurt to finally reveal the untold story. "I was going to tell you, but then you said you didn't love me anymore. So I stayed quiet."

She looked up at him, expecting an interruption, anticipating a rebuttal, but he remained silent. She continued. "There was nothing else to do but tell my parents and ask for help. They didn't help, though." Her eyes went to the fire. "They kicked me out.

"My father wanted me to get an abortion, but I didn't want one. I'm glad I had a choice, but I still didn't want one. I went to Uncle Jack, and he took me to a friend's home in Dallas. I stayed there until the baby—Kit—was born."

Cara heard her voice, but it sounded like it was coming from a computer it was so stilted and flat. It was the only way she could get through the story, though, without breaking down. "I wanted to keep the baby, but Uncle Jack kept telling me how impossible that would be. I didn't really understand, until he died, that I could never have made it on my own." Her voice started to falter, and she had to stop a minute before she could continue. "He t-took her away. I never even saw her."

She realized that she was gripping Tye's hand. She didn't know if she'd reached for him or he'd reached for her, but it didn't seem to matter. "Uncle Jack told me he knew a family who needed a child, a family who...who would love a child and take care of it."

Her eyes left the fire and came to rest on Tye's face. If it were possible, his expression was more pained than she knew her own must be. "Obviously you've had her. Why did Uncle Jack lie to me like that?"

She watched Tye swallow, the strong column of his throat moving in the reddish glow. "He did what he thought was best, Cara. For everyone, including the baby." He was holding her hand as hard as she was holding his, both sets of knuckles white. "He'd already found Monty and Jerilyn at that point, and they'd agreed to keep Kit until I could get out of prison. I think Jack thought everything would work out—for the two of us—after I was released. In fact, he even tried—" Tye stopped, a fresh wave of pain crossing his eyes.

"What?" Her voice was an anguished cry. "Tried what?"

He waited a moment, then began to speak again. "Jack took Kit to your parents, Cara. He was hoping to change your mother's and father's minds about what had happened. He thought if they saw her—their only grand-child—they'd relent and let you come home." His eyes pleaded with hers for understanding. "He thought that even Elizabeth and Phillip would be unable to resist a grand-daughter."

"Granddaughter." Cara repeated the word and let the images flood her that she had never allowed before. A little girl in a ruffled dress and polished Mary Janes. A little girl in muddy overalls and scuffed tennis shoes. A little girl in printed shorts and fancy-colored Jellies . . . sitting on Phil-lip's knee. The fire popped and Cara came back. "But they did resist, didn't they?"

Tye nodded as if he couldn't speak, and Cara thought her fingers might snap, he squeezed them so hard. When he finally spoke in a breaking voice, it wasn't her fingers that cracked—it was her heart.

"Yes. They resisted just fine. Said they didn't even want to see a bastard child of mine."

Cara stared numbly at Tye. She hadn't thought her heart could handle more, but she hadn't even known the meaning of the word *pain* until now. Pain *and* guilt. It rolled over her in an enormous black tide, and she felt herself slipping under, drowning in its vile and murky depths. "I should have—"

"No." The one-word answer came instantly. "There was no way you could have done anything, Cara. My God—you were seventeen. You had no job, no family. Nothing. What do you think you could have done?"

"I don't know," she cried. "But something—I could have done *something.*"

He shook his head. "Not on your own." Taking a deep breath, his chest rising with the motion, Tye continued, every word the painful truth. "The night Jack was supposed to give the baby to Monty and Jerilyn was the night he was killed, Cara. They were on their way to pick her up when they heard on the radio that Jack had been shot. Apparently, he'd gotten the call and had to leave the baby with his neighbor. Monty and Jerilyn never even met him."

"Oh, God." She floundered in the depths of her emotion. "Why didn't I . . . I do something?"

His voice was tortured. "What? What could you have done?" He answered for her. "Nothing. You couldn't have done any more than I did. We were both locked up—in different ways, but we were both locked up."

Pain sliced through her, not with the sharpness of a knife, but with the jagged edges of a dull ax, chopping at the last of her reserves for comprehension. "Then you got out?"

"Yes. I got out, and Monty helped me put the pieces of my life back together again. Kit and I even lived with them for a while. All I knew about being a parent was that I wanted to do it differently than my mother had. Monty and Jerilyn taught me how to be a father."

"So you learned parenting and I went on to college." The words were empty, devoid of any emotion.

"I went to your mom and dad, but they wouldn't tell me anything about you. I begged them to at least let you know that I'd been there, but they didn't, did they?"

She shook her head. *He'd actually tried to contact her.* The thought was incredible but it simply took its place beside the other, even more unimaginable revelations that were piling up inside her mind like so many rocks.

"I didn't think they had," he said, obvious regret deepening his voice. "When I didn't hear from you, I figured as much."

By now, Cara was simply insensate. She spoke automatically, repeating herself. "They never told me."

"Why should they? You were planning to marry. Your new husband knew nothing about the child, and you seemed happy with him. There was no point in telling you." Unlike Cara, Tye had spoken with deep emotion coloring his voice and words—until this point. Now, for the first time, his voice turned blunt. "I hired a private investigator, though. It took a few years, but after he found you in New York, I went to see you, anyway."

"You came to New York?"

"Yes. I saw you outside your apartment—you and your husband—and I knew I didn't have a place in your life anymore." He looked down at the floor.

A knot swelled up inside Cara's chest, and suddenly she couldn't breathe. She wondered if it was some kind of delayed reaction from her tumble into the lake, but just as quickly she dismissed the idea. This had nothing to do with her accident and everything to do with Tye.

"I came back to Angelton and filled my life with Kit. She . . . she was a beautiful baby, and she grew into a gorgeous child. Always happy. Always sunny." He turned his head and stared out the window, a soft smile playing against his face. "She had a miniature fishing pole, and her favorite thing to do was to go fishing. She was the only kid I'd ever seen that could just sit there for hours. It was incredible."

"So you've had her all this time. Fourteen years."

"Yes. Fourteen years. At times, being alone, it got pretty hairy, but without Jerilyn it would have been impossible. She was a perfect mother, though."

At the word *mother,* the fierce pain that had been building inside of Cara suddenly exploded. She'd given up Kit, she'd denied herself emotions, she'd done everything she'd thought was right, and this is what it had come to. Tye had raised their daughter, and another woman had served as mother. Without another thought, Cara lifted her hand, and she slapped Tye Benedict as hard as she could.

Wordlessly he stared at her, his hand going to his already reddening jaw. "How dare you say that to me?" she cried.

"What are you trying to do? Twist the knife a little? Make me hurt even more than I already do?" She threw the covers off the bed and jumped up, ignoring the sweep of dizziness that hit her. She had to get away from him, put physical distance between them. She stopped on the other side of the room in front of the fireplace, then swirled and spoke again. "You can't make me feel any worse than I already do. I don't need you to dish out punishment. I do it quite well myself, thank you very much."

With three strides, he crossed the room. In her bare feet, Cara came to just under his chin, and he stood so close now she had to crane her neck to see his face. When she did, she saw anger and shock and something else that she didn't want to see—something that looked suspiciously like sympathy.

He grabbed her upper arms with a hard grip—one she could not escape. "And do you think you have the sole rights to those feelings, Cara? Do you think you're the only person in this world who thinks they've made mistakes in their life? Mistakes they wish they could call back and undo?"

Wrenching sideways, Cara sought freedom—freedom from Tye's piercing blue stare and from the pain of his words—but he only held on tighter. He jerked her around to face him and shook her slightly. "How many times do you think I cursed myself for telling you I didn't love you? How many times, Cara?" His fingers dug into her arms so hard she could feel his touch all the way to the bone. "I'll tell you. Try every day of my life, dammit. *Every damned day.* I get out of an empty bed every morning, then I go in the bathroom and shave, and I think, 'You could have had it all, you stupid bastard. But you blew it. You blew it big time.'"

Tye's image wavered as Cara stared at him through tear-filled eyes. The agony in his voice racked her, tore her apart, ripped her to shreds, because she recognized it—it was *her* pain, too. And suddenly she couldn't hold that pain any longer. It was bigger and stronger than her—more power-

ful than either one of them—and before she could even try
to contain it, it spewed from her in a hot, molten flow.

She began to pound on his chest with fists full of anger.
"That's right!" she screamed. "That's right. You blew it,
and I've spent years wondering why. Years asking myself
what I did, years asking why you didn't love me anymore,
years trying to think what I could have done differently that
day to make you change your mind. You *should* have loved
me, Tye. You should have stuck by me . . . by me and Kit."

"I would have if I'd known," he cried. "You didn't tell
me."

"Because you said you didn't love me!" she screamed.
"Do you think I have no pride at all? I wasn't going to
throw myself at you. Pride was the only thing I *did* have
left."

With those words, the last of her control evaporated, and
her fury took over, Cara's hysteria reaching a fever pitch.
Obviously, Tye had no idea what he'd done to her, no idea
whatsoever, and as she continued to hit at him and release
the rage and wretchedness of fourteen years, she suddenly
realized she hadn't fully known herself. She'd buried her
feelings so deep and kept them there for so long that even
she was shocked by the intensity of them as they poured
from her. Shocked but incapable of keeping them within her
a second longer.

Tye seized her hands, but the strength of her agony was
too strong, even for him, and there was nothing he could do
but follow her movements as her arms swung wildly out and
away from his chest. For what seemed like an endless moment, they scuffled in front of the roaring fire. Finally, he
brought both her hands behind her. Cara arched her back,
then fell helplessly against him. With her chest rising and
falling rapidly from the efforts of her exertion, she looked
up into his eyes. "Let me go," she cried. "Just leave me
alone."

"I did that once, Cara." His blue eyes bored into hers,
sapphire bright and diamond hard. "And by God, I don't
intend to do it again. Ever."

His lips came down in a crushing kiss. There was nothing gentle or loving about it. It was a kiss born of desperation, the kind of kiss that told her he'd been thinking of this moment as long as she had, regretting what he'd done and regretting what he'd left undone. And despite all her anger, despite all the years, she responded.

Her fists were still between them, but as Tye's mouth continued to make its demands on her, Cara lifted her hands and threw them around his neck. Using every bit of her strength, she pulled him to her. A perverse side of her wanted to make him know that this is what he could have had if he hadn't spoken those hateful words so long ago.

He answered exactly as she expected. His hands left her shoulders and flattened against her back. Warm, almost hot, hands burning through the thin silk of her nightgown. Burning but searching, seeking yet pulling—drawing her even closer. As she opened her mouth to his tongue, he dropped his hands even lower and roughly cupped her buttocks, almost lifting her off the carpet.

Deep in the very back of Cara's throat, a moan started and built. Nothing had changed between them, yet everything had. The passion, the flare of desire—that was identical, but now they were adults, and they knew exactly what they were doing. Of course, there'd been no fumbling in the back seat with Tye, because even as a teenager, he'd been more than a competent lover, but the feelings he was creating in her now were unlike anything Cara had ever experienced.

There was a wild desperation in Tye's touch, a kind of recklessness that told her he didn't care about the consequences. They'd already cut each other as deeply as they possibly could. Their actions now would either join them once and for all, or fling them into separate corners of the universe.

Tye tore his mouth from Cara's, then began to kiss her face, her neck, her ears, murmuring all the while. The words were incoherent, but it didn't matter because Cara was, too. The pain of tonight's revelations had done more than tear her apart, they'd seemed to carve a deeper ability in her to experience pleasure, as well. Every touch of Tye's hands was like the first, every kiss of his lips was like the last.

Her fingers left the tight cords of his neck and threaded through his hair as his hands came around and cupped her breasts. Through the thin silk, he brushed her nipples into taut awareness, and Cara knew now there was no going back. They'd reached the point of no return. Even if she'd been able to stop, Tye wouldn't have. His hard arousal between them proved that point without a word.

He continued to drop kisses across her bare shoulders, then the thin straps of her nightgown gave way to his insistence. The gown fell down and revealed her breasts.

In another time and another place, Cara might have worried about her body. She might have wondered what Tye thought about the tiny blue veins or the slight slope that gravity had wrought in fourteen years. But Tye didn't give her that chance. He buried even the barest hint of concern with his overwhelming attention, kissing first one breast and then the other, his hands dancing over their sides with the lightest of touches.

Instantly she had to have his bare skin against hers, and her fingers dropped to the buttons of his shirt. Whimpering against their stubbornness, she persisted until every last one was undone, then she peeled the shirt back over his shoulders and pressed her hands against him. Under her fingertips the beat of his heart entered her soul and went straight into the core of her existence. They were connected, connected in a way that no ordinary relationship could sustain.

Tye must have felt the moment, too. He stopped kissing her and seared her with the blue flame of his eyes. "There's no going back now, Cara." The words came from him as if they had been pulled painfully from his heart. "If we do this, there's no going back."

Her pulse thundered as she clutched his arms. "It's already too late for that."

A second later, his clothing dropped to the floor, and Cara saw she wasn't the only one whose body had changed. The years had brought more than maturity to his physique, they'd brought a hardness, a kind of impenetrability that said he could handle whatever came his way. It was, she realized with startled awareness, the body of a man and not a boy. And not just any man, either, but a man who'd known bad times, when his strength had been all he could depend upon.

He poised beside the edge of the bed. "Are you protected?" She shook her head, sudden desperation in her eyes. "Then I'll take care of it," he said instantly. "Like I should have before."

He left, then rejoined her an instant later, and the touch of his hands against her skin forced everything else from her mind. They flitted over her cheeks, down her neck, along her breasts, then lower to the tender flesh of her stomach. Once there, he stopped and flattened his hand over the barely visible white lines that her pregnancy had caused. He didn't say anything. He didn't look at her. He simply studied the paleness for several long seconds, then replaced his hand with his mouth, kissing the marks tenderly and softly as though he both regretted and reveled in them.

He gave her no more time to think about that action either, as his hands traveled lower to tease the softness of her inner thighs. His touch was magic—feathery soft yet insistently demanding—and even if Cara had wanted to stay still she couldn't have. She responded to his every move. Her own hands brushed across his chest, and she followed them with her lips and tongue, presenting her own demands to him as she took his nipples into her mouth and bit gently.

He groaned against her touch, a deep agonizing groan, then his hands began to stroke her. How many nights had she lain in her bed and wanted his touch, remembered his touch? Closing her eyes, Cara arched against his fingers and lost herself to the sensations flooding her. She had no memory of this kind of intensity, this kind of power. Had he always been able to make her feel this way—as if she were riding a roller coaster that had no end and no beginning?

There was no time to consider the question.

His weight shifted; she knew he was poised above her. She tensed, her body begging for the final release she knew he could bring to her, but it didn't come.

"Open your eyes, Cara. I want to see you."

She did as he instructed, and Cara knew at that moment that no matter what had happened between them in the past, and no matter what *would* happen between them in the future, she would take the sight of his piercing blue eyes with her to her grave. It was a moment frozen in time, a moment that crystallized for her everything between them.

He studied her for two seconds, as though making sure she wanted what he was about to give. At this point there could be no question, no ambiguity. They'd made mistakes before, big mistakes, and Tye obviously didn't want this to be one of them.

Cara's fingers dug into his shoulders, and she spoke as though he'd voiced the question. "Yes," she whispered. "Yes."

He closed his eyes and entered her with a single stroke.

She felt as though time had collapsed, and a deep piercing sweetness rocked her with each of his thrusts, a sweetness her body remembered and responded to. Locking her ankles over Tye's back, Cara let the feelings and the emotions sweep her into a place that she'd forgotten even existed.

A place she'd only shared with Tye.

For endless minutes, she clung to him, moaning incoherently and urging him on until she finally lost what little control she had left, waves of pleasure radiating outward from the center of her body. A second later, he collapsed against her, his heavy weight no burden against her damp breasts.

She could feel his heart. It was pounding in a rhythm that matched her own, and when he lifted his head and looked at her, she knew the past had finally caught up with them.

Chapter 10

At first light, Cara slipped out of Tye's arms and into the robe that matched the gown she wore. Easing away from the bed, she padded softly to the bedroom door. In some ways, his touch was almost painful, and she didn't want to compound that by being there when he woke up. She couldn't.

They'd made love all night long, and a part of her wondered if they were trying to make up for the years they'd lost. It was hopeless, of course. Nothing would ever bring that time back. It was gone, lost, forfeited, never to be seen again.

Just like Kit's childhood.

Unsure of which way to turn, Cara stepped into the spacious corridor outside Tye's bedroom and stopped. Underneath her bare feet was parquet floor, warmed by stripes of sunshine spilling through wide arched windows. On the walls, lined with padded silk, a variety of oils, prints and watercolors hung. Outside, a spacious lawn stretched down to the turquoise blue of a gleaming pool.

Tye had come an awfully long way from the house where he'd grown up.

Cara looked to her left and then her right. She had absolutely no idea where the kitchen was, so she simply turned left and headed down the hall. A second later, after she'd peeked behind two doors and found pristine guest rooms, she realized her mistake—this was obviously the bedroom wing of the house. She turned around, then stopped. There was one more door at the end of the corridor. It had to be Kit's room.

Cara told herself she shouldn't, but her feet paid no heed. On their own accord, they took her toward that last door. When she reached it, she stopped and slowly lifted her right hand. With one finger, she pushed the door open, then stood on the threshold, suddenly petrified to take this final step.

Her eyes swept the room and took inventory. It looked to Cara like a typical teenager's haven, even though she had no idea what was really typical. In one corner, a desk waited, its surface piled with schoolbooks and papers. Against the other wall, a short bookcase bulged with paperbacks, a small TV resting on its top. Twin beds, neatly made with canopies covered in matching lace tops, stood side by side, one filled with stuffed animals of every color, size and shape. An open door across from where Cara stood obviously led to a bathroom and dressing area. A window between the beds looked down toward the pool.

Pulled by a force greater than herself, Cara walked inside, the warm wood of the corridor giving way to pale pink carpet, the light scent of a floral perfume surrounding her. Stopping in the center of the room, she paused uncertainly. She wasn't looking for anything in particular—she just wanted to see what she had missed.

She continued until she reached the desk, then stopped beside it and looked down at the open notebook perched precariously on one corner. It was a report of some kind, obviously for school, about the changing state of the world's boundaries.

Cara's breath caught in her throat, and a murmur came out that sounded suspiciously like a sob. *The changing state of the world's boundaries? How about the disappearance of your own boundaries? How about total anarchy—of the heart?*

With a quick swirl, she turned away from the desk, her feet taking her across to the room and to the open door of the bath. Expecting a confusion of bottles and makeup and curlers, Cara was surprised to see a remarkably clean and orderly countertop. Obviously Kit had inherited a penchant for neatness. The only sign of disturbance was an open box of bandages, its contents apparently spilled in haste. From the pink tiled floor, Minnie Mouse winked up at Cara.

Stepping into the bathroom, she bent down to pick up the scattered strips of plastic. The floor was cold under her toes, and quickly she gathered each bandage, stuffed it back into the box, then rose. Returning the package to the countertop, Cara went back into the bedroom. She needed to leave, needed to get out of the room before Tye found her. Having him see her here, her naked longing completely exposed, was somehow even more intimate than what they'd shared last night.

Once again, though, she found herself stopping in the middle of the room, her gaze drawn to the small window between the beds. The pool outside was framed in the center of the glass, and Cara's designer eye appraised it for what it was—a perfect way to emphasize something that must be important to Kit. *Was she a swimmer? Did she like the water?* She obviously liked to fish.

Drawn to the window, Cara found herself grasping the daintily carved post of the twin bed on the left. A second later, her knees gave out, and she sank to the mattress. *This was her daughter's room. Her daughter.* Who liked to fish and swim and write reports for school.

Tears welled into Cara's eyes in a blindingly hot rush, and her throat closed against the pain. What had she done? What had she given away fourteen years ago? At that very moment, she'd have mortgaged her soul to have a second chance with her daughter.

Not even knowing what she was doing, Cara reached out toward the nearest stuffed animal and pulled it to her. Working the soft, plush fur beneath her fingers, she cried silently, the tears running down her face in a torrent of sorrow.

Oh, God! What had she done?

A fresh wave assaulted her, and she doubled over with her sadness and pain, clutching the stuffed animal. Even though she'd given Kit away fourteen years ago, Cara had never grieved. She'd never allowed herself the luxury of giving in to what she considered a weakness, and now that pent-up mourning was punishing in its intensity. It racked her with a physical agony that she felt all the way down to the bottom of her heart.

For every nursery she'd wanted to see but avoided, she cried.

For every toy she'd wanted to buy but didn't, she sobbed.

And for every baby she'd longed to hold but wouldn't, she wept.

The tears came from a well inside of her, a well so full, so deep that it seemed to be bottomless. She wept inconsolably, great waves of sobs that stole her breath, robbed her sight and plundered her soul.

And that's when Tye found her.

At first, he didn't know what the sound was, but with a father's instinct, he leapt from the bed, threw on his robe and hurried out into the hallway, his feet automatically going toward Kit's room until he remembered that Kit wasn't even there.

But the sounds *were* coming from Kit's room...and slowly he realized what they were. Kit wasn't at home—but Cara was.

He approached the doorway, unsure of how to proceed. Cara had absorbed a tremendous shock last night, and intruding on her was the last thing he wanted. In fact, he wondered now if their lovemaking had been the smartest thing to do. At the time, that question hadn't entered his mind, though. They'd both been in pain, and it had been the only way to offer comfort. Comfort that had blazed into something much, much deeper.

He paused at the open door, his bruised and battered heart taking another hit. Cara was sitting on Kit's extra bed, a stuffed elephant in her hands, tears streaming down her face. There was so much pain, so much grief, coming from her that it was a palpable, living thing. It reached out and tore at Tye, too. He immediately went to her, pulling her into his arms to absorb the silent gush of tears.

Wiping her face with the back of her hand, she attempted to minimize her emotions, her sobs dissolving into hiccups. "I—I'm sorry to fall apart like this," she said. "I shouldn't have—"

"Hush." He captured her hands in his. "There aren't any more *shouldn'ts*, Cara. It's way too late for that now." Clearing his own tight throat, he looked down her and spoke. "Besides, if anyone should be saying that, it ought to be me. I...I should have called you a long, long time ago and told you what was going on."

With tears staining her pale cheeks, she stared at him with dark, accusing eyes. Her voice was blunt, and her question even more so. "Then why didn't you?"

His gaze went to the floor and stayed there, pulled by the weight of his guilt. "I was scared," he said simply, finally raising his face. "Scared to death."

"Scared?" she repeated, her eyebrow knitting. "Scared of what?"

"Of you."

The dark eyes that had closed in passion beneath him the night before now opened in amazement. "That's ridiculous. Why in the world would you have been scared of me?"

He stood and walked to the window, his back to her. "Not past tense, Cara." Turning slowly, he stared. "I still am scared—even more so now."

She rose. "But why?"

"Isn't it obvious?" He lifted one hand and indicated the room they were in. "I have something that belongs to us both. I've had it for a very long, very selfish time, and I don't want to give it up." He crossed his arms. "Kit's the only thing I care about, Cara. I'm not prepared to relinquish her."

Cara reached behind her, her fingers fumbling against the bedpost. "Wh-what makes you think you'd have to give her up?"

"I'm a former con, Cara. The only reason I got Kit in the first place was because of Jack. Otherwise I wouldn't have had a chance in hell. If you wanted to take her away, I'm sure the court would see things your way." He pushed back his shoulders and moved another step closer. "But before that happened, you'd have a helluva fight on your hands, I want you to know."

Cara looked up at him, her eyes open so wide he could distinguish the lighter centers of her irises from the darker rims. "I understand how you'd feel that way, Tye, but—"

His heart cramped. "Look, I know how bad this sounds, and believe it or not, I'm not completely cold to your feelings in this, but there's no negotiation on this issue, Cara. If you wanted to take Kit from me, I'd fight you until hell freezes over. She's the one person in this world who has *always* loved me. Period. Unconditionally. She's asked absolutely nothing in return for that love, and it's the most precious thing in the world." He loomed over Cara, his own hands grasping the bedposts beside hers. "I'd never give her up—"

"Stop it, Tye." Cara shook her head furiously, then pushed him out of her way and stood. "Just stop it."

He blocked her with his body. "No, Cara. Nothing would make me—"

"Tye, listen to me, for God's sake." She put her hands on the lapels of his robe and shook it slightly until he fell quiet. "You're putting words into my mouth. I would never take Kit away from you. Never."

Relief flooded over him in a giant wave, and he felt years of fear wash from him. Just as quickly, however, confusion took its place. "You . . . you don't want her?" he asked in a dazed voice. The thought was so incomprehensible to Tye, that he didn't stop to analyze exactly what it meant to him, nor did he give Cara the time to respond. "How in the world could you not want her?" he said in a puzzled voice. "She's the brightest, the cutest, the most loving kid in the world. Are you crazy? How could you not want her?"

Cara stepped back as if he'd slapped her, her face freezing into a mask of something he couldn't define. "I didn't say I didn't want her. It's just that I . . . I have absolutely no experience with children." She moved to the end of the bed and picked up the stuffed animal she'd been holding earlier. With precise movements, she put the fluffy gray elephant back into the exact position it had held before. "I wouldn't have the first idea of how to handle a teenager."

He didn't understand, especially when the expression of longing on her face was totally incongruent with her words. Fear came over him again, and he wondered if he'd made a horrible mistake. He reached out, grabbed her arm and turned her to face him. "If you feel that way, then why all the tears?"

Her eyes flickered with an emotion he couldn't read. "I don't have to explain myself to you or to anyone, but if you've got to have a reason, then use this one. Last night was one helluva shock. I've spent half my life pretending I didn't have a child, then boom! In the middle of a dinner party, my own . . . daughter walks up to me." She looked down at the floor for a moment, then back at Tye. "I know it's hard for you to understand this, but giving Kit up for adoption was the hardest thing I've ever done."

She swallowed, and he watched the column of her throat move. It was a sight that reached down into him and twisted his gut because he suddenly caught a glimmer of how confused, how tangled she must feel. She continued to speak. "I wanted to keep her, thought of nothing else for the months that I carried her, but in the end, I finally accepted the fact that I couldn't. Giving her up took courage and guts and sacrifice, even though there was nothing else I could have done at the time. Nothing. For fourteen years I've told myself I did the right thing—that was the only way I could keep going. I can't second-guess that decision now. It's way too late for that.''

Breakfast was awkward. Very awkward.

''More coffee?'' Tye said politely.

''Yes, please.'' Cara held out her cup. ''Thank you very much.''

Last night could have been a dream for all the intimacy they shared now, she thought with a grimace. They'd made another terrible, drastic mistake.

''Another roll?''

''No,'' she said, shaking her head. ''They're delicious, but I like to watch my weight.''

''There's not a thing wrong with your figure,'' he said gruffly. ''It's perfect.''

Cara felt the heat rise in her face. *God, this was so tough!* Abruptly she set down her coffee cup, and his startled eyes met hers over the breakfast table. ''What are we going to do, Tye?'' she said. ''We have a real situation here, and we can't just ignore it.''

Last night's rain had washed the Texas sky into a bright morning, and outside the open window beside them, Cara could hear the strident call of a crow in the distance. It sounded like he was mocking their plight. Sighing, Tye put down his own coffee cup and looked at her. ''This is all Monty's fault,'' he said without preamble. ''We ought to make that old son-of-a-bitch come over here and unravel it all.''

Confusion made Cara shake her head. ''What on earth are you talking about?''

''If Monty hadn't insisted on you coming here, this would never have happened.''

''But he had no idea—''

Tye shook his own head. ''I'm afraid that's not exactly the truth. He *does* know who you are, Cara. In fact, he actually planned all this.''

Cara fought to keep her world on track as disbelief rose up once more. What else was going on she knew nothing about? With trembling fingers, she brought her cup to her lips and sipped. The scalding-hot coffee barely registered. "I don't think I understand," she said tightly.

"Jerilyn *did* see your work in New York. She thought you were marvelous and told Monty all about it. But he procrastinated like always, and the building was finished without any kind of interior touches done." Tye looked up. "Frankly, I think he was halfway scared, too. He and Kit are very close, and . . . well, I guess he was afraid that things might change if you came around."

This situation was so far out of control, Cara suddenly felt like she'd never recover from it. With a tremendous effort, she blanked out her feelings and kept her face neutral. "Then why did he do exactly that?" she asked, her fingers tearing her limp bread into tiny pieces.

"Jerilyn made him." Tye's voice was tense. "She told him she . . . she didn't want to die leaving Kit without a woman to turn to." He poured more coffee into his cup, dumped in a spoonful of sugar, then stirred it vigorously. "They thought you were the right woman for that job."

Cara swallowed and turned her head to stare out the window. Out on the lawn, beneath a huge spreading oak, a bird feeder was under attack by two squirrels. She felt as if she were, too, with endless confusion digging into her just like animal claws.

Part of her wanted to break down and confess her fears, but she'd spent so many years lying to herself that she couldn't even begin to think about voicing the truth now—especially to him, and especially *this* truth, the truth slicing through her like a heated blade.

She'd give up her right arm to have Kit.

But it would never work.

Never.

Because no matter how badly Cara might want it, no matter how badly she might *need* it, the three of them could never be a family. Tye had hurt her, not once but twice, and both of them had made Kit suffer. Families didn't come out of situations like that, and Cara knew it. She'd suffered through one of the worst ones, and she'd die before she'd make Kit experience that kind of life, too. Besides all that— what if Kit hated her? Cara would if she were in the teenager's shoes.

All she could do was look at Tye. His dark blue gaze was sympathetic, and, giving in to her pain, she covered her eyes, anguish radiating behind their lids with comets of light. A few seconds later, she dropped her fingers and looked at him wearily. "Let me just make sure I understand." She paused, her mind clutching at the slippery details. "Monty hired me to do a fake decorating job so that I could come back here and be a mother to a daughter I gave away fourteen years ago. Because his wife is dying. And because Kit's at the age where she needs a woman in the house. Is that about it?"

Tye nodded. "The decorating job isn't fake—we need the work done."

Cara raised one eyebrow. "Is that the only part I got wrong?"

"Yes."

She leaned over the table and stared at Tye. He had missed a spot right over the left side of his lip when he'd shaved that morning. "And did you approve of this plan?"

"No." He ran his finger over the rim of his cup. "In fact, I was as shocked as you were that day you walked into my office. I knew how Jerilyn felt, but I didn't think she'd actually make Monty take any action on it."

"But he did."

"Yes, he did. And I couldn't stop him."

Cara's anger edged forward. "You're his CEO, for God's sake. Don't tell me you couldn't do something."

He looked at her skeptically. "He's my uncle, dammit! What would you have me do, Cara. Fire him?"

"I don't know, but the whole situation is like Pandora's box," she retorted. "You should have thought of something."

With a screech that set Cara's teeth on edge, Tye pushed his chair back from the table and grabbed his plate. "We both should have thought of something—fourteen years ago when we were rocking your father's boat."

His hasty words brought forth an image so powerful, so compelling, that Cara instantly fell into silence. He was right. What else could she say?

In obvious frustration, he spun around and went into the kitchen where she heard him scrape the plate, then drop it into the sink with an angry crash. When he walked back into the breakfast nook, his boots clattered against the tile. He stood behind the chair he'd just vacated and gripped the wooden back with fingers whose knuckles were white. He looked angry—angry but as confused as she was. "If you're so all-fired smart about everything, what do *you* think we ought to do now?"

Cara breathed deeply, and thanked God for Tye's reaction—it made her strong, forced her own feelings back under control. Seeing him lose his restraint simply strengthened her resolve not to get too emotional. "I think the first question—" she took another deep breath "—is what does Kit know?"

The words hung between them, suspended like Cara's own heartbeat.

Tye met her gaze, then sighed. "Everything."

"Everything?"

"Everything but who *you* are." He walked to the curved window behind the table. Above the opening, the ceiling was lower, giving the area a cozy, enclosed feeling. Tye lifted his hands and braced them on this overhang. He spoke with his back to Cara. "She knows we weren't married, she knows you had to give her up, and she knows I'm her real father."

Cara's pulse froze. "And she's never asked about me?"

"Oh, yes," He turned slowly. "She's asked, and I've tried to explain, but I don't know what kind of job I did."

"Wh-what did you tell her?"

"The truth," Tye said bluntly. "That we were young and didn't know any better. That you got pregnant, and I didn't know it. That you had no way of supporting her so you gave her up for adoption.''

"And what did she say?''

"She wondered why you didn't want her."

Cara sucked her breath in. Closing her eyes and swallowing her pain, she blinked rapidly and looked away from Tye. "Did you tell her it wasn't a matter of *want?*"

He moved around the table and sat down, not meeting her eyes. "Yes," he said. "I tried to explain about your parents. About Jack's death. I don't know if she understood or not, but I tried." He put his hands on Cara's. "I really did try."

Cara spoke again, her voice a hollow whisper. "Did she ever ask to see a photo of me?" The question came from a long way away, from a place so far outside of Cara that she couldn't acknowledge this was what *she* had always longed for. Some kind of visible, tangible proof that a child *had* existed.

"Yes. I told her I didn't have one." Across the expanse of table, his eyes asked her to understand what her heart couldn't accept. For a moment, their gazes locked, then he dropped his bright blue stare, and that's when she realized he was more than confused or even angry. He was still scared. Totally, unequivocally scared.

It wasn't an emotion she had *ever* associated with Tye until the last twenty-four hours, and even though he'd told her last night that he was worried about her taking Kit, his *fear* had not registered until this very moment. The thought brought her up short, turned her around, and slowly she realized there *was* one thing missing in this revelation.

Cara leaned across the table, her elbows against the cold, wooden planks. "Tell me one more thing, Tye," she said softly. "You said you told our daughter the whole story." She deliberately stopped speaking until he raised his eyes to hers again. "Tell me—did that story include the fact that I didn't know you've had her all these years?"

Chapter 11

Her heart ticked off the seconds as she waited for his answer. Behind her, a breeze bearing a touch of coolness came through the open window.

The sapphire blue of his eyes darkened momentarily, then his lips narrowed into a slash of defensiveness. "What's that got to do with anything?"

Cara slowly released her breath. "You didn't, did you? You let her think *you* were the only one who loved her, that cared for her."

He crossed his arms over his chest. "I told her you weren't able to keep her. I didn't make you out as someone who didn't care." He paused, then spoke again, his voice softer, more compelling. "You've got to understand how much she means to me, Cara. Kit is my whole life. She's everything to me." He dropped his gaze, and when he looked at Cara again, the emotion behind his eyes was almost more than she could bear to see. "The love I have for her is something I didn't think I'd ever have—not after I sent you away that day. Being her father is all I've got. I've never wanted to share that, because I was afraid to." He shook his head.

"That's why I just don't understand—how could you possibly not want her?"

His question rang out in the breakfast nook, and an emotion escaped from the locked confines of Cara's heart, an emotion she'd guarded for a long, long time. Under different circumstances, she might have called it a maternal instinct, but at the moment the only way she could think of it was as a small crystal thought that shattered and split into a thousand diamonds of anger, pain and regret.

She rose from the table and drew up to her full height, the incongruous wish flitting through her mind that she should be wearing something more than a slightly wrinkled jumpsuit without a belt and no shoes.

"I said I wouldn't take Kit *away* from you, Tye." She spoke each word slowly and precisely. "But there's a difference between that and not *wanting* her. Maybe you ought to think about that."

He jumped to his feet and opened his mouth to interrupt her, but she continued, meeting his gaze without flinching. "No—no." She stopped and took a deep breath. "For once—*for once*—I think someone around here needs to think about what's best for Kit. She's not a piece of property or a used car. She's a person, and she has a right to some consideration here. Some consideration and the truth."

On Monday morning, Cara told herself she shouldn't do it.

But by that afternoon, she couldn't stop herself.

At 4:00 p.m. she eased the Cadillac down the street that fronted Angelton's only middle school and let her eyes skip over the milling teenagers as they waited for the school buses to ferry them home. It didn't take long for her to spot Kit. Over yellow-striped leggings, she wore a bright purple top that hung past her hips and a crocheted vest. On her head, again, was the bright blue hat she'd worn at the lake the first time Cara had ever seen her.

Cara's heart accelerated as she peered through the windshield. *That's my daughter! My daughter.*

She whispered the words out loud, a sense of wonderment coming into her voice. "My daughter...my daughter, Kit. Hello, Kit." Her voice cracked slightly. "You don't know me, but I'm your mother...and I love you very, very much."

For a second, tears blurred her sight, then she rubbed her eyes and refocused. Kit stood beside a boy, a tall, lanky teenager, and as Cara watched, Kit laughed at something he said and clutched her books protectively against her chest. He reached over and playfully tugged on her hat, then she jerked her head away and pretended to hit him.

Hungrily, Cara stared at them. What was his name? Were they friends? How had Kit's classes gone today? Did she have any tests tomorrow?

For just a second, Cara let herself think about what it would be like to ask Kit those questions, to be waiting for her at home, to hear her teenage problems and concerns. The need to be there for Kit almost overpowered Cara, and with a deeply felt physical ache, she realized that she wanted nothing more at the moment than to leap from the car and enfold Kit in her arms.

But she couldn't. Wouldn't.

Because doing that would only hurt them all, and Kit especially.

Cara realized suddenly that she'd inadvertently maneuvered the Cadillac into the line of mothers waiting to pick up their children, and as the cars snaked forward and she didn't move, the auto behind her honked impatiently. She sent one last fleeting look in Kit's direction, then pulled out and drove away—her heart cracking into tiny broken pieces.

The next few days passed in a fog for Cara. She had no idea what she was doing, no idea what she was thinking, no idea how to proceed. Somehow, though, at the end of the week, she had a portfolio of paint and wallpaper samples to show to Monty, who'd been out of town until today. She sat numbly in his office after lunch on Thursday and waited for him.

She hadn't seen Tye at all. Peggy had said something about a meeting in Austin, but Cara had tried not to listen. She didn't *want* to know where he was. Just like she didn't want to think about him holding her in his arms and making love to her.

There was so much emotion, so much confusion, hanging between her and Tye. All their feelings contained too much past and too much heat. And now there was Kit to think about, too. Cara's brain spun with all the possibilities.

She'd been telling Tye the truth—she *didn't* want to take Kit away from him, despite the love Cara had for her. What kind of woman would want to unleash turmoil like that in a child's life? Obviously, until Cara had arrived, they'd had a perfectly calm life. As Tye was so fond of pointing out, Kit was happy, and they'd gotten by just fine without Cara, thank you very much. Even with Jerilyn gone, they wouldn't really need Cara. So where could she possibly fit in?

The answer was more than clear. Nowhere. There was only one thing she could do, she thought, lifting her head from the glass and staring out to the lake.

She'd have to give Kit up a second time.

She'd have to leave immediately and return to New York, make it a clean cut before this situation got even messier, and Kit was hurt, too. With a little luck and a lot of effort, someday Cara might be able to put herself back together and put this all behind her.

But it would be like cutting her heart out with a dull knife.

The door to Monty's office opened, and Cara swirled around. With a briefcase in one hand and a small laptop computer in the other, Monty entered, his suit crumpled and his tie half-undone. Lines crossed his forehead, and an air of utter weariness trembled around him. Shuffling to his desk, he didn't even notice her until she spoke. "Monty— did you just get in?"

His head jerked up. "Oh—Cara. Yes, as a matter of fact, I did. My plane was late out of Washington, and then we got delayed by bad weather in Atlanta." He dumped his cases on his desk, then lifted his hand to his eyes and rubbed them. "I didn't even stop at the house first. I came straight here." He reached for the phone, then paused. "Would you mind if I called Jerilyn first? Before we had our meeting?"

Cara took a step closer. This was the first time she'd seen him since her world had tilted last week, but suddenly all the anger and frustration she'd held for him drained from her. He looked so worn-out, so fatigued, so worried, that sympathy for him overwhelmed Cara's temper. "Why don't you go on home?" Lifting a hand toward her folders, she spoke again. "This can wait until tomorrow."

He shook his head. "No. I promised you we'd go over it today, and I stick to my promises." He smiled slightly, the corners of his mouth barely lifting. "I imagine you have a few other things you'd like to discuss with me besides wallpaper, too. Let me make a quick call, then we'll talk." He picked up the phone and dialed, speaking all the time. "If you don't mind, would you tell Peggy to get us some coffee? I think I'm going to need a boost here."

Cara nodded, then picked up the silver service from Monty's credenza. She would get the coffee herself and give him some privacy for his call. Five minutes later, she came back with a full pot. He was just hanging up the phone.

"You didn't have to do that yourself," he said, seeing the tray in her hands.

"I don't mind." She put the tray down, then filled one cup and handed it to him before turning back to do another for herself. "I thought you might want to be alone while you talked to Jerilyn."

"After forty-five years of marriage, we have no secrets," he said, sitting down in his chair. Looking up at Cara, he tried to smile but failed. "At least, not anymore." He paused. "I can't say I'm sorry, Cara, for what's happened. Jack and I did what we thought was best, and now I'm doing what Jerilyn wanted me to do. If I had to, I'd do it all over again, though. I'd do anything for Jerilyn."

The thought flashed through Cara's mind that it would be wonderful to have a man care for *her* that much, but she quickly put it behind her. Tye had tried to tell her *he'd* cared that much—and that's why he'd told her he didn't love her—so she'd be free to go on. *What a joke!* Cara carefully stirred her coffee, then moved around the desk and sat down in one of the chairs facing it. "Why didn't you just tell me the truth? Why all the pretense?"

"Would you have come to Angelton if you'd known?"

She looked down into her cup, then finally back up. "No, probably not."

He shrugged his shoulders. "Then there's your answer. I had to get you here. Lying seemed like the only way. I'm not proud of it, but..."

Cara took a sip of her coffee, then set the cup down on the edge of Monty's desk. There was nothing wrong with the brew, but it suddenly tasted as bitter as her feelings. "I'm not exactly proud of what happened to me fourteen years ago, either. So I'm sure you can understand my lack of enthusiasm in your plan for the rest of my life."

His eyes opened slightly, then he ducked his head in what almost seemed, at least to Cara, like an acknowledgment of guilt. "Old men like to think of themselves as important and all-knowing. And when our women ask us for help, well, we bust our butts to do whatever they want." He looked at her over the rim of his coffee cup. "We don't always think about how it affects other people."

"I'm afraid you're going to *have* to think about it this time, Monty. Because I can't give you what you want."

Obviously stunned, he sat perfectly still in his big leather chair and stared at her. Cara stared back.

"You don't want to help raise your own daughter?"

Cara licked her lips. "It's not that I don't *want* to. It's more a question of can't."

"That's ridiculous. You're a woman, aren't you? All women care about kids."

Cara felt her eyes open in amazement. "Being or not being a woman has absolutely nothing to do with this issue. Look at you—you're obviously interested in Kit's welfare and you certainly aren't a woman."

He set his cup down. "Of course I'm not a woman, but that's not what I meant, and you know it. Jerilyn thinks Kit needs a feminine touch during her growing-up years, and I agree." For the first time, his blue eyes turned slightly frosty. "I'll be the first to admit, I didn't think this was the best plan in the world myself, but Jerilyn insisted. I just can't believe that you wouldn't want to participate in raising your own child."

"It's not that," Cara protested almost desperately.

"Then what is it?" he said. "Explain it to me."

"It's a combination of things—my job, my life, my—"

He held up one hand and stopped her. "Why are you lying to me about this?"

Cara's hand went to her throat. "L-lying? What makes you say that?"

"You aren't the kind of woman who wouldn't want her own child. Why, when Kit walked up to you at my house last weekend, I thought you were going to pass out." He nodded as Cara reached out for the back of her chair. "I was watching you—hell, I was holding my own breath."

Cara didn't know what to say, and Monty continued. "Besides that, I trust my wife's opinions explicitly. After she met you the other night, all she could do was talk about how nice you were and how pretty you looked, and what a relief it was to her to know that you and Tye together could raise Kit."

Cara felt her mouth drop open. "She said *what?*"

"You heard me." His weariness settled over him again like a heavy coat, and Cara could almost see the anger drain from him. "She wants what your uncle Jack always wanted—for you and Tye to marry and live happily ever after, Kit by your side." Closing his eyes, he shook his head for a moment, then looked at her once again. "Jerilyn is a hopeless romantic."

Cara rose from her chair, amazement bringing her to her feet. "*Hopeless* is definitely the right word." Holding her hands out in front of her, she took two steps toward the desk. "I . . . I don't know what to say."

"You don't have to say anything right now, Cara." Monty's eyes met hers in an unflinching stare. "Jerilyn isn't going to last much longer. If you could just stay for a little while, then we'll . . . figure out the rest later."

In the outer office, a phone rang, footsteps fell, someone said good-night. They could have been on another planet as far as Cara was concerned.

"Please," he said. "We need your help."

Cara's throat turned tight, and she couldn't speak. Although she barely knew him, Cara was certain of one thing—Monty Montgomery wasn't the kind of man who said "please" often. She met his even stare, but before she could turn away, a spark of understanding flashed and caught between them.

She was no stranger to pain—it was almost an old familiar friend—and she recognized its mark on Monty's face. He was a man about to lose the only woman he'd ever loved, and all he needed from Cara was some time. She didn't want to give it—in fact, didn't have it *to* give—yet something told her she couldn't live with herself if she didn't at least try. And didn't she know what it was like to lose the only person you loved?

She blinked, then looked over his shoulder out the window to the lake. The sun had begun to set and a purple dusk ringed the water. "All right, I'll stay," she said softly. "But not forever."

On Wednesday, when Kit stopped her in the hall outside her office, Cara was not at all prepared. It wasn't just because she was surprised to see the teenager in the office—it was because, Cara realized deep down, she'd been avoiding Kit.

Just like she'd avoided thinking about her for the past fourteen years.

"We're going out to the lake this weekend since it got warm again," Kit said, looking up at Cara. "Would you like to come?"

Kit's face beamed hopefully as she shifted a small purple backpack from one hand to the other, Tye at her side, his own expression inscrutable. Cara couldn't help it. Her own glance lingered on his face.

Kit spoke again, pulling Cara's thoughts away. "The lake's not too rough right now, and the boat's all clean and everything. You might really like it."

Cara swallowed and looked at her daughter. She wore zebra-striped leggings with a sweatshirt so big it drooped to her knees. A floppy hat, its brim turned up and a sprig of violets tucked into it, emphasized her bright blue eyes. Cara had never seen a child look so charming—and she was almost ill with the desire to take her into her arms and never let her go.

"I... I'm not much of a sailor," Cara said, regret thickening her voice. "Maybe some other time."

Kit shot her father a look, then aimed her blue stare back on Cara's face. "That's not what Dad said. He said you liked the water."

Cara smiled. "That was a long time ago."

Kit continued to drill her. "But Dad says some things never change—like riding a bicycle or swimming—you always like to do them."

Tye put one hand on Kit's shoulder, his own eyes punching holes in Cara's insides. "If Ms. Howard doesn't want to go, Kit, then that's okay. We'll take her next time."

"But—"

Tye sent her a warning glance, and Kit's shoulders fell, a veil of disappointment coming over her face. "All right," she said in a low voice, "but we might not get another chance for a long time. It's gonna get cold pretty soon, and then it'll be too late."

Cara was totally unprepared for the guilt that spiked through her. She'd never been the source of unhappiness for someone so young, and she couldn't believe the way it

grabbed her. The irony of the words *too late* didn't pass un-
noticed, either. She spoke quickly before she could change
her mind. "You know, Kit, I think you might be right." She
met Tye's startled glance. "We might *not* get another
chance. What time are you leaving?"

Kit's face immediately broke into a big grin. "At two on
Friday. I'm getting out of school early 'cause it's a teacher
workday. Dad said we'd let them work, and we'd go play."

Cara felt her own mouth turn up, despite her trepidation. "That sounds like a good plan to me."

"All right!" Kit looked up at her dad. "See? I told ya
she'd go." She smiled at Cara once more, then reached up
and kissed her father. A second later, she was heading down
the hall, speaking as she jogged backward. "I'll see ya at
dinner, Dad—I've got band practice till five. Bye, Ms.
Howard."

Kit disappeared around the corner, and Cara felt like all
the energy left the hallway—including her own. This was the
first time she'd been alone with Tye in a week; the last time
they'd been together, she'd just left his bed. *God! Her life
had turned into a roller coaster.*

She looked up at him. "Was this boating expedition her
idea or yours?"

Tye had on a dark blue suit with a paler blue shirt. He
looked every inch the executive, especially with his hands
locked behind his back, his steady gaze searching her face
as if trying to read her. "Does it matter?"

"Yes," she answered. "It does matter—to me."

He tipped his head slightly. "It was hers," he finally ad-
mitted. "She's been bugging me for weeks to take Monty's
boat out, and when I said I had some work to do—with
you—she jumped on it. Said we could do it on the boat." He
let his eyes go to the end of the hall as if she were still there.
"She's no dummy."

But I sure am! Cara's stomach tripped over as she realized what she'd done. An afternoon on a boat with Kit and
Tye? What on earth had she been thinking when she'd said
yes? The closer she got to them both, the harder it would be

when she *did* have to leave. And leave, she would. Sooner or later.

She immediately tried to think of a way out, but when Tye looked at her again, the sympathy in his expression was all she needed to see to know she'd be on that dock Friday afternoon at 2:00 p.m.

It was as if he'd read her mind. "Are you sure it's okay?" he asked. "I could tell her something came up, and you couldn't make it after all."

She squared her shoulders. "That's not necessary," she said. "Kit just thinks I'm a friend of yours, and we're going sailing, right?"

"That's right," he answered, his voice even. "She doesn't know anything else."

Suddenly grateful for the wall at her back, Cara let her shoulder blades rest against it. She trembled at the thought of telling Kit the truth, but she knew it would have to be done. "Sometime soon she's going to have to know, Tye. After all, she's fourteen—that's only three years younger than I was when we—"

"I know, Cara. I know."

Cara's throat suddenly seemed as dry as Bear Lake had been following a drought one year. "I guess waiting a little longer wouldn't hurt. Do—do *I* have to tell her? By myself, I mean?"

For just a moment, Tye's gaze flicked with something that looked like compassion. "Monty told me that you agreed to stay till…well, till things are settled. When the time's right, we'll both tell her."

A feeling of relief swept over Cara, so strong that she felt her knees tremble. Her hand came up to her throat. "Good," she said in a shaky voice. "I—I don't think I'd know what to say all by myself." She gave a laugh that matched her voice. "I always thought if you were a parent, you automatically knew what to say, but that's not true, is it?"

His face softened slightly. "No. But you learn. I was terrified when I first got her, but bit by bit, we muddled through with a lot of help from Monty and Jerilyn." He glanced back down the hallway where Kit had disappeared. "I don't think I've made too many mistakes . . . but I'm not sure."

Cara put her hand on his arm. "I'm sure you've done the best you could. Just like I did."

For a moment, he stood there, pulling his top lip in between his teeth and saying nothing. Finally he spoke. "I...I think I owe you an apology, Cara." His eyes darkened to a shade of blue that made her heart tumble. "I've been thinking about what you said the other day—about not taking Kit away from me. Obviously I overreacted that day and jumped to some conclusions that were wrong. I'm sorry."

Once again, Cara leaned back against the wall, his voice and look making her search for the support that had fled her knees. "It's completely understandable," she answered. "When you're scared, you always think the worst. I do."

He reached up and smoothed a curl beside her ear, sending the scent of his cologne ahead of his touch. "I think I owe you another apology, too."

"For what?"

"For last weekend. I think I took advantage of you."

It would have been easy for Cara to lie, but she couldn't. There was too much between them now for her to deceive . . . or deny. She shook her head. "Don't think that. I needed what you gave me, Tye. It was all such a shock, and what happened between us grounded me, brought me back to earth."

He lifted one eyebrow. "That doesn't sound too good. I thought that kind of activity was supposed to shoot you to the moon."

They'd made love, they'd had a child. They'd shared so many things, but teasing wasn't one of them, and when he smiled down at her, Cara didn't know how to reply.

He smiled, then brushed her cheek with a kiss. "Meet you at the dock on Friday at two. Bring your plans for the conference room . . . and a swimsuit."

The situation was awkward, but Cara didn't know what else to do. Tye *had* to have a major piece for his office, and she couldn't select it on her own. Standing in the middle of the furniture showroom on Thursday, she studied him while he studied a marble-and-glass breakfront.

Part of her wanted to turn around and walk away—like she'd always done and had promised Monty she wouldn't—but another part of her acknowledged that the ties between her and Tye were so strong, so tight, they could never be broken, no matter what.

From a distance, as she watched, he moved to one end of the enormous piece of furniture and ran his hand over the polished marble.

She instantly felt a corresponding ripple down her own back, as if he'd touched her instead of the inanimate piece of furniture. They were linked in so many ways it scared her, but one of the strongest, she had to finally admit, was the physical. When Tye made love to her, the world stopped.

He disappeared around the back of the breakfront, and Cara automatically turned to follow him, her eyes never leaving his form. How had he managed to entrap her so completely, so thoroughly? If nothing else, she would have thought that everything she had learned in the past few days would have set her free from him, but just the opposite had occurred. In a perverse twist, they seemed even closer than before.

And it had nothing to do with Kit.

That realization startled Cara as much as anything since her world had gone crazy. But she couldn't ignore it.

Tye Benedict was the most attractive, the most incredible, the most powerful man she'd ever known, and nothing, including the presence—or lack—of a child between them would ever change that fact. Even if he were a perfect stranger, he would draw her eyes and pull her toward him, just as he was doing right now. To her *and* to another woman who was a member of the sales force at the showroom.

Cara watched as the other woman came over to Tye and began to talk. They were obviously discussing the piece of furniture, but just as obvious, at least to Cara, was the woman's interest in Tye. It was a subtle thing, but one that any woman would recognize. A tilt of the head, a quick smile, a glance down at his left hand. She was an attractive woman, too. Mid-twenties, blond, blue eyes, sharp figure. A woman any man would have looked at more than once.

As Cara watched, Tye and the woman both reached for one of the drawer pulls at the same time. Their hands collided, and they both drew back, laughing. Tye smiled down at her and said something, then the woman brought her fingers to her throat as though to calm a fluttering pulse.

Cara felt a corresponding surge in her own heart, and with amazement she defined the swell as jealousy. She didn't want Tye looking at another woman, smiling at her, making her laugh. He shouldn't be doing that, she thought illogically. He can't be doing that.

And the blonde was out of line, too. *She* had no right to look at Tye like that.

He was hers, Cara thought.

He always had been. He always would be.

Ignoring the implications of that particular thought, Cara put her feet in gear and appeared at Tye's side. "Are you thinking about this for your office?" she asked.

He pursed his lips in a way that reminded her of how the world spun when he kissed her. "I'm not sure, but Marilyn here says marble is the perfect thing for an executive's office."

"Oh, really? That's interesting." Her words said one thing, but Cara was well aware the tone of her voice was giving a much different message. She couldn't seem to control herself, however, and a second later she was glad she hadn't tried. With an envious—but understanding—smile that held a touch of regret, the saleswoman moved away.

Amusement clear in his eyes, Tye looked down at Cara. "Don't you like marble?"

Cara looked at the piece of furniture and tried to regain her semblance of control. She was acting like a schoolgirl, for God's sake. "It's all right, I suppose."

"Marilyn says it conveys a message of strength, of durability." He raised one eyebrow and brought his hand to his chin. "The coldness of the marble and brass imparts a certain detachment from the situation, she said. What do you think?"

"I think that's a salesperson's pitch," Cara said instantly. "But if it *were* true, I don't think it'd fit you, anyway. You aren't detached or cold."

Like a torch, the blue blaze in his eyes turned up another notch, and Cara felt a corresponding heat build somewhere in the vicinity of her lower stomach. "What *do* you see in my office, then?"

She fought her reaction to him, but she couldn't get rid of it. "I—I think something warmer, in wood, with a few scars on it. Something old that meant something to someone once."

"An antique piece, then. Like the one you talked about before?"

"Yes."

He lifted one hand toward her face and brushed his knuckle against her cheek. The touch was incredibly soft and gentle, but it rocked her all the way down to her toes. "And why is that, Cara? Why do you think I'm not cold marble and polished brass after all I've done to you?"

She stared into his face and shook her head. There was no reason to how she felt about this man—no reason, no logic, no analysis that would make sense. There was only emotion. "It's not a crime to love, Tye. If it was, I would have been locked up, too."

Angelton had changed, Cara thought Friday morning as she directed the rented Cadillac into the striped parking spot. Changed a lot. Sitting for a moment, she considered the upscale shopping area in front of her. Tucked into the different nooks and crannies, at least two dozen boutiques opened into a gardenlike pavilion, lined with ficus trees, hanging baskets and giant clay pots filled with mums. Someone with money and taste had designed the area, making it inviting yet professional.

Opening her door, Cara climbed out of the car and headed toward the first shop. When Tye had told her earlier in the week to bring a bathing suit with her today, she'd panicked. She'd only brought a few casual things to Angelton and certainly not a bathing suit. She'd had no choice this morning except to go shopping and hope for the best.

The bell over the shop door jingled pleasantly as Cara stepped inside. Piled high on skirted tables were sweaters, jeans and scarfs, but no bathing suits. A woman appeared from the back. "Hi," Cara said. "I'm a little out of season, but I need a bathing suit. Can you help me?"

The saleswoman shook her head. "I'm sorry, but no. We're totally sold out. But try Nina's at the end of the sidewalk—she usually stocks resort wear all year-round."

"Thanks." Cara stepped outside and glanced up at the signs. A brightly colored pink-and-aqua one, in the shape of a fish, caught her eye. Curlicued letters proclaimed Nina's, and Cara briskly headed that way.

She didn't have the time to be doing something like this, she thought with a frown. Monty wanted to see some revised suggestions for the furniture in his office, and one of his senior vice presidents was giving Cara an exceptionally hard time about the paper in his conference room. Her heels clicked on the bricks as she neared the end of the sidewalk. If Kit hadn't looked so disappointed, this wouldn't have—

Cara stopped abruptly, her eyes drawn by the display in the shop next door to Nina's. Tiny and somewhat forgotten-looking, the antique shop seemed to be an anachronism itself among the bright, expensive stores that were its companions in the area, but that only made it all the more appealing to Cara. She hadn't been lying when she'd told Tye that antiques were her passion. Someday, when she had the time and the money, she'd open a shop of her own, just like this one. Cozy and small and exclusive.

Her fingers rested lightly on the glass as she stared through the plate-glass window. The display needed work, a lot of work. Tossed haphazardly this way and that, a variety of small items caught her eye. Battersea boxes, children's clothing, dusty first editions—they were all thrown together. Cara squinted and looked farther back. There seemed to be a few larger pieces of furniture, but desks and chairs were clearly not the owner's interest. No, every square inch was covered in the kinds of things that rested in the window. Knickknacks.

Cara glanced down at her watch and moaned. She had less than an hour to buy a bathing suit, go back to the hotel and change, then show up at the dock. There was no way she could go in the shop and still get everything done.

Temptation overcame common sense. She stepped over to the door and gave a quick pull on the knob, but it refused to move. The shop was closed.

"Just as well," she murmured with one last look of longing.

Nina's proved bountiful, and thirty minutes later Cara had slacks, tops and two bathing suits. Walking out to her car, she threw the packages into the back seat, then jumped into the Cadillac and headed for the hotel. There would be just enough time to change, grab her briefcase and get to the lake.

Anticipation rippled over her. A day on the water with Tye—and their daughter.

Tye looked up as the Cadillac crunched the gravel near the pier. Beside him, Kit paused, her hands still on the rope he'd just handed her.

"Look. It's Ms. Howard, Dad. There she is."

The excitement in Kit's voice surprised him—she'd never really reacted to the women he'd dated and brought home, but obviously something about Cara pleased her. He tore his eyes from Cara's slim figure to stare at his daughter. "You like her, don't you?"

Kit nodded. "Yeah, I do. I think she's really pretty, and I couldn't believe you'd actually snagged her at Uncle Monty's the other night."

"We were talking, Kit, that's all," he said with what he hoped was a calm voice.

"Yeah, well, it might have been just talk to you, but she was looking at you like she really liked you. Know what I mean?"

Tye bent over and reached for the coil of rope at his feet, trying to hide his surprise. Few details slipped past Kit, but this was one he hadn't considered at all. Would she be able to pick up the tensions that existed between him and Cara? Or the extent of their relationship?

Without another word, Kit left his side and dashed up the rickety boards to meet Cara, leaving Tye to straighten slowly and watch as they walked together toward him.

There was no mistaking the heritage they shared, even though Tye had tried for as long as he'd had Kit. They even walked the same way, their graceful gait matching as perfectly as the highlights in their hair. He was shocked by the startling similarities between them, and he instantly wondered how he'd ever thought he could forget Cara when Kit would always be there. In unison, they laughed, and a catch formed in the back of Tye's throat.

"Look, Dad. Ms. Howard brought a picnic basket. Neat, huh?"

Under the brim of an ivory hat, Cara lifted her face and stared at him. "I hope you don't mind," she said, "but I didn't want to just show up empty-handed. It's not anything special—just some crackers and cheese, a bottle of wine...stuff like that."

Tye's stomach tightened, but his reaction had nothing to do with the food she'd mentioned. "I don't mind at all," he said, his eyes slowly sliding over her turquoise leggings and brightly flowered T-shirt. "In fact, it sounds wonderful."

"Good." She turned to Kit and handed her the hamper. "Why don't you stow this for me, then I'll go back to the car and get my briefcase?"

"I'll do it all," Kit promptly answered. "You're our guest. You just sit here and talk to Dad while I take care of it for you. I insist."

Cara laughed. "Okay, but only if you insist."

Kit grinned, then jumped nimbly from the dock to the gently swaying boat tied up beside them. Cara watched her disappear down a ladder into the below-decks cabin, then turned to Tye and spoke. "Is she always that helpful? That cheerful?"

Mentally shaking himself, Tye forced his gaze to Cara's face. He was acting like a teenager, for God's sake, instead of what he was—which was a father. "Generally, yes. She's an optimist, for the most part."

Cara nibbled on one corner of her lip, her expression puzzled as she studied the boat. "I thought teenagers nowadays were moody, angry. She doesn't seem that way at all."

Tye picked up the rope that Kit had dropped and began to coil it over his arm. "I think you've been watching too much television—but don't be fooled." He lifted one eyebrow and tilted his head. "She's on her best behavior today because she likes you."

Cara jerked her eyes to Tye's face, their dark confusion instantly replaced by wonder and disbelief. She looked like a kid on Christmas morning who'd just caught Santa Claus coming down the chimney, his bag overflowing with presents. "She likes me?"

Tye swallowed hard against the sympathy that welled inside him. He didn't exactly know what Cara was feeling—and something told him she didn't, either—but he was sure about one thing. Cara loved Kit.

"Well, she just said she liked you," he answered. "And one thing she doesn't do is lie."

Cara's hand rested at the base of her throat, and between her spread fingers, Tye watched her pulse beat. "But she doesn't even know me."

"Doesn't matter. She makes snap judgments, like I do."

"And are they usually accurate?"

His fingers poised over the rope. "If you mean, does she believe the same thing a few years down the road, then yes."

Cara nodded slowly, the brim of her hat moving in the breeze off the lake. Kit's head appeared a second later above the deck, then she bounded from the boat and leapt to the deck. "Is your car locked?" she breathlessly asked Cara.

"No, it's open, and my briefcase is on the back seat."

"Great." Her tennis shoes slapping the pier, Kit ran toward the car.

"So much energy," Cara murmured. "She runs everywhere—" She broke off and looked at Tye. "Did you do that when you were a kid?"

He shrugged. "Yeah, only my running took me to the liquor store to pick up a six-pack for my mother." The memory hurt, and as Tye watched his own daughter reach into Cara's car and take something out, he remembered the vow he'd made that she'd never be ashamed of him like he'd been of his mother. He hoped he could always keep that promise.

Before he could give it more thought, a faint ringing erupted on the deck of the boat. Cara glanced toward the deck, then back at Tye. "What's that?"

He grimaced. "My cellular phone. Kit's going to have a fit if that's the office." Glancing up, he saw that she was already coming down the pier. "Keep her busy, would you? I'll see what it is."

In two quick strides he was on the polished teak deck and reaching for the small gray phone. When he answered it, surprise arched his eyebrows. It was Jerilyn.

"Tye, I'm so glad I caught you. Are you down at the boat?"

"Yes, I am." Alarm rippled over him like a breeze before a storm. "Are you okay?"

Her famous laugh sounded, and he felt his tension slip away. "Yes, darling. I'm fine. But I'm wondering if you have Kit with you?"

He watched Kit run down the pier with Cara's briefcase. "Yes, I do. We were just about to shove off. Cara's here, and we were going out for a bit."

Jerilyn's voice dropped. "Cara's with you? That's wonderful."

"We'll see.... Did you want to talk to Kit about something?"

"Well, I don't know what to do. I surely wouldn't want to interrupt your plans, but Maribell's about to have her kittens. Kit's been hanging around that poor cat like a shadow for weeks waiting for the big event. What should we do?"

"Let me ask her." Tye walked to the edge of the deck and leaned over. "Kit, this is Jerilyn. She says Maribell's about to have her kittens. Do you want to go over there?"

Kit's face broke into a giant smile, then clouded as she turned to Cara. Cara said something he couldn't hear, then a second later Kit nodded her head so hard he thought her neck would snap. "I'm afraid we've lost the competition, Jerilyn. Maribell's attractions apparently outweigh an hour on the lake. Shall I bring her or could you have James drive down and pick her up?"

Jerilyn laughed. "He'll be there in five minutes."

Chapter 12

The sun was as warm as Kit had promised, the waters of the lake as smooth, but somehow the day had dimmed for Cara when she'd watched her daughter disappear into the long black Cadillac to go witness the miracle of birth.

She felt Tye's glance on her. "I'm sorry it didn't work out," he said softly. "I can see you're disappointed."

In the stiff breeze coming over the prow, Cara grasped the edge of her hat as she looked over at Tye. He was guiding the powerful boat with two fingers and watching her, sunglasses shading his eyes from her view. "Am I that obvious?" she asked.

He shrugged, a smile pulling up the corners of his mouth. "Well, you look a little down, and since I'd like to think my company's not *that* bad, I made an assumption. Am I wrong?"

Cara turned against the padded cushions to face him. "I was hoping to get to know her better," she confessed. "It seemed like a perfect time."

He turned his glance back toward the water. "There'll be others."

"I hope so."

"In fact, it's Kit's birthday next week."

He continued to talk, but Cara didn't hear another word. Of course, she'd been aware of this and had been trying, unsuccessfully, to put *that* date out of her mind for years. She'd worked until midnight, read until dawn, watched television till it went off the air, yet nothing she'd done had ever let her forget that day.

Tye's voice broke into her thoughts. "—was going to let her have some friends over to swim, eat out…whatever she wants. Why don't you come?"

Tye's hand pulled against the throttle, and beneath her, Cara felt the engines respond immediately, the boat tugging free against the water. Suddenly she felt the same way— without guidance. She didn't know which direction to take. Share a birthday party with Kit? In one sense, it was like a dream come true. But in another, it would be an event to endure—because she knew it would be the only one she'd ever celebrate with her daughter. Emotion won over logic.

"I'd love to," she answered. "Just tell me when and where."

His eyes warmed her. "Good."

They were the only ones on the lake, and in the sudden silence, Cara was almost afraid Tye could hear her nervous pulse. They were alone, totally alone, and inexplicably she'd wished she'd declined his invitation to go ahead with the boat ride after Kit had left. She remembered her feeling as she'd seen the boat her first day back in Angelton. Running away, even for a little while, had appealed to her. Had some part of her known, unconsciously, that the man she'd seen on the boat was Tye? Had she known, but come anyway?

To cover her sudden attack of anxiety, Cara bent over and reached into the hamper at her feet, digging around until she found an apple. She held it out to Tye first, then brought it to her own mouth after he'd shook his head. "Isn't that old man Breshear's farm over there?" she said, nodding toward the shore.

Tye followed her nod, then grinned. "Yeah. Only, now it's his son's."

"No! Really?"

"My God, Cara, Willie Breshear was a hundred years old when we were in high school. You didn't really think he'd still be running the place now, did you?"

She grinned. "Uncle Jack always said the mean ones go last. If that's the case, then Breshear *should* still be alive."

Tye's dark gaze turned thoughtful. "He wasn't *all* that mean, not really. Just lonely, I think."

"I'll never forget how you used to steal his watermelons every summer. You had to clean out his barn all one winter as penance, I believe. Why the sudden sympathy?"

"He was trying to teach me a valuable lesson. I wish I'd learned it." Tye reached over and took the apple from her fingers, his teeth biting into the fruit with a sharp snap. "I met a man in prison that reminded me of him. We shared a cell, in fact. I got to know him, and in a way, I guess I got to know Breshear." Studying the apple, he took another bite.

A tug of something went through Cara's heart. "I asked you when I first got here if prison was really bad. You didn't answer me then. Would you now?"

He polished off the apple, then tossed it over the side of the boat, brushing his hands over his jeans. "That's history," he said grimly.

Cara blinked in the face of his brusqueness, then spoke without thinking. "That's true, but I still want to hear about it." She paused. "I've always felt it was partly my fault that you were there."

His sunglasses hid the blue of his eyes, but she knew instinctively that she'd surprised him—by her honesty or by her feelings, she didn't know which.

"That's ridiculous," he said. "I was the one who held up that store—it was my idea and my irresponsibility that landed me in jail."

"But you wouldn't have done it if my parents had been more reasonable."

He dismissed her words. "I did it. I paid for it." With a nod of his head toward the hamper, he asked, "Did you say you had some wine in there?"

"Yes." She reached down into the basket, but at the same time, he did, too. Their hands collided, and Cara pulled back. "It's in...in there," she said, feeling foolishly nervous again.

He removed the bottle of white burgundy and a corkscrew from the bottom of the hamper. Clamping the bottle between his knees, he began to remove the foil covering on the neck of the bottle. "A lot of people are curious about prison. They have this idea from television that it's either constant brutality or a kind of country club for thieves." He glanced up from his task, his broad hands still. "It's neither. It's simply mind-numbing sameness all of the time. The same food, the same people, the same four walls. *That's* what breaks you—the monotony. The monotony and nothing else."

Cara bit her bottom lip. "I can't imagine what it must have been like. And you were so young."

He went back to work, the aluminum crumpling as he peeled it away to expose the cork. "Every hour seemed like a day, and every day seemed like a month." Using the corkscrew, he pierced the stopper directly in the center, then with quick, deft movements he twisted the opener until the metal rim rested on the glass lip of the bottle. "The only thing that got me through the time was thinking about you."

Cara swallowed her breath, her hand going to her throat. "Me?"

"That's right. In the winter I imagined you sitting by a big fire somewhere, and in the summer I thought about you fishing down here at the lake. I felt very noble because I'd set you free." He gave a quick tug and the cork popped up, a soft sigh coming with it.

From the hamper, Cara pulled out two plastic glasses, her hands trembling. "Instead, I married Bill."

He took one of the glasses from her hands and began to fill it. "How did you meet him?" His casual voice held no more than passing interest, but even in her turmoil, Cara sensed an underlying animosity. Was he jealous? The idea that he could experience what she had felt in the furniture showroom seemed both ridiculous and thrilling at the same time.

"At college, first class, first semester," she answered. "I was majoring in interior design, and he was in the architecture school. We collaborated on a project, then one thing led to another...." She took the glass of wine Tye offered her, then handed him the other empty glass to fill for himself.

His blue eyes studied her. "One thing led to another? That's why you got married?"

She raised her gaze from the drink in her hand and lifted her shoulders in a shrug. "People do it all the time."

"Other people, maybe, but not you."

Startled, Cara quickly swallowed the wine she'd just taken and held back a cough. Tye spoke again. "You aren't the kind of woman who drifts into a relationship. You either believe in it or you don't." He shook his head again, then sipped his wine.

"Maybe I was different back then."

"No," he said again. "I *knew* you back then, remember?"

"I changed after I had Kit."

He set the wine bottle back into the hamper, then leaned against the cushions. "Nobody changes that much."

Her heart protesting, Cara took a deep breath and met his gaze. "The truth is, Bill reminded me of you," she said bluntly. "I married him because I thought it might help."

"Help?"

"Help me forget you," she said, her throat closing. "In some really weird way, I thought marrying him might make me think of you in a different light—might make me stop loving you."

"Oh, God." Tye's blue eyes darkened until they matched the water beneath the boat. Abruptly, he put his wineglass down, then stood and walked to the end of the deck, his long legs covering the small space with two strides. Helpless to do anything else, Cara followed his figure with her eyes. The chilling breeze ruffled his blond hair, picking up the thick curls at the collar of his black Windbreaker and tossing them over his collar. Her emotions were just as tangled. She rose and went to his side.

"You asked," she said almost defensively.

"I know." He looked down at her. "But I didn't expect the truth."

The silence of the lake wrapped around them, and Cara found herself stepping closer to Tye. "I didn't, either," she answered, "but somehow when I get around you, the truth just seems to come out—whether I want it to or not."

Slowly, as if he were afraid he might frighten her off, he reached out for her, his hands going to her face. Cradling her cheeks, he studied her. "I think it *is* time for the truth between us, Cara. We've made too many mistakes by lying. I don't want that to happen anymore."

Her mouth suddenly dry, Cara nodded. "You're right, but... I'm not always real good at facing the facts."

"There's one thing you can't ignore."

She stared at him, his mouth inches from hers, so close that she could feel his warm breath as he spoke. "What's that?" she asked, her stomach tightening.

"I think you know."

His mouth came down on hers, and this time there was no anger, no hesitation, no point that either one of them had to prove. They couldn't use the excuse that they were comforting each other, and they couldn't say it was an accident that shouldn't happen again. They couldn't even say they were teenagers, and they didn't know any better.

Because only the truth would do—the truth that told them this kiss meant more than anything that had happened between them since Cara had returned to Angelton.

His lips closed over hers, gently at first and then a bit more desperately, as though he were trying to make sure she understood what was at stake. After only a second, he lifted his mouth, then immediately he brought it back, kissing her again.

It was a kiss that reached down into Cara's soul and pulled out a response so deep, so heartfelt, so immediate, that she could do nothing but raise her arms, twine them about Tye's neck and give in to the storm of emotions now rocking her. His mouth tasted of the wine they'd shared, and behind that was a faint, clean apple scent. Beneath her closed eyelids, flashes of desire sparked and flared into longing.

His hands slipped from her face to the back of her neck, one cupping her head, the other tangling in her hair. Before the sharp wind had seemed cold and cutting to Cara. Now it wrapped them together, the chill meaningless as the warmth from Tye's body merged with hers.

His mouth increased its demands, and Cara eagerly opened to them, molding herself against him as if he could protect her from what she was feeling inside as easily as he did from the wind. Her fingers curled into his hair, his soft, thick, blond hair, and in the back of her throat, a moan began, then died.

Finally Tye raised his head. His own eyes seemed slightly dazed and Cara realized with amazement the kiss had affected him as deeply as it had her.

She met his stare, her voice as shaky as her legs. "You're right," she said. "I can't ignore that."

As if he were on a diet, and allowing himself only a taste of the forbidden, Tye leaned back down and took the corner of her mouth in his. The touch was butterfly quick and soft, but the impact on Cara wasn't. She leaned against him, the gently moving deck under her feet unaccountable for her wobbly knees.

"I...I don't think you should keep doing that," she said.

"Why not?" he murmured against her mouth. "Is it bothering you?"

"Yes," she breathed. "It's bothering me a lot, and I think you better stop."

Obligingly, he released her lip, but his mouth continued its torture, dropping kisses over her cheeks, her eyelids, along the line of her hair. His hands went to her back and he pulled her even closer. "Are you cold?" he whispered. "Should we go down to the cabin?"

Cara shook her head. "No...no, I don't think that'd be a good idea, either."

He kissed the tip of her ear, his mouth so warm, so tender against her skin that it made her squirm. "Why not?" The rasp of his breathing matched her own, and Cara knew they couldn't continue this way much longer. "I think it's a great idea. There's a heater, and hot brandy, and lots of blankets...and a nice big bed." Leaning back from her, Tye seared her with his eyes. "Come with me, Cara. Let me make love to you like I've wanted to for the past fourteen years."

She sucked in her breath. "What was last weekend?"

"That didn't count. We were both too needy, too hurt to give each other pleasure." He caressed the small of her back, his hand warm through the sweater she'd put on earlier. "Let me love you, Cara. Love you like you deserve."

Cara couldn't answer. She couldn't even speak, and with the decisiveness that made Tye who he was, he picked her up and turned around. A second later, they were in the cabin.

It was just as warm as he'd said it would be...and the bed was just as big.

He stopped beside it and tenderly set her on her feet, his eyes never leaving her face. "I want you to know something," he said, slowly releasing each tiny pearl button of her sweater. "Through the years, I've thought of you many, many times. On New Year's Eve, I wanted to dance with you." He gently peeled the wool away from her shoulders and dropped it on the floor. "On Valentine's Day I wanted to send you flowers." Reaching under her T-shirt, he took the waist band of her leggings and gently tugged them down. Mesmerized by his words, she silently stepped out of the pants and kicked them aside, her own eyes incapable of leaving his face.

"In the spring, when the bluebonnets bloomed, I wanted to bring you out with me and drive through the countryside to see them." He lifted her T-shirt over her head, and she stood beside him in the warmth, her silk bra and panties gleaming in the dusky twilight that filtered through the porthole. "And at Christmas," he said, his hands pressing against the sides of her breasts, "when I'd be sitting by the fire, you were the only woman on my mind."

He brought her hands to the buttons on his shirt, and without a word, she began to undo each one as he continued to talk. "What I'm trying to tell you, Cara, is that I never stopped thinking about you, even though I'd told you I didn't love you. It's very important to me that you realize that."

She pushed his shirt off his shoulders, then pressed herself against him, the rough hair on his chest scratching against her bare skin. Holding on to him as if he could keep her from feeling any more, she spoke, her mouth moving against him. "I do know that now," she answered softly, "but back then, I didn't." She looked up at him. "I thought you meant what you'd said... and if I hadn't been pregnant, I... I don't know what I would have done."

She saw his throat move as he swallowed convulsively, and when he pressed her head against his chest with one hand, she could hear his heart thumping wildly. "God, don't tell me that," he said in a frenzied voice. "I can't bear the thought of you being that desperate—and just because of my stupidity."

Cara shook her head and looked up at him. "I didn't tell you that to make you feel guilty, Tye. I told you so you'd know—I never stopped loving you, either."

"Oh, God." He wrapped his arms around her and hugged her even closer. If he could have, she thought, he would have brought her under his skin—and that would have been fine with her. What he did instead was kiss her.

Suddenly Cara realized she couldn't hold on to the constraints of her emotions *and* to Tye, too. As his mouth came down on hers, she felt the beginnings of release well up from deep inside her. Their cards were really on the table, and all the lies were gone. The frozen wall within her—the one that

had protected her heart for so long—was breaking down
with frightening swiftness.

Returning to Angelton had chipped the first piece from
the barrier. Another piece had cracked and fallen down
when she'd first seen Tye. And when she'd met Kit, the
barricade had shattered. All that was left now was an empty
shell, and in the overwhelming warmth of Tye's embrace
and his confession, the last of that piercing numbness fell
away. With dazzling clarity and pain, Cara realized how very
long it'd been since she'd shared such complete and utter
intimacy with another human being.

With one swift move, Tye bent down and lifted her into
his arms. A second later, he placed her on the bed and fell
down beside her. She reached blindly for him, her hands
urgent with need, her mouth bereft until his came down on
hers once more. A flurry of clothing—his and what was left
of hers—flew from the bed.

He'd said he wanted to make love to her like he'd dreamed
of for the past fourteen years, but Cara didn't want to wait
for that. She couldn't. The wall of her loneliness had come
crashing down, and replacing it was a passion, a need, a
desire, bigger than any she'd ever felt before.

"Please, Tye," she said, her voice hoarse with effort.
"Please." Her nails bit into his shoulders, but he didn't
seem to mind. In fact, her wantonness seemed to free the last
of his own need for control. With a savage cry, he tore his
lips from hers and rolled over on his back, taking her with
him.

She followed his move, her breasts pressing against his
chest, her hands gripping the hard muscles of his shoulders. In the dwindling light, she could barely see his face,
but she didn't need to. He guided her with his hands, with
his mouth, and with his body.

Unable to wait another minute—every second was torture—Cara lowered herself to meet Tye's hips, her body
moist with desire, Tye's breath rasping in the utter silence
around them. There was no more control to be had. It was
gone. The only thing left between them now was passion.

With a savage thrust, he took her.

For one frozen moment, Cara suspended herself and her emotions. All that she felt, all that she knew, all that she *was*, was Tye. He filled her completely. At that very single second, she needed nothing else to survive, nothing but Tye.

Even the gaping loneliness that had been part of Cara's existence since she'd given up Kit was suddenly no longer there.

Tears sprang into Cara's eyes as the enormity of what was happening registered, but she had no time to give them their due. Tye's hands seized her waist, and he began to rock her back and forth. There was suddenly no other thought but one.

Behind her tightly clenched eyelids, explosions of color and passion swirled Cara away. They took her to a place she'd only glimpsed before, and as she reached the peak, she cried out the name of the only man she loved. "Tye—oh, Tye."

He answered her the only way he could—with a final thrust of his hips. A heartbeat later, Cara collapsed against his slick chest, her own face wet with tears.

Tye's fingers drifted down her shoulder to the curve of her hip. The soft sound of water lapping against the boat mingled with the music coming from a radio behind them. He'd turned it on after calling home and telling Jerilyn they'd be late—they were going to dinner. He'd winked at Cara lying in the bed, and she'd felt an undeniable thrill, as if she were staying out way past her bedtime. Now, wrapping her arms around Tye's neck, she met the heat of his gaze. "Thank you," she said.

"For what?"

"For this." Her hands threaded through his hair, her eyes taking in the crumpled bed.

"Anytime." One corner of his mouth lifted. "But you don't really have to thank me."

"Well, actually, that's not exactly what I was thanking you for," she said. "But since it *could* apply, I'll thank you for it, too. And possibly take you up on that offer."

He lowered his head and kissed her forehead, the scent of his after-shave bringing a sharp ache to her throat. "I'll be here," he said. "Waiting."

She pushed against his chest and stopped his kisses for a moment. "What I really meant was thank you for showing me something—for making me realize how...lonely I've been. Even though I was married, even though I was working, had people all around me, I was isolated. Is it really possible to cut yourself off that way?"

His hand traced a line on the side of her cheek, this simple touch almost unbearable in its pleasure. "Of course it is. People do it all the time. It's called survival."

Cara pulled herself up and stared at him, her fingers clutching the sheet to her chest. "I can understand denying Kit—that part hurt so bad that it's easy to understand." She threaded her fingers between his. "After I gave her up, I did some reading about adoptions. A lot of birth mothers handle the situation that way, but I think I might have gone beyond that."

She let her eyes wander to the porthole. The only light relieving the inky blackness, besides the oval cast on the water from the window, was a solitary twinkling on the distant shore. Cara felt the rest of the world had disappeared, leaving only her and Tye, wrapped in darkness, cradled in water.

"I know," he said softly. "You cut yourself off completely. All of your emotions dried up." He paused, and his fingers tightened on hers. "I know because I did it, too. It was the only way I could make it through prison."

"I feel like I've been in prison, too."

"You have been—a self-imposed one, but it doesn't have to be that way anymore. You've been released, you know. You're out. You don't have to go back to that kind of life ever again."

Cara smiled, but there was no pleasure in it. Tye didn't know what he was saying, and with bittersweet regret, she leaned over and kissed him, the touch of his mouth enough to arouse her once again. She'd been set free, yes, but what good would it do her?

There was no place for her in Angelton—not permanently, anyway. She had a life in New York, a business, a career. Angelton held absolutely nothing for her but Tye and Kit—two pieces of her heart that she'd never really be able to have back.

And even if, for some outlandish reason, she thought she'd try living here once again, where would she fit in? She and Tye had made love—and yes, the world had moved—but that didn't mean they could build another relationship. No matter how much she might love him, sometimes love just wasn't enough.

Because Kit stood between them. She'd never understand why Cara had given her up, and they'd never be able to be a real family. There was simply too much pain and not enough trust. And if there was one thing Cara understood, it was that families had to have more than love.

Tye's touch broke into Cara's thoughts as he put his hand against her cheek. She turned her face into it and kissed the center of his palm.

Their lovemaking had shattered the wall of ice around her heart, and stepping out into the warmth, Cara realized now just how much she'd really missed. The wall was gone—there was nothing to hide behind anymore.

For a little while, Cara could stand in the warmth. She could share Kit with Tye, she could feel needed, she could love and be loved. The process had begun the day she'd driven into town, and as much as she'd hated to do it, Cara had given in to it, step by step. Making love with Tye had been the natural conclusion.

But thawing, like any change, was painful. Deep, agonizingly painful. It brought the kind of hurt a person would do anything to avoid, but that she hadn't been able to. The kind of hurt she'd felt in Kit's room that day. The kind you never wanted to repeat.

But she knew she would.

In fact, she knew before this was all over, she'd experience something even more painful, if that was possible.

And that would happen when she had to leave Kit and Tye again. When she had to return to the cold. Alone.

Chapter 13

She looked like a completely different person.

Tye studied Cara from across the conference room. She wore her professional hat, so to speak, but he found himself wishing instead for the real floppy-brimmed ivory one she'd worn on the lake last weekend. Oh, she was beautiful, as always, but he much preferred her leggings and T-shirt over the coral business suit she wore now.

Actually, he amended, he preferred her in nothing at all. No matter what happened in the future, he'd never, as long as he lived, forget Cara lying in the bed on the boat, her eyes black with emotion, her lips bruised from his kisses, her voice telling him the words he'd wanted to hear for so long...that she loved him, had always loved him. It was an image burned into his memory, etched by love and polished by desire—an image he would always keep in his heart.

"And so," she finished, catching his eye with a look that said *Pay attention*, "with Mr. Benedict's approval, I'll be placing my initial work orders this afternoon. You may be somewhat inconvenienced for a while by painters, paperers and other workmen, but I'll try to see that the disruption is minimal. The second phase of the project will begin on Monday when I start selecting the accessories for the senior VPs' offices plus all the conference rooms.''

She gathered her papers, then looked around the table. The five top managers, plus Monty, looked suitably impressed, Tye thought, and so they should be. Cara had done an outstanding job directing everyone toward a look that was uniquely their own, but managing to blend it together into a stunning whole. Tye had been shocked at how easily she'd seemed to do it—and equally amazed at how the building had already been transformed by the changes she'd made.

''I've gotten to know most of you pretty well, but accessories are what really pull a look together.'' She smiled at each one of the managers in turn. ''I confess I'm partial to antique touches, so I'll be looking around shops in the area, but if there's something you like in particular, please let me know. I'd hate to put an étagère of Battersea boxes in your office if you're not an anglophile.''

Tye had absolute no earthly idea what an étagère was, and he'd never heard of Battersea boxes. He'd have been willing to bet his next week's salary, too, that the managers around the conference table didn't, either, but they wouldn't give a damn if Cara put one in their office. They only knew, as he did, that every room she worked on came out looking like something from the pages of *Architectural Digest*, while still managing to be functional and comfortable.

As Cara walked around the table, the men and women seated around it rose and began to mill about. The weekly meeting was finished—Cara had been the last to speak. Tye started toward her, then stopped when Monty stepped next to him and put a hand on his arm.

''Jerilyn told me you and Cara took the boat out on Friday.''

Tye met Monty's inquisitive look. ''Yes, we did,'' he said easily. ''It was nice—a little chilly, but nice.''

''Do you mean chilly between you or chilly as in weather?''

Before Tye could answer, Cara walked up, her folders tucked under her arm. "I think it went quite well, don't you?" She looked up at Tye and smiled.

"Yes," he answered. "It went perfectly, but why not? You've done a great job."

Tye could feel Monty's eyes on him, but he refused to meet the older man's stare. He could think what he wanted—at this stage in the game, Tye didn't really care.

Monty cleared his throat and spoke. "Yes, Cara, I'm very pleased with everything, and I know my managers are, too. In fact, after I told Jerilyn how great the offices look, she asked me to find out if you might have time to stop by the house later on. I think she wants to fix something up—I'm not too sure what."

"I'd be happy to," Cara answered. "I've wanted to talk to Jerilyn about...well, about a few things, anyway. I'll drop by whenever it's convenient."

"Great." Monty shot Tye another puzzled look, then ambled off when Tye ignored him.

Tye focused on Cara. "You really did a nice job on the presentation, and I am *very* pleased with my office. If your work in New York was half as good as this, I can see why Jerilyn was impressed."

Cara smiled warmly, her dark eyes sparkling from the praise. "Thank you. I enjoy it, and I guess that always helps. The fun part is about to begin, though. I like to juxtapose older things in contemporary offices, and I think a few good pieces would look great around here." She glanced around the conference room, then back at Tye. "Haunting the antique shops to look for them is really fun, too."

"Could I go with you?" Tye suddenly asked. "I've been wanting to add something to my study at home, but I don't really know what. Maybe you could help me?"

She smiled. "I'd be happy to, but first I need to see the room."

"That makes sense. You're still coming for Kit's party, aren't you? You could look then."

A flicker of something passed over Cara's face. If Tye had known the adult Cara better, he might have understood it, but as it was, all he could do was ask. "You do still want to come, don't you?"

Cara dropped her gaze for a second, then raised her face again. "Are you sure that's a good idea, Tye?"

"Yes," he said instantly. "I *know* it's a good idea because I asked Kit if it was all right, and she was thrilled."

Cara's eyes rounded into ovals of surprised delight. "She wants me there?"

"Yes. Definitely." He paused. "And so do I."

Behind them, a loud laugh rang out over the murmur of the managers as they waited for lunch. Tye glanced up, then looked back down at Cara. He'd told the truth, he realized with a start. He *did* want Cara there to celebrate Kit's birthday. It was appropriate in more ways than one, and all at once, his former fear that she'd take Kit from him seemed outrageous and ridiculous.

Cara was a warm, loving woman, and in the past few weeks, Tye had begun to learn exactly how deeply she'd been hurt by the past they shared. She'd made the supreme sacrifice—she'd given up a child so that child could have a better life. And what had he done? He'd raised and loved and lived with the child Cara had had wrenched from her arms. Kit, Monty and Jerilyn had formed a cordon of love around him, and he'd finally had a family.

In contrast, Cara had dealt with her pain by cutting off her emotions. By living totally alone in a world of strangers. By denying herself a family to love and be with.

But that could change.

He could change it.

And, by God, he would.

He took her arm. "Please say you'll come. Kit would be very disappointed if you didn't."

Cara licked her lips. "I want to be there, but..."

"But what?"

Her dark eyes searched his face as if for understanding. "I think I'm afraid."

"Of Kit?"

"Yes, in a way." Cara shrugged her shoulders almost helplessly. "I think I'm scared of how to act around her. I don't know what to do around teenagers, and besides that, I'm afraid I'll slip and say something. I'd hate for her to accidentally find out everything—I want to plan it, be prepared when it's time to tell her who I am."

Tye moved his thumb up and down the inside of her arm. It was the only physical way he could reassure her at the moment. He didn't care who knew, but Cara would. She was that kind of woman, and he wanted to respect that.

His voice was low. "In the past fourteen years, have you ever 'slipped'?"

"Of course not."

"Then what makes you think you would now?"

Two vertical lines formed between her slender eyebrows. "I'm not the person I was when I drove into Angelton six weeks ago. I've changed."

He squeezed her arm. "You'll do fine—just be yourself."

Just be yourself.

The advice rattled in Cara's mind like a box full of marbles. She wanted to be herself, but she wasn't sure who she was anymore.

Easing the Cadillac into the circular drive of Monty's house, Cara put the car into park, then twisted the keys and killed the engine. She'd been one person when she'd left Angelton fourteen years ago. When she'd returned more than a month ago, she'd been someone else. And now? Who was she now?

Her hands curled over the steering wheel as she stared through the windshield. So much had happened, so much had changed. How could she deal with all of this?

For the first time in a long time, despite all she had found out, she wished for Uncle Jack—the Uncle Jack she'd known as a kid, the man who'd stood by her when no one else had. Even though he'd kept the truth from her, she understood now that he had done what he thought was best. With longing, she remembered his steady understanding, his quiet support, his calm suggestions. Her eyes grew hot with unshed tears. Like a lot of things she'd wanted through the years, this was one she wasn't going to get, either. That man was gone.

And she wasn't a kid anymore.

Even though Tye had made her feel that way on the boat this weekend.

She brought her trembling fingers together and laced them over her lap as if holding herself together. She loved Tye. She loved Kit. She wanted, more than anything in the world, to live here with them and be a family.

But that could never happen.

And by wanting it, Cara was only hurting herself.

Above the car, the branches of the live oak moved, the wind teasing the leaves into a dance. She should have run away the minute Tye kissed her the first time. They'd been sitting right here in his Mercedes, the night of the party, and she'd let him kiss her and she'd enjoyed every minute of it. And like most kisses, that one had gotten her into more trouble than she'd ever thought possible.

It had made her feel again. And nothing but bad was going to come out of that, because when all this was over, she'd have to go back to New York, and once again she'd be leaving a piece of her heart in Angelton. Pretty soon, she wasn't going to have a heart left—there would just be a hole.

The front door to Monty's house opened, and Cara saw a uniformed woman staring at her with puzzled eyes. With a startled glimpse at her watch, Cara realized she'd been sitting in the car for more than ten minutes—they probably thought she was crazy. And she was definitely beginning to feel that way, too. With a quick curse, she grabbed her briefcase and purse and got out of the car, heading toward the door.

"I'm Cara Howard," she said, reaching the steps. "I'm here to see Jerilyn. She knew I was coming."

The woman, obviously a nurse, smiled and nodded, her concern leaving her face. "Oh, yes. Mrs. Montgomery told me to look out for you. I should have opened the door sooner, but I was upstairs."

"And I was woolgathering." Cara smiled and extended her hand. "You're . . ."

"Grace Pepperdine."

They shook hands, and Grace pulled the door open farther. "Please come in. I'm so glad you could drop by." Cara entered the foyer, then followed the nurse's glance up the stairs. "She's not doing very well today, I'm afraid."

"I hate to hear that." Cara took her purse off her shoulder, then stopped. "Maybe I should come back—"

"Oh, no, no." The nurse shook her head, then reached out for Cara's briefcase, obvious concern darkening her hazel eyes. "On days like this, it's much better if she does have visitors. That way, it gets her mind off the pain. Lets her focus on something else."

Cara felt a flutter of disquiet. "Are you sure—"

"It's fine, believe me, Ms. Howard." The nurse tilted her head toward the kitchen. "I was just about to make us some tea. Why don't you go on up? It's the third door on the right. I'll be right there as soon as the tea's done."

With an unsteady smile, Cara nodded and started up the stairs. Two seconds later, she was lightly tapping on a carved wooden door. "Jerilyn," she said softly. "It's me—Cara Howard. Can I come in?"

"Cara—please do, my darling."

Pushing the door open, Cara stepped into a beautifully feminine room. Lace swags hung over double French doors. A pink marble fireplace warmed one end. And in the center of an enormous bed, Jerilyn Montgomery rested against the headboard, a pink satin bed jacket covering her shoulders.

Cara's heart plunged to the floor.

It had only been a few weeks since Cara had seen Jerilyn, but the woman had grown drastically thinner. Those famous cheekbones, so high, so patrician, were like blades across her face, and the eyes that had made men swoon were now too bright, too feverish. "Come in, my dear. Please come in." Her voice still projected like an actress's always would, but behind it, Cara heard the trembling of a person who knew she was dying.

Cara wanted to weep.

Instead, she smiled and walked quickly to the edge of the bed. Taking Jerilyn's birdlike hands between her own hands, Cara leaned over and kissed the paper-thin skin of the older woman's cheek. The scent of lavender rose up to meet her.

"It's so good of you to come, Cara." Jerilyn's fingers fluttered up to Cara's face, briefly touched her cheek, then went back to lie on the pink sheets. "I know you have much better things to do than visit with me, but I do appreciate you stopping by."

Cara took the chair that Jerilyn nodded toward. "I *wanted* to come see you, Jerilyn. In fact, I was planning on it even before Monty told me you wanted to talk about doing something here at the house."

Jerilyn's hand rose in a clearly dismissive gesture. "I can't believe he fell for that. Why in the world would I want to redecorate something? Where I'm going I certainly don't need new wallpaper and paint."

Cara reached out and patted her shoulder. "Now, don't say that, Jerilyn. You know—"

Jerilyn held up one hand and stopped her. "I'm dying, Cara. I know that. I've made my peace with it."

Her bluntness turned Cara inside out. She'd grown up with people who ignored the truth, who denied reality, and to see someone address an issue so matter-of-factly was disconcerting. For a moment, she could only regard Jerilyn in stunned silence.

"It's all right," the older woman said softly. "Don't be shocked and don't feel sorry for me—because *I* don't. The only reason I lied to Monty about getting you here was to protect him. He's . . . not handling all this too well. In reality, though, there's only one thing left I'm worried about, and *that* is why I wanted to see you."

"And it's not a new bedspread, is it?" Cara smiled tentatively.

"No." Jerilyn's own mouth turned up. "I think you know what it is—or rather, who it is. Your daughter."

Unable to sit still, Cara rose and drifted to a tall bookcase near one of the French doors. On one shelf were books—an eclectic mixture of bestsellers, romance novels and mysteries. On another, all Jerilyn's playbills, ranging from Broadway shows to Shakespeare. Cara turned and looked at the woman in the bed. "It's still difficult for me to even realize I *have* a daughter. I wish more than anything..."

"You did the only thing you could." Jerilyn lifted her chin a notch and stared at Cara almost defiantly. "What in the world would you have done with a child? You were a baby yourself."

Cara's heart cracked open a little farther. "You...you think I did the right thing? By giving Kit up?"

"But of course you did, my dear." Two faint spots of color appeared on Jerilyn's face. "What else could you do? Seventeen, homeless, loveless. I don't see any other options."

"I...I guess I'd decided you would have disapproved."

Jerilyn closed her eyes, then moved her head against the pillow. "Why would I do that?" Opening her eyes again, she stared at Cara. "Come here," she said softly. "Come closer."

Cara started back toward the bed, but her steps stopped when the bedroom door opened. Grace Pepperdine walked in, a full tea service spread out on a silver tray in her hands. "Here we are," she said brightly. "Shall I pour?"

In a surprisingly strong and regal voice, Jerilyn answered quickly. "Cara shall pour, Grace. And that will be all, thank you."

Obviously surprised, the nurse stopped in the middle of the room, her eyes flicking uncertainly from her charge to Cara, then back to Jerilyn. "I'd be happy to—"

"I know you would, Grace, but I would like to be alone with Cara. Put the tray on the table."

Her mouth puckering into a tiny moue of disapproval, the nurse deposited the silver tray at the side of Jerilyn's bed, shot Cara a stare, then flounced from the room. Cara turned away to hide her amusement. Jerilyn could still act the grande dame when she wanted to, and for a moment, Cara saw a glimpse of the woman who must have captured Monty with a single look.

The door closed, and Jerilyn laughed delightedly from the bed. "Ah, I do love to rile Grace sometimes. It's my only pleasure left in life."

Cara abandoned her effort to remain quiet and let out the chuckle that had been building. Moving toward the tray she poured one cup of tea and extended it to Jerilyn. "I'm sure Grace doesn't mind," she said.

Taking the cup in trembling hands, the older woman sipped. "Well, I certainly hope she does. It's like I've always told Katherine—Kit—if you can't ruffle a few feathers, why bother to even fly?"

Cara smiled again, then took her tea and sat down once again. Somehow she felt more relaxed, more at ease. If Jerilyn could give her nurse a hard time, then surely this conversation wouldn't tire her too much. The thought flashed through Cara's mind that that was exactly why Jerilyn had done what she'd just done, and she suddenly felt even more respect for a woman she already admired.

And that's why it meant so much to her that Jerilyn didn't hate her for what she'd done.

"Katherine?" Cara said finally, rolling the name over her tongue with pleasure. "Is that Kit's real name?"

"Yes," Jerilyn said quietly. "Somehow it got shortened to Kit."

Cara took one sip of her tea, then looked at the frail woman in the bed. "You know I didn't want to come back to Angelton," she confessed. "I was afraid of what I would find."

"I would be, too," Jerilyn answered. "It took a lot of courage."

"No, it wasn't courage," Cara said with a smile. "My boss said come or else. Then your husband said he had to have me and no one else. By the time everyone was finished, I didn't have a choice. It didn't require courage, believe me."

"Nonsense." Jerilyn shook her head, her silver hair shining in the light now coming through the doors. "Everything you've done requires courage, and you shouldn't look at it any other way." She took another sip of her tea, then focused her green eyes on Cara. "I've had to make some very hard decisions in my lifetime, too, and believe me, I know that what you did took courage." She paused, then spoke again, more slowly, more distinctly. "And what you have left to do is going to take even more."

Cara's fingers clenched the delicate handle of the china. "I told Monty that I would stay for a while, and that was it. Beyond that, there is nothing left for me to do."

"You're wrong." Again, that note of steel beneath the silk. "You have a daughter to raise. Tye's done it long enough, and now it's your turn."

Suddenly afraid that the teacup would shatter if she held it a minute longer, Cara set it down on the bedside table. "I can't do that."

"Why not?"

"Because Tye doesn't need me here, for one thing. And for another, he's made it perfectly clear that he doesn't want me to come between him and Kit."

"I'm sure he said that at first when he was threatened by your presence. I can't believe he feels that way now."

"Nothing's changed—why wouldn't he feel the same?"

"Because things *have* changed." Jerilyn's stare nailed Cara to her chair. "Right?"

Flustered, Cara looked down. Jerilyn's feathered house shoes peeked out from under the dust ruffle. "Well?" Jerilyn's voice rang out, even more clear than before, as if the conversation were giving her more energy rather than sapping it. "Can you sit there and tell me that you and Tye aren't lovers again?"

Cara jerked her head up, one hand going to her throat. Jerilyn smiled and nodded in obvious satisfaction. "Of course, you can't—because it'd be a lie, and you don't lie." Smiling sweetly, she lifted her hand and raised it toward Cara. "I'm not trying to be mean, darling. I'm just trying to make you face things a little faster than you'd want to on your own. I'm a selfish old woman who wants to die happy."

Instantly, Cara rose, and taking Jerilyn's fingers, she sat on the edge of the bed. "What exactly would make you happy, Jerilyn?"

"The same thing that would make you happy. To see you and Tye and Kit together as a family. As you should be."

Cara frowned. Six weeks ago she hadn't even known this woman, but there was something so remarkable, so intense, about the way she manipulated everyone's lives, that Cara found herself fascinated rather than angry. "Why do you care so much?" she asked. "To you, Tye was a complete stranger. You've helped him raise my daughter. And now you're trying to get us all together to be a family. Why?"

"Can't I just care?"

"Yes, I guess so," Cara answered. "But I think if you were to tell the truth, it'd be more than that."

For a moment, Jerilyn met Cara's eyes. There was a look of measured judgment in the older woman's gaze, a look that clearly said she was wondering if Cara deserved the truth. Cara found herself holding her breath until Jerilyn began to speak—and then she couldn't breathe at all.

"I was found on the steps of a Catholic church when I was two days old. It didn't seem to matter until I became famous on the stage, and then my publicist made up an entire family and background for me." Her eyes met Cara's. "He told me I should never tell anyone the real truth, and I haven't. You're the first."

"Monty—"

"Doesn't have a clue."

For two seconds, Cara was completely speechless. Years before, when she'd seen Jerilyn on stage, there had been talk of her "mysterious" European family, hints of some kind of tragedy too sad to be told. *This* was the reality?

Jerilyn's fingers pulled the sheet into a knot. "I didn't really want to lie, but my career had just begun, and I couldn't jeopardize it. After a while, I'd told the story so many times I believed it." She laughed softly. "Who wouldn't rather be a lost French princess than an abandoned kid from the Bronx?"

Outside, a lawn mower started, the muffled sound of the engine intruding into the room. Jerilyn glanced toward the window, then faced Cara once again. "We share a unique connection, Cara. We're tied together by circumstances and by fate. A woman who was given up and a woman who *gave* up. Don't you see it?"

Cara wet her dry lips and nodded. "And how did you feel about your mother—the woman who gave you up?"

"Once I grew up, I imagined her to be a selfless, loving woman who did the very best that she could by leaving me on the church's doorstep—a woman just like yourself. It took me many years, however, to see my abandonment as an act of supreme sacrifice, probably because I could never have children of my own. As a child I thought much differently." The green of her gaze was so piercing, Cara felt it as an almost physical touch. "You *can't* let Kit think that. She must know how much you love her."

"Is it that obvious?"

"Yes, my dear." The famous voice softened slightly. "Your eyes light up, your expression changes—you love that little girl, just like I always have, and you *must* let her know how you feel."

She reached out for Cara's hand and took it, her fingers so thin and fragile Cara was afraid to even hold them. "You asked why I cared, and this is why. I can't let Kit grow up thinking, like I did, that she wasn't wanted, and I knew a woman that Tye would love wouldn't want that, either."

Her green eyes drilled Cara. "He's been a wonderful parent, but it's your turn now."

The park was smaller than Cara remembered, but her heart was pounding as loudly now as it had been the last time she'd been there. That time, one of many, she'd stood in the same spot, beside the swings, and waited in the dark for Tye, her parents at home, sleeping safely, and thinking she was, too.

She raised one shaking hand and grasped the metal pole beside the play gym. She'd spent a restless night, Jerilyn's words repeating over and over in her mind like a song she couldn't forget. Her life was as confused and anxious now as it had ever been. Why did things have to be so damned complicated? Was it too much to expect some semblance of peace by this point?

Apparently so, she answered herself, because peace was the last thing she was getting. Instead, she had a new lover, a new daughter and more new worries than she knew how to handle.

Families streamed into the small park in groups of threes and fours, calling out to one another, the fathers laden with chairs and picnic hampers, the mothers holding hands and leading children. They were all there for the same reason as Cara—a fund-raiser and band concert—but there the similarities ended. *They,* she was sure, had even, level lives with no drastic pronouncements or unexpected upheavals every time they turned around.

Cara shifted her own hamper to her other hand and let her gaze drift over the small green area. Fall hung in the air like a promise as the laughter of children rang out. Mums brightened the tiny bandstand, and someone had strung lights along the gazebo that stood near the perimeter of the grounds. The entire scene looked like something from a Norman Rockwell painting, she thought, even down to the smallest detail.

Only, Rockwell had never painted a family group like the one she and Tye and Kit made up.

For that reason alone, Cara had almost not shown up. They would never be a *real* family, and it was foolish to even pretend they could be. She couldn't explain that to Kit at this point, though, and no other excuse had sounded adequate when the teen had called and invited her. In addition, refusing Kit anything seemed impossible. She was every bit the charming, bright girl that Tye had said she was, and when she'd asked Cara to come with them to the concert, there was no way Cara would have refused.

And a second later, when she saw the smile on Kit's face, Cara knew whatever else happened, she'd done the right thing by coming.

"Cara—you made it!" Kit danced up to her and smiled broadly. "I'm so glad you could come."

Cara responded the only way she could. "I wouldn't have missed it for the world." She glanced at Tye as he stood beside their daughter, and the sight of the two of them—so similar, yet so different—almost stole her breath. *This,* a tiny voice inside her said, is what you gave up. *This* is what you could have had.

Tye smiled gently at her as though he knew what she was thinking, then reached out for her hamper. "Let me take that," he said, relieving her of the burden, "and we'll go find us the perfect spot."

Kit bounded ahead of them, greeting her friends and yelling across the park, as they moved away from the swings and nearer the edge of the area. "What have you got in here?" Tye asked, swinging the hamper. "It's heavy enough."

She glanced up at him and told her heart to be steady. He wore a faded chambray shirt that made his blue eyes even bluer and jeans that had seen better days. For anyone else, the casual wear might have resurrected memories of a younger image; for Cara, it had the opposite effect. She immediately thought about what a handsome *man* Tye had turned into.

With a start, she realized he was waiting for her answer, and she had to struggle to remember the question. "It...it's just the usual," she finally managed. "A baked chicken, some pasta salad, sandwiches. I stopped at the bakery and got a carrot cake and some cookies. Then, let's see...oh yes, a bottle of wine and some diet drinks, too."

He laughed, the deep tones ringing out. "The usual? What kind of picnics do you have in New York? That sounds like a feast."

She shrugged her shoulders and felt a blush ride up her face as they came to a stop near a live oak tree. "I wasn't sure what Kit would want, and I thought I'd cover all my bases."

He set down the basket, then looked at her, his expression a mixture of compassion and amusement. "She'll eat anything, Cara. You didn't have to go to that much trouble."

His instant understanding of what she'd done—something she hadn't even realized until this very moment—unsettled her. "Well, I wasn't sure if..." she started stiffly, then stopped. "That is, I wanted to..."

"Do it right," he finished for her. "And you did. So don't worry about it."

She pulled her bottom lip in between her teeth and nodded her head.

Changing the subject, he indicated the area with a tilt of his head. "Is this spot okay with you?"

"It's perfect," she answered. "We can see the bandstand, but we're not right in the middle of things."

At Cara's side, Kit suddenly appeared. "Is this where you're going to sit?"

Tye glanced at Cara with a grin. "If it's acceptable to you."

"It's perfect. Not too close to the middle, but you can still see the bandstand."

Startled, Cara let her eyes meet Tye's, and they both laughed at the same time. Kit grinned as Tye explained. "I knew I liked you for some reason," she said to Cara. "We think alike, right?"

"I guess we do at that," Cara answered, somewhat shyly.

Tye's contribution to the party was a blanket and lawn chairs, and for the next few minutes he arranged things as he liked them while Cara and Kit chatted about the concert. Kit had only joined the band the year before, and she was full of enthusiasm for the music and the school's director.

"When I'm sixteen, the band is going to Paris," she told Cara with a sideways look at her dad. "We'll be gone for almost ten days, touring places and playing concerts. I can't wait to see the Eiffel Tower."

Cara glanced at Tye and tried to hide the flash of distress she felt. "To France? For ten days? That's quite a trip for a group of teenagers, isn't it?"

"Yes, it is," he answered for Kit with a pointed stare. "And I'm not too sure you're going, either."

"Oh, Daddy." With her face screwed into an expression of disgust, Kit made the two-syllable word into four. "I'll be sixteen then. That's practically grown-up."

Tye sat down on the blanket he'd just spread, then indicated Kit and Cara should join him. "It's far, far from being grown-up, and two years away to boot, so let's discuss it when we get closer to the date."

For a second, Kit looked as though she wanted to argue, then obviously she thought again and decided this wasn't the time. "Okay," she said with resignation, "but I *really* want to go, and Jerilyn said that anytime anyone *really* wanted something that bad, they should do everything they could to get it. I'm just trying to prepare you, that's all."

"Well, thank you so much, sweetheart." He reached over and took her chin between his fingers, then pulled her face to his and kissed her soundly on the cheek. "I can see you're just thinking about your poor old father and trying to give him a break. I really appreciate that."

She squealed with laughter, then jumped up and ran off as a friend nearby called out her name. Cara let her eyes follow her, then slowly her gaze came back to Tye's face. "Oh, Tye," she said softly. "I can't believe she's actually our daughter." Her eyes filled up with unbidden tears. "She's so wonderful."

He looked startled for a moment, then his own gaze automatically went down the park to where Kit stood with a group of her friends. "Yes," he finally answered, "she is. I try not to take it for granted, but life gets complicated, and I guess sometimes I forget."

"You forget?" Cara focused on him, her amazement coloring her voice. "How could you ever take something like that for granted?"

He reached over and covered her hand with one of his. "Day-to-day living with a teenager isn't like the movies, Cara. It's just life, like everything else. You hope for the best, then pray they make it into adulthood."

"But to take her for granted?" Cara shook her head. "I don't see how you could ever do that. She's so great, so perfect."

Tye laughed out loud at that. "Now *there's* a fantasy. There is no such thing as a perfect teenager—that's an oxymoron if I ever heard one."

Cara knew he was teasing, but she persisted. "No, it's true. I've made every effort I could to never listen to other people's stories about their children, but I've got friends back in New York that tell me real tales of horror. None of them have kids like Kit, believe me."

"That may be true, but living in Angelton could have something to do with that."

She met his gaze. "It didn't keep us out of trouble."

The smile slowly left his face, replaced by an expression of seriousness. "It may have been trouble then, but that's not what I'd call it now. Would you?"

Time seemed to hold still, and even the trees stopped their rustling in the fall breeze as Tye waited for her answer. "I... I'm not sure what I'd call it now," Cara answered slowly. "But it isn't going away, is it?"

He shook his head, then lifted a finger to her cheek. "No, sweetheart. This time it's not."

* * *

Time passed swiftly, and Cara was shocked three hours later when she glanced down at her watch. She'd had no idea how late it was. The food had been marvelous, the music surprisingly good and the company the best. And Kit—she'd played so well that Cara had thought her heart would break with pride. She couldn't believe the talented young girl was really her daughter. After the band had finished, she'd bounded to their side, then told Tye she was going home with a friend. Now they were alone again. In the dark sky above them, stars had begun to come out and dot the velvet darkness.

"It's almost ten," she said, glancing over at Tye. He was stretched out on the blanket, his head cradled in his arms. "Don't you have to get home?"

"Nope." He shook his head, then looked at her, his profile a shadow. "Tomorrow's Saturday. I can sleep late." He paused. "And so can you."

All around them, families were beginning to pack their hampers and make the first treks back to their car. Across the park, in the distance, Cara could hear the plaintive cry of a child exhausted by too much fun. It wasn't enough to distract her, though, from the implication in Tye's voice.

She took a deep breath and mentally stepped back. "I thought I might go into the office, anyway. I want to see how the wallpaper looks in the dining room, and those painters from Austin are supposed to be—"

Tye rolled over and put one finger against her lips. "You don't have to do all that at the crack of dawn."

"But I like to get an early start on the day," she said automatically.

On their left, a sudden movement caught Cara's eyes. It was a father walking by with a small child cradled in his arms. A woman stepped beside him, her arm around his waist, her eyes on his. They were speaking softly, and Cara couldn't hear the words.

"How about this instead . . ."

Tye's words drifted into the background of her consciousness as Cara watched the young couple. Did they have another child in the band? Had they just come to listen to the music? Was the park a favorite place of theirs, like it seemed to be with all the other families?

Something about them held her gaze as they threaded their way to their car. The mother opened the back door first, and the daddy gently deposited the sleeping child into a car seat. Once he had the child buckled in, the man quietly closed the car door and turned to his wife. In the dim light, Cara watched as he put his hand on the woman's shoulder, and they exchanged a look of love and promise so intense that it took away Cara's breath.

Behind her, she could hear the last of the families call goodbyes to each other, their voices drifting over the crisp night air. A radio started then died, and the faint smell of barbecue lingered. It was a perfectly normal situation, but suddenly it was like one of those crazy drawings in the newspaper with the words *What doesn't belong?* written underneath. The answer, in this case, was plain to see—Cara.

For the past few hours, she'd let herself pretend. She'd shown up with every kind of food she could think of and watched Tye and Kit eat it with gusto. She'd seen Tye kiss Kit and tease her, and thought about doing the same. She'd even let herself be concerned about Kit's future and the proposed trip to Europe. Like the people who had just climbed into their car and driven off, Cara had imagined the three of them—herself, Tye and Kit—as a family.

But they weren't. And they never would be.

She turned her head and studied Tye, and despite every effort, a slow burn of resentment started in the pit of her stomach. He was saying something about Saturday, about how he wanted to show her something, but the words didn't register. All she could think about was how many picnics he'd gotten to share with Kit through the years.

He'd probably brought her here before she could even walk. In the spring, when the new birds were out and the sun just beginning to warm the days, he'd probably pushed her in her stroller along the path by the gazebo. He'd stopped and talked to the mothers along the way, and they'd compared diapers or formulas or baby powder.

In the summer, Kit could have taken her first hesitant steps over by the fountain. Cara's eyes went to the bubbling water near the center of the park, as though she could see into the past. Tye would have stood beside Kit, her fat, chubby fingers grasping one of his as she'd made her way around the watery hazard.

Cara closed her eyes, but she couldn't escape the montage of speeded-up images that were now assaulting her senses. Kit at two, screaming with delight as she went down the baby slide. Kit at four, yelling to be pushed higher and higher on the swings. Kit at six, propelling herself on the merry-go-round. A final image, the one she'd actually experienced only hours before—Kit at fourteen, sweetly drawing her bow across her violin and looking over at Tye and Cara for approval—was more than she could bear, and Cara suddenly stood, her hand at her throat.

Her unexpected movement brought Tye's eyes to her face, and when he saw her expression, he jumped up to stand beside her. "Cara?"

Her throat closed down, and she had to force herself to breath. "I . . . I've got to leave," she managed to get out in a strangled voice. Turning, she took two steps.

He was beside her in an instant, stopping her with one hand on her arm, his eyes searching her face in the darkness. "Why? What's wrong?"

She didn't know what to say or how to describe the black feeling of lost years, and her eyes filled up with tears. "I've got to go," she repeated almost desperately. "I can't stay here any longer. It was a mistake to come in the first place."

"No." His protest, and his voice, grew in strength. "It *wasn't* a mistake, Cara. What in the world would make you say that? I thought you were enjoying yourself."

"I was," she said. "That's the problem."

He shook his head, wrinkles crossing his forehead. "What—"

"Don't you see what we're doing, Tye?" She tore her arm from his grasp and motioned around them. "This isn't real. It isn't forever. We're kidding ourselves by doing this."

"You're making too big a deal out of it, Cara. It's just a picnic."

"No. It's much more than that. It's what we aren't and never can be, and if we keep letting Kit see us together like this, she's going to think things are possible that aren't."

"You're jumping to conclusions—"

"No. I'm telling you the truth, and you're too blind to see it. Just like you take Kit for granted. *You've* had all this, all these years, and you don't even appreciate what you've held in your hand. I do. I know what I've missed, and being here tonight has only brought that point home."

He started to say something, but she held her hand up to stop him, her jaw tightening with indignation. "It makes me angry when I think about it, Tye. You've had so much, and I've had nothing. All these years while I was alone, the two of you were together. Giving up Kit was a choice I made, but I'd be lying if I told you I could ever forget you've had her while I didn't." Pausing, she drew a deep breath, then stepped away from him even more, the physical distance between them something she had to have. "And I'd be crazy to set myself up for that kind of pain all over again."

Cara wanted nothing as much as she wanted to leave Angelton the next week, but she couldn't. There was work yet to be done, and she'd promised Monty. At the time she'd made that promise, she'd had no idea how much it would cost her. The picnic had been sheer torture. But a promise was a promise. Now, exhausted and more stressed-out than ever, Cara found herself at the mall where she'd purchased her bathing suit. She had no idea what to do or say, but one thing was for sure—she had to buy Kit a birthday present, and it had to be special. And to Cara, special meant antique.

The shop was as dusty inside as it had appeared to be from the window, but when the bell over the door sounded, a young man appeared promptly from the back. Cara quickly introduced herself to him, explaining that she was a decorator and would be looking for some larger pieces.

"I'll be needing some things for a job I'm working on," she said, "but today I'm interested in a gift for a young girl—a teenager."

He sent a clearly bewildered look around the shop. "I have absolutely no idea what's in here. This was my great-aunt's shop, and she just passed away. I'm here trying to sort out her estate and catalog the inventory." He lifted a hand to indicate the clutter. "Help yourself, but don't ask me about anything."

Cara smiled in sympathy. "It must be a bit confusing if you don't know anything about antiques."

"It all looks like junk to me," he said with a quick grin, "so I hope you're honest. Otherwise you could offer me fifty cents for some of this stuff, and I'd probably be delighted."

"I'll try not to take advantage," she answered, her eyes roaming over the room, then back to him, "as long as your prices are reasonable. I'll warn you, though. Antique buyers like to horse-trade. It's part of the process."

While she spoke, she stepped toward a low table covered with different pieces of silver. Littering the top were everything from snuff boxes to letter openers to what looked like christening cups. Surprised by the quality of the items on display, she ran her fingers over the smooth top of an art-deco cigarette box, then looked up at the young man.

He rolled his eyes and answered her, clearly in distress. "I'm a math teacher—I don't know the first thing about bargaining." Taking a red bandanna from his pocket, he wiped his face. "And if you think it's bad out here—you ought to see the warehouse in back. It's so full I can hardly walk around at all. I have no idea what I'm going to do with this."

Taking her completely by surprise, a ridiculous idea jumped into Cara's mind. She'd always wanted a shop just like this. A dusty, out-of-the-way, unique kind of place that she could take over and spruce up, polish into a real gem. Quickly, she stuffed the outrageous idea into the back of her mind. Picking up one of the christening cups, she ran her fingers over its elaborate repoussé, then automatically flipped it over to check out the price.

"Say—" he stuffed the bandanna back into his pocket "—you wouldn't want to help me, would you? I'd pay you to go through all this junk and tell me what it's worth."

With her heart pounding so loud it almost drowned out the owner's words, Cara lifted her eyes to his face. He looked at her hopefully. "I've only got another week of my vacation left, and then I have to go back to Austin. I wanted to put the shop up for sale as soon as possible, but I'm going to run out of time—and I still don't have the foggiest idea of what to ask for it. If you could help me, it'd be great."

"I...I don't know," she stammered. His suggestion, so close on the heels of her preposterous thoughts a minute ago, was uncanny. "I don't live here, either," she said by way of explanation. "I'm just here doing a job, and this looks like it'd take quite a while."

"Tell me about it," he said wryly. "And it takes even longer if you don't know what you're doing." He reached over to a desk practically hidden under a variety of first-edition books. "Here's my aunt's card with the phone number for the shop." He paused a second, then bit his bottom lip. "I'll pay you whatever you want. I'm desperate here."

Cara took the card and stuffed it into the pocket of her blazer. "I'll think about it," she promised. "In the meantime, if you don't mind, I think I'll look around."

"Help yourself," he said, heading toward the back, "but don't expect any bargaining...."

Cara leaned weakly against the table that held the silver. Talk about opportunity knocking! This was incredible. But why, of all the places in the world, did it have to knock here in Angelton? Looking around the quaint shop, she felt like a kid in a candy store. There wasn't one item her eyes fell upon that her fingers didn't itch to pick up and examine. She could spend hours here.

With a start, she realized she was still holding the christening cup she'd first picked up. The silver had warmed in her hand, and now as she looked down on the embellished cup, her heart began to hammer. The silversmith had used a pattern of roses and leaves, twining them about a trellis-like design. The relief was still quite high, the workmanship superb. The details registered dimly, though, like voices from another room, lyrics from a forgotten song, as she read the sentiment so lovingly engraved on the side of the cup. *For Katherine—pure child of my heart, sweet child of my dreams.*

She clutched the cup to her breast and told herself she didn't believe in portents.

She was almost asleep when the phone rang.

"Did I wake you up?" Tye's voice was a husky whisper over the line as she clutched the receiver to her ear.

Normally she would have lied, would have pretended to be wide-awake and alert, but with Tye she couldn't do that. Not when his voice sounded like the silver moonlight pouring through her window and memories of his touch weren't far behind. "I *was* dozing," she confessed, throwing a glance toward the clock beside the bed. "It *is* after midnight, you know."

"I know." He paused, the silence on the line filled with emotions. "But I couldn't go to sleep, and I had to talk to you. I hope you don't mind."

His voice held a wistfulness that she'd never heard before, and Cara eased up in the bed and put both her hands on the receiver as if she could get closer to him by doing so. "I don't mind at all. Are you still in Dallas?"

"Yes. The negotiations aren't going as smoothly as I thought they would. We may not get the company we're trying to buy."

"I'm sorry to hear that. What's going wrong?"

A sound came over the line, half amusement, half despair. "Everything, if you want to know the truth. They want more money, more time and more concessions." He paused. "That's not the real problem, though. The real problem is the negotiator. He can't keep his mind on the task at hand."

"Why not?"

"Because he's too busy thinking about the woman he left behind."

Drawing her knees up, Cara closed her eyes in the darkness and listened to her heartbeat, her reply coming out before she could stop herself. "Then maybe he ought to come home to her."

"He can't."

"Why not?" she repeated.

"Because he's not too sure she wants him."

"What makes you think that?"

"Isn't that what you were telling me in the park?"

She didn't answer right away; she couldn't. He kept going. "I hope it isn't, but the more I started thinking about that conversation, the more worried I got." His voice turned deeper, huskier. "You have every right to be angry, Cara. Every right in the world, but I love you. I always have. I always will."

Her throat closed up at his words, and she dropped her head against the tops of her knees, unable to speak.

"Are you still there?"

"Yes."

"Then say something."

"I don't know what *to* say."

"Then let me say it." She heard him draw a deep breath. "You faced an impossible situation all alone. You were seventeen, had no family and thought I didn't love you anymore. You had no choice except to do what you did, and

I've never even said thank you. All I did was take advantage of the situation and reap the benefits from it. I think it's time I said those words, Cara. Thank you. Thank you for my daughter, and thank you for loving me.''

She brought her hand to her eyes and covered them, even though she could see nothing in the darkness. "You're welcome," she whispered.

Again there was silence on the line before he finally spoke. "Almost everything you said in the park was right. There's one big point that you were wrong about, though."

"What's that?"

"You said you'd be crazy if you set yourself up for that kind of pain again. I think you'd be crazy if you *didn't* give love a second chance.''

Chapter 14

Cara spent the rest of the week going over the details of each manager's office, making lists of the pieces each one wanted to see, and trying to turn some of the more outrageous requests into more reasonable ones. By Friday afternoon, she was exhausted and grateful that Tye still hadn't returned from Dallas. She didn't think she could cope with the demands of the job, her thoughts about the antique shop *and* his presence. Especially after the concert in the park. Especially after his phone call. *Especially* knowing that in only two hours, she'd have to face Kit's birthday party.

Rising from her desk, Cara headed into the hall for a cup of coffee, then stopped when she saw Monty hurrying toward her. "I need to talk to you," he said, taking her arm and steering her out of the way of the hall traffic.

She looked at him in alarm. His face was flushed, and something about his eyes made her stop and take notice. "What's wrong?" she asked.

"It's Jerilyn," he said without preamble. "She's bad—real bad. All week long I've thought she was getting worse, but she insisted she was fine. This morning, though, she hardly responded to me, and just a few minutes ago, Grace called and said she's ordered an ambulance. They're on their way right now to the hospital. I told them I'd meet them there."

A wave of dark foreboding came over Cara, and she found herself squeezing Monty's arm. "I'm so sorry. Is there anything I can do?"

"Yes—that's why I came to you. I know this may be a baptism by fire but you've got to handle Kit's party alone. I promised Tye I'd go early if he didn't get back in time, and now I can't." He looked down at his watch. "I'm sorry, Cara, but there's going to be ten fourteen-year-olds at Tye's house in less than two hours, and someone's got to be there besides Tye's cook." He smoothed one hand over his hair, then stopped and looked at her, as if he were finally realizing what he was doing. "I'm sorry, sweetheart, but—"

She shook her head and gave him a gentle push. "Forget it, Monty. Just go—and call me from the hospital."

Beneath his worry, he dug out a final grateful smile, then hurried off down the hall. Peggy dashed out from his office with his coat and a briefcase.

Cara sent up a small prayer for Jerilyn, but her initial feeling of hopelessness didn't leave. As she watched Monty fly around the corner, Peggy trailing behind him, Cara knew this time might be the last. Jerilyn had simply looked too frail to continue her battle much longer.

Taking a deep breath, Cara returned to her office, picked up her briefcase and followed Monty's path to the parking lot, her heart beating painfully. She wanted to make a good impression with Kit, wanted to do it right, and now she'd just been appointed to supervisor first time out. What if she embarrassed Kit? Or did something hideously wrong? Teenagers were so tricky.

By the time Cara got to Tye's house, her palms were sticking to the steering wheel, and her stomach felt like it was about to rebel from the stress. The picnic had been one thing—Tye had been there to act as a buffer between them— but this was the first time she and Kit would be by themselves. Before Cara had a chance to try and calm herself, Kit burst from the front door and ran out to the car. She opened the door and grinned at Cara.

"Hey—you're the first one here. Come on in."

Trying to force her own fears aside, Cara smiled tentatively at Kit and climbed from the car, her gaily wrapped package tucked under her arm. "I'm afraid I have some bad news, Kit. Jerilyn's gotten worse . . . and Monty had to take her to the hospital."

Kit's face instantly crumpled. "Oh, no. We'd better cancel the party. I should go to the hospital—"

Gently, Cara shook her head. "That wouldn't do any good, and I'm sure Jerilyn would want you to go on and have it." She looked into Kit's blue eyes and read the indecision. "Don't you think she'd want that?"

"I . . . I don't know." Kit sucked in her bottom lip and stared at Cara. "Will she be okay?"

"I'm not sure," Cara answered honestly. "She's very ill, and they took her to the hospital in an ambulance." She paused, shifting her purse to her other shoulder, feeling awkward, wishing she were somewhere else. This wasn't how she'd envisioned her first real conversation with her daughter, a talk just between the two of them. "I hope you don't mind me being here," she tried again. "I know you don't really know me or anything, but I'll try not to embarrass you."

"Well, I don't *mind* you being here—I *wanted* you here—but . . ." Her face tightened for a moment, and then she blurted out, "Didn't Dad trust me enough to be on my own? After all, I *am* a year older."

Cara stopped and looked down into Kit's blue eyes—eyes so much like Tye's they made Cara's heart stop. "I'm sure your Dad trusts you implicitly—wholeheartedly—but Monty got worried because he couldn't come and he knew your dad wasn't going to be here, either. So he asked me to show up a little early, that's all."

Kit nodded slowly, the sun glinting on the silver beads that decorated her earlobes. Last week in the park when Tye had kissed Kit's cheek, Cara had almost died with the need to do the same. Giving in to temptation now, she raised her hand and moved aside one long lock of blond hair, her throat almost closing with a flood of emotion.

It was the first time she'd touched her daughter—ever. Moments after her birth, they'd bundled her up and whisked her away. "What neat earrings," she said, hiding her choking voice and smiling into Kit's eyes. "Are they new?"

Kit smiled shyly. "Yeah. Dad gave them to me for my birthday. He said I was old enough to wear real jewelry now. They're silver—sterling silver. I like silver so much more than gold, don't you?"

Cara's breath caught in her throat. "Yes . . . yes, I do. It's my favorite, too." She held her present out. "In fact, here's a little something I picked up for you that I think you might like."

"Oh, wow. Thanks a bunch." Kit took the box, then opened the front door and held it back for Cara. "Can I open it now?"

"Sure. Why not?"

They went inside, and Kit immediately began to rip off the wrapping paper. A second later, she opened the box and gasped, the overhead light shining on the softly polished silver christening mug. "Oh, my gosh—this is gorgeous." The tissue paper crinkled as she reached in and picked up the cup. "I can't believe it." She brought it closer to her. "It's even got my name on it! Oh, thank you, Cara. I love it." Immediately, she reached out and hugged Cara.

For a moment, all Cara could do was stand stiffly in Kit's embrace as shock rippled over her. This was her daughter—*her daughter*—who had her arms around Cara. As her paralysis broke, she responded, wrapping her arms around the teenager and letting her hand stroke Kit's hair for a heartbeat. Cara realized, as she'd never realized before, just how empty her arms had always been.

"I—I'm glad you like it," Cara said, her voice husky with emotion as Kit finally pulled back. "I found it in an antique shop, and I hoped you would like it as much as I do.

Obviously it was done for someone who loved a 'Kather
ine' very, very much.''

Kit's eyes shone. "Well, I love *it*. Thank you very much—
I can't wait to show it to everyone." She carefully placed i
on the mantel, then turned back to Cara. "Are you going t(
stay for the whole party?'' she asked.

Taking a moment to recover from the emotions assault
ing her, Cara slowly began to pull off her blazer, the
draped it over a nearby chair before speaking. "The whol(
party? I . . . I guess so. How long will it last?''

Kit shrugged her shoulders. "Usually everybody's gon(
by noon.''

"Noon?" Cara squeaked. "Noon tomorrow?''

"Well, yeah—it's a slumber party. Didn't you know?''

Grinning weakly, Cara shook her head. "No, actually
didn't. I thought since Monty was coming—''

"Oh, he and Jerilyn always come for cake and ice crean
and everything, but they don't stay the whole time.''

Cara reached for the back of the sofa in front of her an(
told herself not to panic. "I guess that's one of the reason
he asked me to come—since your dad isn't going to be here
You couldn't exactly have sleep-over friends without some
one here.''

"No, I guess not." Kit grinned. "We might set the hous(
on fire or something, huh?''

Cara smiled back. "I doubt that. You don't look like ;
firebug to me . . . but then, you never know.''

Kit walked around Cara and collapsed into one corner o
the wraparound sofa. "You want some dip or something?'
She pointed to the spread Maria had already prepared fo
the party. "The kind in the pink bowl is shrimp—it's reall}
good.''

"Maybe in a minute," Cara answered, slipping out of he
shoes and settling into the other side of the sofa. "Wh}
don't you tell me about your friends that are coming?''

"Well, there's Mindy—she's the girl across the street, an(
she's really neat. We've been friends forever and . . .''

As Kit rattled on, Cara allowed herself the luxury of staring at her daughter. She truly was a beautiful young woman, Cara marveled, with Tye's gorgeous blue eyes and Cara's own bone structure. Cara had always been proud of her high cheekbones, not that she'd had anything to do with them, but to see them replicated in her daughter sent a thrill of pride through her. Had her own parents felt that way the first time they'd seen her?

Kit finally ran out of steam and reached for a potato chip. Nibbling on it, she stared at Cara. "Do you have any kids?"

Cara's breath stopped, trapped in her chest by surprise. "Uh, yes, I do," she finally answered, "but she lives with her father."

Kit nodded sympathetically. "Yeah, a lot of my friends have to do that, too. Their parents are divorced, and it's tough." Her head tilted slightly, and Cara prepared herself mentally for whatever was coming next. "I guess you know my dad's not divorced. I live with him because...well, he is my real dad and everything, but it's kinda complicated."

Complicated! If you only knew, Cara thought suddenly. "Yes," she answered, reaching for a cracker in her nervousness. "I understand."

"Do you think—" Kit stopped suddenly, breaking the chip she held into tiny pieces.

"Think what?"

Kit hesitated. "Dad says I talk before I think sometimes."

"Believe me, Kit, everyone does that."

"Even you?"

"Especially me." Her heart thumping inside her chest, Cara grinned.

"Well...I was just wondering if you and my Dad are serious or anything." The words came out in a rush, one long thought. "I mean, I saw you at Monty's party, and you two went out on the boat when I couldn't go with you, then you came to the park with us, and I just wondered if you liked my dad, because if you did, I think it'd be cool."

Cara didn't know whether to laugh or to cry. "Cool?" she said in a strangled voice.

"Well, yeah. See, my dad never dates. I mean *never*. That's why it was so neat when I saw him standing next to you at Monty's party that night. A lot of my friends don't like it when their parents go out, but I think it'd be great for Dad, and, well, I just wanted to tell you that."

"I'm happy you think that—"

"Listen," Kit said suddenly, jumping up from the couch and running to the door. "Somebody's here. I bet it's Mindy!"

Totally stunned, Cara leaned back into the couch cushions and took a deep breath. She'd been so worried, so terrified, and all for no reason. Kit *did* like her—just as Tye had said. Cara couldn't believe it, but for the third time that day, she issued a small prayer, this one of thanksgiving.

On the heels of it, though, came another heart-stopping question.

When Kit found out who Cara really was, would she still feel the same way?

By 10:00 p.m., the party was in full swing, and Cara was having as much fun as any of the kids. She couldn't remember the last time she'd giggled as much as she had in the past few hours, and she found herself wondering why she'd been so nervous.

She didn't even have anything to do, actually. Maria had prepared a feast, and Kit had scheduled activities practically down to the minute. The other girls teased her good-naturedly about it, but secretly Cara was very impressed. At ten-thirty-five, when the horror movie came on, Cara ducked out.

She wanted to see more of Tye's home, but without him there, she felt slightly uncomfortable wandering around and exploring. It didn't stop her, though. Going from room to room, touching tables, straightening pictures, she saw that it was definitely a man's home. Without even thinking about what she was doing, Cara mentally rearranged the furni-

ure, rehung the pictures, painted walls. It would be so much
un to do it in reality, she thought suddenly. To turn it into
home for all three of them.

In his office, a pair of French doors beckoned her down
o the pool. Grabbing a navy sweater off Tye's desk chair,
Cara hesitated long enough to listen for the shrieks from the
ving room, then stepped outside, knowing the girls would
e entertained for at least another hour.

As she made her way to the pool, Cara lifted her head and
rew a deep breath. A cold front had blown in earlier in the
eek, bringing with it the first of the really chilled air. Now,
s she pulled it into her lungs, Cara smelled the familiar tang
f fireplace smoke, fallen leaves and rain-soaked earth.

The pool at the end of the well-lit path gleamed like a gi-
nt blue topaz when Cara leaned over to dip her fingers in
. Expecting cold water, she was shocked when the warm,
elaxing current kissed her fingers. Tye must have heated it
or the girls. Another bonus of living in Texas, she mused—
wimming almost all year round.

Shaking her fingers off, she rose and made her way to a
rouping of lounge chairs at one end of the deck. When she
at down and looked back toward the house, she realized she
ould see straight into the den. All ten girls were present and
ccounted for, their faces turned toward the blue light of the
elevision, their expressions ranging from hysterical to pet-
ified. Kit must have picked out the perfect movie, Cara
hought with a grin.

Pulling Tye's sweater closer around her shoulders, Cara
rank in his scent that lingered in the wool and continued
he fantasy she'd started back at the house. For just a mo-
ent longer, she let herself think about what her life could
e like if she lived here. She'd buy that little antique shop
nd rename it something really clever. After school, Kit
ould stop in and help her. Cara could teach her all about
ld silver, let her rearrange the displays, polish it, learn to
ove it as she did. At the end of the day, they'd close up, then
ome home—home to this beautiful house on the hill with

the heated swimming pool and spreading oak trees and Ty
waiting for them both.

Cara closed her eyes and slipped deeper into her mind
Tye liked to cook—he'd told her that on the boat—so in he
vision she saw him in the kitchen, pots and pans all ove
everywhere, an apron over his jeans. He'd kiss her, their lip
lingering, longing, promising. And after dinner, she imag
ined herself in Tye's bed again. In that wide, generous be
where they'd first made love. Where he'd comforted her
Sighing, she let out a small moan of grief for what wouldn'
be.

"It can't possibly be that bad this soon."

Cara's eyes flew open, and her hand went to her throat
"Tye! You scared me half to death. What are you doing
here?"

Grinning, he took the chair beside her. "I live here."

"That's not what I mean," she said, leaning forward t
receive his kiss. With one hand along her jaw, he caresse
her skin with his thumb, then his lips warmed hers. In
stantly she thought of the fantasy she'd just completed. *Thi
is what it could be like,* her mind screamed, *if things ha
only worked out differently.*

She pulled back abruptly and ignored his puzzled eyes
"I . . . I thought you were going to be in Dallas until tomor
row," she finished lamely. "That's why I'm here
Monty—"

"I know about Jerilyn," he broke in. "In fact, that's wh
I decided to come back early. That and Kit's party, o
course." He tilted his head toward the house. "Did the
drive you out? They can get pretty wild sometimes."

She smiled. "Heavens, no. I've loved every minute of it
until they popped Stephen King into the VCR. I can't han
dle him."

"You're doing pretty good, then. Most people woul
think ten fourteen-year-olds to be worse than anything *h*
could dream up."

Cara relaxed against the cushions and shook her head
"They've been perfect. Believe it or not, I was actuall

looking forward to the sleep-over part. It's been a hundred years since I went to a slumber party, but with you here..."

Putting his elbows on his knees, he leaned forward and took one of her hands in his. "You don't have to leave just because I came back." With his thumb, he rubbed the tender spot on the underneath of her wrist. "We could have our own slumber party."

Staring at him in the darkness, Cara felt his touch radiate down her hand, up her arm and straight into her heart. "I don't know if that would be such a good idea."

"I think it's an excellent idea."

"With all those kids in there?"

Even in the darkness, she could see his blue eyes twinkling. "Those kids know the score better than we do, believe me. They know what goes on behind their parents' closed doors."

Cara's chest clutched. "*Parents,* yes. *Lovers,* no." She reached out and traced a line down Tye's jaw. "I don't think we'd get the *Good Housekeeping* Seal of Approval as far as parenthood goes."

Tye captured her hand and brought it to his mouth. One by one, he kissed each fingertip while his eyes seared hers. Finally releasing her gaze, he looked down at her hand and kissed her palm, his tongue tracing lightly across it. "We could do something about that, you know," he murmured against her skin.

"About what?" she said, half-dazed by the eroticism of his touch.

Raising his face, he studied her for a moment, then spoke. "What would you say if I asked you to marry me?"

Cara's heart stopped, then tumbled to the deck, her emotions joining it to lie stunned and numb.

"Marry you?" she repeated, her mouth refusing to close. "Marry you?"

He arched one eyebrow. "Is the idea that revolting?"

"Revolting?" She shook her head, stunned and speechless. "It's not revolting at all, but I'm in shock. I just never..." Overhead, the moon came out from the clouds and lit Tye's face with silver light, and with even more shock, Cara read the nervousness in the tightness of his expression. He was scared!

He dropped her hand and rose. "While I was in Dallas, I started thinking about everything—that's when I called you—but since then I've been even worse. I realized how much I looked forward to seeing you in the office every day. I realized how close we've grown in the past few weeks." He took two steps away, then two steps back. "I realized how much I love you, Cara. How much I've always loved you." Kneeling beside her, he took her hands once more. "I want to do what I should have done but couldn't fourteen years ago."

Cara jumped up from the lounge chair so abruptly that it fell backward and splashed into the pool. She never even looked over her shoulder. "Are you sure about this, Tye? Absolutely, positively sure?"

He wet his lips. "Like I said, you're all I've thought of for the past few weeks, Cara. Every meeting I went to, every manager I talked with—it was all pointless, because you were on my mind every minute of the day. I haven't been able to get you out of there." He held out his hands and waited for her to take them. "I want us to be a family, Cara. *I* want it. This isn't for Jerilyn. This isn't for Monty. It isn't even for Kit. It's for me and for you."

Cara had lived for this moment—in her dreams, in her fantasies, in her memory—for so long that now when it was actually happening, she could do nothing but stare into Tye's midnight eyes. He was offering her exactly what she wanted, exactly what she'd given up years ago. A life with the man she'd loved and with the daughter she'd lost. At her side, her hands clenched.

"I ... I can't."

Two deep lines of confusion instantly etched across his forehead. "What do you mean, you can't?"

She shook her head and stepped away from him. "There's too much between us, Tye. Too much history. Do you really think we could base a family life on that?"

"Why not?" His voice was bewildered. "This is real life, Cara, not 'Leave it to Beaver.' People hurt each other, they make mistakes, but if they're smart, they learn from them and go on."

"I don't think—"

"I love you, Cara," he interrupted, "and you love me. For God's sake, don't let your fear come between us."

The air left her lungs, as surely as if he'd hit her in the stomach. "My fear?"

He moved closer and took her hands in his. "You said yourself that you survived by *not* feeling, by freezing your emotions." His breath hung as a white mist in the cold air. "You're afraid of feeling, of loving, and I have to confess that maybe I am a little, too. But you don't have to be. I'll help you. We'll do it together. We could be a family like we were at the concert."

Cara stared at Tye with uncertainty, confusion and hesitation pulling her lips together. Could she do it? Could she release her fear? Exchange it for love? Step out of the shadows of her existence and into the sunshine of a family?

Tye waited, his strong hands never wavering, their fingertips reaching out to her. All she had to do was take one step, say yes and be in his arms. All she had to do was relinquish her loneliness and grab the lifeline he was offering. Everything she'd been dreaming of only moments before he'd arrived could then be hers. It was like taking the first step out of an airplane with only a parachute on your back—all she had to do was trust and reach for it.

Slowly, inch by inch, she began to raise one hand. Eyes never leaving his. Turning her hand over as she lifted it. Fingers opening up, then stretching out. Reaching. Touching. Committing.

Their fingers met, and with a single cry, Tye pulled her into his arms, his mouth murmuring against her hair, his hands bringing her closer and closer. "Oh, God, I love you," he said over and over. "I love you so much, Cara. I promise nothing will ever come between us again. Nothing."

She lifted her shining face to his and, smiling through her tears, she spoke, conviction and determination making her voice a husky whisper. "Nothing," she agreed. "Nothing but love."

Chapter 15

As if she'd brought back some of the moonlight that had bathed them outside, a subtle glow surrounded Cara minutes later as she talked and joked with Kit's friends. Tye couldn't take his eyes off her.

Kit came up beside him and put one arm around his waist. "Thanks for coming back, Dad. It's always more fun when you're here."

He tore his eyes from Cara and looked down at his daughter. "I'm glad you feel that way, baby. Next year, when you're a grown-up lady a whole year older, you may not want your old dad hanging around like this."

She grinned, her blond hair swinging down her back. "Oh, I'll still need you 'cause next year I think I may want boys at my party, and if they got rowdy then we'd need you to throw them out. Would that be okay? Cara said she had her first boy-girl party when she was that age."

He raised his face and met Cara's gaze. Even from across the room, her eyes could warm him. "And what else did Cara say?"

"She said when she was seventeen she'd met the man she'd always love. Isn't that romantic?" Kit drew her lips into a line. "I guess that means you're out of the running, huh?"

He glanced down. "Don't you think you can love more than one person in your lifetime?"

"Not like that—that's what Cara said. She said you only love one man like that."

"Then she's probably right." He squeezed Kit's shoulders. "Are you having a good time? Was Cara a good chaperon before I got here?"

"Just fine. She didn't embarrass me or anything."

Tye laughed out loud. "What on earth would make you think she would do that?"

"I didn't, but she did." Kit turned her head in Cara's direction. "That was one of the first things she said when she got here. She hoped she didn't embarrass me."

Tye's heart cramped. Cara wanted so badly to do the right thing—especially where Kit was concerned. Even after his proposal, a moment neither of them would ever forget, Cara's first thought had been for Kit. "We have to tell her the truth," she'd said. "As soon as possible." They'd both agreed on tomorrow.

He tightened his arm around Kit's shoulder. "I'm glad you like her," he said. "Now you better go join your friends or you'll get a rep as a bad hostess." Kit grinned, then followed his advice.

Two seconds later, the phone rang, and Tye's heart stopped. He ran to his study, the doors still rattling behind him as he rushed to pick up the phone. The voice on the other end was exactly who he'd expected, and the news was exactly what he had feared.

"She went about an hour ago," Monty said, his voice thick with grief. "I started to call you, to tell you to come, but I didn't want to leave her. You couldn't have gotten here in time, anyway."

An hour ago, Tye thought, his heart cracking in two. *An hour ago when he'd been proposing to Cara, when she'd been reaching out to him and taking his hand.* The tears slipped down his cheeks unbidden.

"It...wasn't hard for her at the end," Monty continued. "I was holding her hand, and she opened those damned green eyes of hers and said 'I love you,' clear as a bell. A second later, she was gone." Monty's voice cracked and Tye could hear him start to cry. "Just like that, she was gone." Over the line, his sobs snuffled back, as if he were trying to regain control of himself. "She was gone."

Cara knew immediately that Jerilyn was gone—all she had to do was look at Tye's face. He'd done the best he could, and he could have hidden his real emotions from a stranger, but not from Cara. The lines had deepened on either side of his mouth and the pinched tightness of his shoulders, hunched as if he were cold, told her the truth. She crossed the room and entered the hallway where he stood, taking his hands in hers.

"That was Monty, wasn't it?"

"Yes." He nodded once, then spoke, his voice hoarse. "She went about an hour ago. She told him she loved him, then she died."

Tears filled Cara's eyes, and, slipping her arms around his waist, she rested her head against Tye's broad chest. Covering the back of her head with his hand, he patted her, comforting her even as she tried to do the same for him. Her breath caught in her throat. She hadn't known Jerilyn all that well, but the woman had left an indelible mark on Cara's life—a mark Cara would thank God for every night the rest of her life. She tightened her arms around Tye, then released him reluctantly. "Do we tell Kit now or wait?"

He brushed his fingers across his eyes, then glanced into the living room. "I don't know. What do you think?"

She glanced at her watch and shook her head. "We'd have to take everyone home, and it's almost one-thirty. Let's get them to bed, then we'll explain it to Kit in the morning."

He nodded. "That's probably a good idea." Looking down at her, he smiled weakly. "Jerilyn wouldn't want Kit's birthday party spoiled. She'd be the first one in there telling ghost stories if she was here."

Cara tucked her arm inside Tye's and linked her fingers with his. "I have a feeling you're right. She wasn't a mother, but she seemed to know exactly what to say to Kit. Maybe we need to remember that."

Cara couldn't contain the small feather of jealousy that brushed over her when Tye led Kit into the living room late the next morning, after all the girls had left. *She* was her mother. *She* should have been the one sitting beside her, explaining everything. Even as she had the thought, however, Cara realized how foolish it was. To Kit, she was simply a friend, and it would take years to develop the kind of bond that Kit shared with her father. For the time being, all Cara could do was take a chair opposite the couch and look on helplessly as Tye gently broke the news.

"Wa-was she in a lot of pain?"

"No, sweetheart. She wasn't in pain at all." Tye looked over Kit's head at Cara, and she realized that he didn't really know, any better than she did, what to say. He struggled on. "Monty was with her—right beside her, holding her hand—and he said she looked really peaceful in the end."

Kit sobbed against her father's shoulder. "Jerilyn said she didn't want me to cry, but...but I can't do that, Daddy. It's so sad, and we'll never see her again." The last words dissolved in a fresh wave of tears. "Never again."

He patted her back. "I know, sweetheart, I know. And yes, it's sad, but I think the most important thing for you to remember is that Jerilyn had been sick a long time. Sometimes when people are sick for that long, they want the release that death brings. I know that's hard for you to understand now, but when you get older—"

Rubbing her eyes, Kit tore out of her father's arms and stumbled to her feet. "When I get older, I won't like it any better. She's still dead, and nothing you say is going to change that." With a cry, she dashed out of the room, her nnis shoes slapping the wooden floor. A second later, her edroom door slammed shut.

Tye dropped his head into his hands. "Oh, God. I did a retty bad job on that, didn't I?"

Cara rose and went to him, her heart breaking at the rustration in his voice. "You did fine. Just fine. There's no asy way to say something like this, and you did it per- ctly."

He lifted his face and stared at her with hollow eyes. "I'm ot cut out for this kind of thing, Cara. I . . . I don't under- and how teenage girls think. Do you . . . Could you . . . ?"

Cara's chest tightened. A second ago, she'd wanted to andle the situation, but now she was suddenly terrified. Vhat she said to Kit would be the foundation of their rela- onship. It was as important as the words she'd have to redge up when it came time to tell Kit the truth of who she as.

Cara wanted to run out of the room, just as Kit had done, ut instead, with her heart in her throat, she nodded. I . . . I'll try," she said.

Seconds later, with a trembling hand, Cara rapped lightly n Kit's bedroom door. "Kit? It's me, Cara. Can I come ?"

A muffled reply came back, and Cara wasn't sure what it as. Her mouth dry, her stomach a nervous, rumbling reck, she opened the door, anyway, and stepped inside the oom. Kit was stretched across the bed with all the stuffed nimals on it, her arms wrapped around the rattiest of them l, a gray-and-black monkey who had cotton coming out ne arm and was missing an ear.

Kit stared at Cara with red-rimmed eyes. "Nothing you y is going to make me feel any better."

Cara reached out for one of the bedposts and hoped she oked more confident than she felt. "I know that," she id quietly. "When I get mad, I feel the same way."

Kit's expression registered surprise, then suspicion. Mad?"

Cara moved over to the other bed and sat down. "Sure
Isn't that what you're feeling right now?"

Kit looked down at the dilapidated monkey in her arms
"I thought you were supposed to be sad when someon
died, not mad."

Instantly Cara remembered what Tye had said to he
when she'd said virtually the same thing to him. "Ther
aren't any supposed-to's with feelings, Kit. Whatever you'r
feeling, you feel. That's all there is to it."

"Are you mad?" Kit's voice trembled slightly.

Cara wet her lips. "Yes, in a way, I am, but you knew
Jerilyn a lot better than I did. I'd guess you're probabl
more mad than I am."

One huge tear slipped down Kit's cheek before she coul
angrily brush it aside. She thought for a moment, the
looked up at Cara. "It's not fair."

"No." Cara made her voice gentle. "It isn't fair. Not a
all. Jerilyn was a wonderful woman."

"Somebody mean should've died—not her."

Cara smiled through her own tears. "I can see how you'
feel that way. I would, especially if she'd been like a mothe
to me."

Kit snuffled. "She wasn't my *real* mother."

"I know that." Cara's throat closed. "But she loved yo
as if you were her daughter . . . and you loved her."

Kit picked at the stuffing escaping from the animal in he
arms. "Is there going to be a funeral?"

"I assume so."

"When?"

"I don't know."

Kit looked up, her eyes two brilliant pools of sparklin
blue. "Can I go?"

Cara couldn't help herself. She stood up, crossed the sma
space between the beds and took Kit into her arms. Th
teenager resisted for only a second, then abandoned her ef
forts and wrapped her arms around Cara, sniffling and cry
ing. "Of course you can go to the funeral," Cara said

patting Kit's thin back and holding her tight. "Why would you think your father wouldn't let you go?"

Between sniffs, she spoke. "Daddy treats me like such a baby sometimes. I...I was afraid he would think I was too young or something."

Cara raised her hand and cradled the back of Kit's head. Under her fingers, the silky blond hair felt warm and soft. "Daddies always think of their daughters as babies. It's part of being a daddy, I guess."

Kit continued to cry softly, and even as Cara grieved herself, another part of her thrilled at having her own daughter in her arms. It was a bittersweet emotion, though, because she also realized, for the first time in her life, that when a child hurt, the mother's pain was even greater. If it were possible, she'd have done anything—anything at all—to take away the hurt. She wanted to say so, even opened her mouth but just as quickly shut it once again.

Now wasn't the time to tell Kit the truth.

Slowly, her sobs began to abate. "Wh-what about Maribell?"

Cara drew a complete blank. "Maribell? Who's that?"

"Jerilyn's cat. She just had kittens. Who's g-going to take care of her with Jerilyn gone?"

Cara brushed a strand of Kit's hair away from her face. "Monty's not going anywhere. I'm sure he'll take care of them."

"No." Kit shook her head vigorously. "Monty hates cats. He always said that he'd never have them in the house if Jerilyn wasn't there." Her eyes refilled. "He'll throw them all out, and Maribell's scared of everything. She won't know how to take care of her kittens *and* herself, too."

Another giant tear slipped down Kit's face, and Cara's heart cracked open a little farther. She knew Kit wasn't really worried about the cat, but it was something for her to focus on—something less painful than the reality of Jerilyn's death—and Cara definitely understood that technique well enough.

"I doubt very seriously that Monty would do that, but just to make sure, let's ask your dad. I bet he'd let you bring Maribell here to live. How would that be?"

Kit smiled through her tears. "I'd like that...it'd kinda be like having Jerilyn around, because she and Maribell were always together. I...I could look at Maribell, and I'd remember Jerilyn."

Cara hugged her daughter one more time, her own tears falling over her cheeks. "I think that's a great idea, sweetie."

Cara had never seen so many white roses in one place. Their fragrance filled the chapel and even followed the mourners to the small cemetery next to the church. As she watched Monty accept the condolences of everyone as they passed by the casket, Cara couldn't help but wonder what Jerilyn would think of it all.

An hour later, at Monty's house, Cara had decided Jerilyn would probably approve. Everyone in town had known her, and they each had a special story to share. A planeload of friends from her years in show business had even arrived from New York. Every room was packed, and the noise was almost overwhelming. Cara looked for Tye and then for Kit but could find neither in the crowd, so she slipped outside.

The weather had warmed again, and as she made her way toward a swing near a huge oak tree in Monty's backyard, the last of the sun bathed the area in a golden glow. Overhead, a dove called to its mate. Cara hadn't been sitting for a minute when the back door opened and Tye stepped out. She waved at him, and he came down off the steps and headed her way.

Cara watched him cross the expansive yard, and a yearning built inside of her chest that was almost too big to contain. *He loved her. He really loved her. And they were going to be a family.* It was like a dream come true, and she was halfway afraid to even acknowledge it for fear that something might happen. What if he changed his mind? What if it didn't work out? What if...

He reached the swing and stopped. "Got room for one more?"

"Only if the one more is you."

Sitting down with a sigh, he reached over and brushed her cheek with his lips, wrapping his fingers through hers. "Kit told me what you said."

"Uh-oh." Cara rolled her eyes. "I said a lot. What specifically did she say?"

He closed his eyes and rested his head against the back of the swing, the dying sunlight playing across his features. He spoke softly. "Basically it was all praise. She thinks you're smart."

Cara tried to make light of the compliment, but inside she was thrilled. "Got her fooled, huh?"

Tye shook his head. "I don't think so. She's a pretty sharp cookie."

Tightening her fingers around Tye's hand, Cara looked at him. "Of course she is. Look at her parents."

Slowly he opened his eyes, and Cara felt their blue promise all the way down to her heart. "Do you want a big wedding?"

Cara's heart flipped. A wedding. It was really going to happen. "No," she whispered. "It's not necessary, especially with Jerilyn passing. I think just something simple—maybe even down at the courthouse."

He raised her hand to his mouth and kissed the back of it. "I think we can do a little better than that."

"It doesn't matter to me." She turned in the swing and met his gaze full on. "The most important thing is that we're family. As soon as possible."

His eyes narrowed. "And what about your career?"

Cara answered without thinking. "There's a little antique shop on the edge of town that's for sale. I talked to the guy who owns it the other day." She stopped and looked down at the grass. Until now, she hadn't *really* thought about it, but she'd begun to answer Tye's question automatically. Shocking herself, she realized in the back of her mind that she must have been considering it all along. She looked up at him. "What would you think if I wanted to buy it? Run it myself? I've got some debts back in New York I'd have to pay off first, but afterward . . ."

"I imagine I could swing a loan for you." He smiled broadly, then reached out and touched her cheek. "Or would you like a business partner?" Dropping his hand, he shook his head. "I have to confess I've been afraid to ask what you wanted to do. I thought you might want to commute or something like that."

"No way. I've got you now. Do you think I'd chance leaving you again?" She smiled. "Besides, I'm ready to be a real mother to Kit. I want to be there for her when she needs me."

Tye's expression sobered. "I wish there was an easy way to tell her about us."

"I know." Cara looked back toward the house. "Do you think we should wait? Maybe let her recover from Jerilyn's death?"

The breeze ruffled the leaves above them. "I don't know." He sighed heavily. "I never know exactly what to do." Looking at her sideways, he smiled. "Are you sure you're ready for instant motherhood?"

Cara wet her lips. "I don't think of it that way. In the back of my mind, even though I denied it, I've *always* been her mother. Now I'll take an active role." She hesitated, then looked over at Tye. "Do you think she's going to hate me?"

He smiled gently. "Why would she hate you?"

Cara shrugged. "You said yourself she asked you why I gave her up." The memories swept over her before she could push them away, forcing a noise from her throat that sounded like laughter but held no humor. "*Gave up.* That's such a curious phrase, don't you think?" She met Tye's understanding eyes. "It implies a voluntary action, and there was nothing arbitrary about my decision. I think if I could have cut off my arm and made a life for the two of us, I would have."

Tye opened his arms to bring her closer, and Cara automatically moved into his embrace, already addicted to the

omfort it could bring. Before she could do so, however, his
ands froze in midair, his expression a mixture of shocked
isbelief and horror as he stared over her shoulder. Cara's
aroat instantly closed. Something told her, before she could
aove, what he saw. Slowly she turned around.

Kit's face was as white as the clouds that had drifted over
ae sun, leaving them all suddenly chilled. "You—you're my
aother? My *real* mother?"

Cara's heart crashed to the ground at the expression of
unned disbelief Kit wore. She rose to her feet. "Kit!
Where...? How...?"

"I was behind the tree," Kit cried. "I heard every word
aat you two said." Her accusing eyes went to Tye's face.
Why didn't you tell me?"

Tye jumped to his feet, the swing going out behind him.
What were you doing eavesdropping? You ought to
aow—"

Cara reached out and grabbed his arm. "Tye—"

"What were you waiting for?" Like a frightened animal,
it swung her head wildly, looking first at one of them and
aen the other. "Why didn't you tell me when you first got
are? I should have known. You should have—"

Tye's face flushed and he moved toward Kit. "Now just
minute, Kit—"

"Tye, stop it." Cara stepped between them and held up
ar hands. "She's right—we *should* have told her sooner."
ae bit her lip and turned to Kit. "We didn't know *how* to
ll you, and we didn't know if I was going to stay or not.
'e thought it best to wait until—"

"Until you decided if you liked me or not? Were you go-
g to run off again if I was ugly or something? I guess it's
good thing I don't have bad teeth or crooked legs or you'd
obably—"

"Kit!" Tye's angry voice stopped the tirade, but he
uldn't hold back the pain sweeping over Cara at Kit's ac-
usations.

"It wasn't like that," Cara said. "You're talking about
ings you don't understand." She moved forward to take

Kit's arm, but the girl jumped back, away from Cara'
touch, and Cara's heart cracked open at the gesture.

"What's to understand? You gave me away like . . . like
dress you didn't want anymore. Nothing you can say coul
explain that."

Pain rolled over Cara like a dark storm cloud. She shoo
her head. "That's not true, Kit. It wasn't like that at all.
She swung around and looked at Tye. "Tell her, Tye. Te
her I couldn't do anything else."

He stepped forward and reached out for Kit just as Car
had, but again Kit jumped back. "Don't touch me," sh
yelled. "And don't talk to me. You'd just lie, anyway." Sh
dashed a hand across her already-reddened eyes. "You'r
both liars. I've got liars for parents. I wish both of you ha
left me alone and let someone else adopt me. I would hav
been better off!"

Her pain a physical ache in the middle of her heart, Car
reached out again. "Kit, please—"

Kit's anguished expression stopped Cara's plea, but whe
the teenager spoke, Cara's heart stopped, too. "This is a
your fault," Kit cried, her blue eyes shafts of pain that in
stantly stabbed Cara. "If you hadn't come back to Ange
ton, this would never have happened." She swirled aroun
and took off running, and a second later, the dusk swa
lowed her up.

With a desperate, hollow pain, Cara turned helplessly t
Tye. And in the growing darkness, she read the same acc
sation in his expression.

Chapter 16

Cara took two steps back, as another part of her detached instantly—a part of her that now looked down from a distance. A part of her that wouldn't have to feel the pain.

His face shifted instantly. "She didn't mean it, Cara. She's just..." He reached out to her, but she stepped back again. "Please, things are so crazy..."

She brought her hand to her throat, her fingers trembling. "Things *are* crazy," she said in a voice that was totally cool, totally removed, "but she's right. If I hadn't come back, this would never have happened."

He held out his hand, his voice a desperate cry. "Cara, don't do this to us. You know that's not the truth."

"No." She shook her head, her hair moving against her cheek in the evening breeze. A second ago, it'd been warm, but now it chilled her like an arctic blast, and she couldn't contain a shiver. "No. I could see it in your face—you agree with her."

"That's not true," he cried. "I don't think that at all."

"It's okay."

"No. It's not okay... because you're wrong."

Turning away from him, she stepped around the swing, putting it between him and her. "I was an idiot to ever think that this could work out, anyway. You and Kit are already a family. You don't need me, and it's pretty obvious that Kit doesn't want me."

"She's shocked, that's all. She wasn't expecting this. If we'd told her the way we were going to, it would have gone a lot smoother."

"Don't be ridiculous." Cara's voice came out sharper than she wanted, but at this point, what did it matter? "*How* you give someone bad news doesn't matter."

"You being Kit's mother isn't *bad* news."

Cara's bitter laugh slashed the evening air. "Right. Tell Kit that."

"I will—the minute we find her." He moved around the swing and tried to take her into his arms, but Cara held out her hand to stop him. "Don't do this," he said. "Don't cut me off like this."

An hour ago, his voice would have broken her heart, but now the wall that had always protected Cara was back in place. Instantly. A part of her was amazed that it could come up that fast, but at the same time, another part of her knew it was fragile protection. Once she was alone and the reality sank in, it'd probably come tumbling down. She wasn't about to show that to Tye, though.

"This was a major mistake, Tye." Her eyes swept over his face, but didn't connect with his pleading gaze as a giant wave of guilt washed over her. "And it's all my fault. How can I—"

"It *isn't* your fault, Cara. It's *our* fault. *You* aren't totally responsible for Kit being here, you know. I had something to do with it, too. And if you recall, every time you wanted to tell her the truth, *I* was the one that said let's wait. If anyone should take responsibility for this, it's me."

"That's ridiculous—"

"Us arguing is what's ridiculous," he shot back. "We're all upset. We're all saying things we don't really mean. Let's go find Kit and work this out."

"She won't want me to find her." Cara's throat convulsed, but she kept her expression as flat and tight as she could make it. "*You* go. I'm going back to New York—where I belong."

She made it into the house to tell Monty she was leaving. She made it to her car and all the way into the hotel room. She even made it into the bathroom of her suite.

But when she saw the pale oval of her face in the mirror, the deep lines that went from her nose to her mouth, the two black pools that were her eyes, she broke down. The tears came in a hot, angry flood, and when that finally finished, they came in a steady stream. A stream of sorrow and agony that cut into her heart and carved off an island of pain greater than she'd ever known before.

Giving up a child once was one thing. Doing it a second time was almost inconceivable.

But there was no other way.

She didn't belong here, and part of her had always known that, but she'd shoved that part away from her. She'd shoved it away because she'd wanted so badly to be a mother, to be Tye's wife, to have what had always been denied her. Now, with a teenager's unerring accuracy, Kit had shown Cara just how wrong she'd been to ever think she could have those things. Kit would never forgive her, no matter what the circumstances had been.

And without that understanding, they couldn't be a family. Rejection destroyed families; it didn't created them.

Raising her head and staring at her bleak reflection, Cara watched the tears roll down her cheek and drop to the marble countertop. There was nothing left to do but pack and leave.

Leave another part of her heart in Angelton.

The day Cara was ready to leave, the temperature dropped into the forties. By five that evening, when she'd finished packing and had paid her bill, it seemed even colder. Shivering, she stowed her briefcase into the trunk of the rented

Cadillac, then slammed the trunk and headed back into the hotel room to see if she'd left anything behind.

Her throat caught as she stepped back into the now-empty room, the winter wind ripping the door from her hand and thumping it closed behind her. The only thing she was leaving in Angelton was her heart.

But that was nothing new, was it?

Crossing the carpet, she moved toward the window and placed her fingers on the cold glass. Bear Lake was a mirror of the leaden sky above it, a smooth, flat reflection that looked as frigid as she felt. She should have known, she told herself. She should have quit her job, run away, done whatever was necessary to spare herself the grief of the past few months. Instead she'd returned to Angelton, and once again she'd found nothing but heartache.

Leaning her head against the window, Cara closed her eyes. She couldn't cry; she had no more tears. All she could do was hold her anguish inside of her, let it sit like a rock in the place her heart had been.

Tye had attempted to see her twice since Jerilyn's funeral. Once he'd come by her office and tried to talk to her, once he'd stopped by the hotel. Each time, she'd refused to see him. There was no point in it. What had been between them was now gone. And if she did nothing else with her life she would make sure that it stayed that way.

She hadn't seen Kit at all.

It didn't seem to matter, though, because superimposed on every thought of Tye was another one of Kit, and together the images had a strength that far exceeded what Cara had fought before. She saw Kit playing the violin, Tye watching proudly in the park. She saw Kit in Tye's arms, her tears wetting his shirt over Jerilyn's death. She saw Kit shocked as she'd learned who Cara really was.

The images haunted Cara's thoughts like the aftereffects of a nightmare, and nothing that she'd been able to do had blotted them out. All she could do was tell herself that time would help. Time and distance. Two things she intended to put between herself and Angelton as soon as possible.

Lifting her head, she stared out the window a final time and unconsciously memorized the picture of Bear Lake. The dark pines ringing its perimeter had an almost bluish cast to them in the evening dusk, and the rickety dock where she'd fished as a teen appeared even more fragile than usual. She'd never see it again, she told herself, and never was too soon for her.

It was time to leave. With a deep breath, Cara turned and headed for the door.

She crossed the room, her vision blurring from tears she didn't know she had, and opened the door with a quick twist of her wrist. Before she could take a step outside, however, her feet—and her heart—faltered to a stop.

Kit stood on the sidewalk.

She wore a pair of ragged jeans and a bright green sweater that almost hit her knees. A low-brimmed black hat perched on her blond hair, and black Dr. Martens covered her feet. On her shoulder, a navy backpack rested. She looked confused, angry and very uncertain.

Cara was the first to recover her voice, but even as she spoke, her heart hammered inside her chest with an incredible rhythm. Part of her was absolutely thrilled at seeing Kit one more time, and another part of her was screaming for her to leave and spare herself the pain.

"Kit! What are you doing here? I was just about to leave."

"I—I know. Can I come in?"

"Of course." Stunned and not quite sure what to think, Cara stepped aside and let the teenager enter the room. A whiff of the floral perfume Cara had smelled in Kit's room came with her. Before she could stop herself, Cara looked into the parking lot, wondering if Tye had come. His Mercedes was nowhere to be seen, and she told herself to ignore the drop her stomach took. Turning back to Kit, Cara spoke. "How did you get here?"

"I caught a ride."

Cara's hand went to her throat. "You hitchhiked?"

Bright blond hair flashed as Kit removed the hat. Her voice held more than a twinge of defensiveness. "I knew the guy who stopped. If I hadn't recognized him, I wouldn't have gotten in the car."

How stupid, Cara wanted to scream. *How could you do something so stupid?* They stared at each other a few moments, and Cara realized Kit was waiting, almost daring her to say exactly that.

Seeing the mad but guilty expression on her daughter's face, Cara felt her own anger dissolve. Better than anyone, she should know exactly what it was like to be a teenager and in trouble. Of course, Kit's situation was very different from Cara's a thousand years ago, but that empty-stomach, empty-heart look told Cara the emotions were all there just the same. Kit hadn't had time to think. She was too busy feeling.

Feeling betrayed and all alone.

"I had to come and see you," she finally said. "I couldn't just let you leave. I . . . I have too many questions."

"Questions?" Cara met Kit's blue gaze. It reminded her instantly of Tye, and *that* brought a sharp pain to her heart. "What kind of questions?"

Kit dropped her backpack to the bed and walked over to the window, her back to Cara. "I want to know why you gave me up," she said, her voice small but clear. With a rebellious expression on her face, she turned around, crossed her arms, and met Cara's gaze. "I want the *real* reason, not some made-up answer."

The words sounded tough and demanding, but behind them—in Kit's eyes—Cara saw an open vulnerability that broke her heart in two.

"You might not really want that, Kit," Cara answered, a catch in her voice. "The truth isn't always pretty."

"Neither are lies," she said with a maturity that rocked Cara. "But I'm tired of them."

Cara realized she was, too. "All right," she said, taking a deep breath. "I'll tell you exactly what happened, then. When I was barely three years older than you are right now

I met your father. We fell in love. My parents hated him, but I didn't care. I snuck out at night to meet him and did everything I could to be with him. We were young and very foolish, and we made love without protection." Cara stopped to catch her breath, and Kit's eyes widened. She'd heard part of the story, Cara knew, but obviously not as completely—or as bluntly—as she was hearing it now. Cara kept going before she could reconsider.

"We knew my parents wouldn't help us or support us in any way. In fact, my father had already smacked me once for seeing Tye against his wishes. It was only going to get worse. So after a few months, we decided we would run away to Austin and live together. We didn't have any money, so we robbed a convenience store first. I was already pregnant with you, but your father didn't know that. At the last minute, when things went wrong, I jumped out of his car. My uncle was the local policeman. He arrested your father, and a few months later, he went to jail."

"For two years."

"That's right. For two years." Cara brought her hands together and knit her fingers into a knot. "When my parents found out that I was pregnant, my father tried to get me to have an abortion, but I refused."

Kit's face paled, and she sat down on the bed behind her. Cara forced herself to continue. "They kicked me out. I had nowhere to go, no job, and I was all alone. Remember that I was seventeen—three years older than you."

"Wh-where *did* you go?"

"My uncle arranged for me to live with some friends of his. The entire time I was there, I argued with him about keeping you. I thought I could do it somehow, but he kept saying it'd be impossible." Cara let her gaze go out the window. "In the end, he was right."

"He brought me to Uncle Monty and Aunt Jerilyn?"

"That's right. He'd told me that an adoption had been arranged, and that was all I knew. He had made these plans without telling me. Obviously he was hoping that we would all be together one day. Before he gave you to Monty and

Jerilyn, though, he took you to my parents' house. He was hoping that they might relent when they saw you and let me come home. They were hard and unforgiving people, though, and they turned him away."

"Your parents—my grandparents—where do they live?"

"My father is dead. My mother lives in Florida."

"Did she ever ask about me?"

"No." Cara saw the flash of pain her answer brought, but there was nothing she could do about it. "She's remarried, and I haven't seen her myself in many years."

Kit rose from the bed and took two steps toward her. "Why didn't you wait for my father to get out of jail?"

Cara briefly closed her eyes, then reopened them. "There was no point." She waited a moment, then spoke. "He had told me he didn't love me anymore."

"He said that?" Her expression told Cara that Kit wasn't quite sure she was getting the truth.

"Ask him yourself, if you don't believe me. He thought he was freeing me to love someone else, but he didn't know about you."

"And you didn't tell him?"

"No."

Kit's pinched face registered anger. She didn't want any blame to go to her father, but she was too smart not to realize some of it had to. She tried, anyway. "You should have told him. You should have kept me."

"How?" Cara's hands went back into fists. "You're old enough to have a baby. How would you do it?"

Kit's stare dropped to the carpet, and her expression shifted. "I would have found a way."

"That's what I thought, too." Cara moved toward a nearby chair and sat down heavily. "But the reality of the situation is this. When you're young, when you have no job, no husband, no family—you can barely take care of yourself, much less a child." She turned toward Kit and faced her head-on. "I gave you up so you could have a better life than I could provide for you, and until you've faced that kind of

ain—and I pray to God you never do—then you shouldn't
dge me."

"But what you did was wrong."

"I disagree." Cara arched her eyebrows. "How is it
rong to do what you think is the best thing? I might say
aat hitchhiking to get here was wrong."

"I didn't have any other way."

"And neither did I."

She stood and went to Kit's side. "We do the best we can,
nd try not to hurt anyone, but sometimes it just doesn't
ork out that way. No matter how hard you try." She raised
ne hand and tucked a fine strand of Kit's hair behind one
ar. "Look at your father. He loved me, but he told me he
idn't. Someone might say that was a mistake, but he did it
ecause he thought he was doing the right thing."

As Cara watched, Kit's face betrayed her struggle, and
ara's heart twisted for her. "And are you doing the right
ing now?" Kit asked.

Cara's fingers stilled. "What do you mean?"

"Going back to New York. Is that really the right thing
 do?" Blue eyes drilled her.

"I—I don't know, Kit. I wanted to stay here and marry
our father, but—"

"But I screwed that up, didn't I?"

"No." Cara's answer was immediate. "You screwed up
othing. I'm not staying because I think you'd both be bet-
r off without me."

Again an expression flitted across Kit's face. She was
oming to a conclusion, Cara realized, and she found her-
lf holding her breath as she wondered what it was.

"You're wrong," Kit finally said. "I mean, *really* wrong."

The words hung between them. "What makes you say
aat?" Cara asked slowly.

"Dad is miserable without you. He's moping around the
ouse, working later and later. He never says anything to me
nless I ask him a question. It's awful."

Despite herself, another piece of Cara's heart broke away.
urning away from her daughter, she spoke, not believing

what she was saying, but realizing there was nothing else sh
could say. "We'll both find someone else, Kit," she said i
a thick voice. "He'll fall in love again, and he'll forget me.'

"Maybe." Kit's voice was so soft that Cara could hardl
hear it. "But I won't."

Cara's heart stopped. Her breath quit. The very blood i
her veins stopped rushing through her body. She couldn'
move.

"It—it's kinda silly, but I've always thought about m
mother and wondered stuff about her. Like what she looke
like, and what her name was, and if she had a funny doubl
joint on her little finger like I do."

Startled, Cara turned her head and raised her left hand
Two sets of eyes went to the smallest finger, then met i
widened surprise.

Kit looked down first. "I just wanted my *real* mothe
around. Jerilyn was wonderful, but she wasn't my mothe
Do you know what I mean?"

Cara nodded soundlessly.

"Daddy was there, but he couldn't do it all." Her fac
screwed into a combination of resentment and confusior
"He didn't always understand, and there were just som
things I couldn't tell him. Boy stuff and private stuff an
clothes stuff."

Her voice began to rise as she continued, and the ange
she'd been holding on to bubbled out. "I wanted some
body to help me dress when I was a little kid and tie my ha
bows just right. I wanted to take homemade cookies t
school, not store-bought. I wanted a mother to teach m
how to sew and to go shopping with and to read to me a
night." Her blue eyes watered into bright sapphires of pain
"I wanted you here!"

Cara's throat burned with instant tears. "Dammit,
wanted that too, Kit. Just as much as you did. But I didn
think it was possible. I did the best I could."

Cara hadn't meant to curse, but the word had just slippe
out, and an instant later, she was glad it had. The harsh
ness seemed to stop Kit in her tracks, the realization con

ng into her eyes that her mother was a person. A person who had feelings, just like her.

They stared at each other a second longer, then without even thinking, they both moved at the same time, Kit's arms going around Cara's waist, Cara's arms cradling Kit's now shaking shoulders. They cried together, their tears rising and falling like the cold wind now whistling around the pines outside.

Cara couldn't tell who turned loose first, but Kit was the one who went into the bath and brought out the box of tissues. Grabbing a handful for herself, she thrust the rest of them in Cara's direction. The reversal seemed strange to Cara—her daughter was trying to take care of *her*. Then slowly she realized that was good. Kit needed to feel needed. Just like Cara.

Kit finally met her eyes. "I don't want you to leave. You *do* belong here, and I think I was probably wrong to say what I did the other day at Monty's." She looked down at the carpet. "Do you think you could stay? Just a little longer?"

Cara felt a fresh wave of tears, but these were tears of joy. She took Kit's chin in her hand and lifted it so she could look into her eyes. "I'll stay for as long as you want me, sweetheart."

"And you'll be my mother?"

"Always."

"And go ahead and marry Daddy?"

"Oh, Kit." Confusion and sudden anxiety washing over her, Cara dropped her fingers and turned away from her daughter. "I . . . I don't know about that."

"Do you love him?"

"Yes."

"Then go tell him. Believe me, he'll be thrilled."

A spark of hope flared inside Cara. "Do you think so?" Kit nodded, her blond hair bouncing. "I *know* so. He's been incredibly miserable thinking you were going back. He didn't tell me that or anything," she added hastily, "but I could just tell. To be honest, that's one of the reasons I came here today. I couldn't stand to see him so unhappy." She took a deep breath. "I didn't really know what I was going to say, but I had to have some answers, and I figured one way or another, we'd get around to him."

Cara reached for Kit's hand and squeezed it. "I don't know too many teenagers that would think of their dad like you have."

A dark blush spread up Kit's cheeks. "He's been a pretty cool dad." She suddenly looked worried. "You wouldn't tell him what I said, would you? About wanting a mother? I wouldn't want him to think—"

Cara cut the question off with a shake of her head. "You don't have to worry about that, Kit. Your father knows exactly how much you love him." She stopped and wet her lips. "Now I guess I'd better go see if I can convince him do, too."

Cara took Kit back to Tye's sprawling house, but his Mercedes was nowhere in sight. "He's probably still at the office," she'd said hopefully. "Try there." They'd exchanged a quick kiss and hug, a tentative but definitely strong connection growing between the two of them, then Cara had left.

Now, as she pulled into the deserted parking lot of the Marshall companies and spied his car, Cara tried to talk her crazy heart into slowing down. *You can do this,* she said softly. *You can tell him how you feel, and be honest about it. Nothing could be worse than Kit's expression last week and see how that turned out?*

An almost unnatural silence filled the car as she switched off the engine and stared through the windshield at the building in front of her. The conversation with Kit had left Cara reeling, a mixture of pride, fear and surprise still hitting her. On top of everything, however, was a feeling of anticipation. What could be better than getting to know such a wonderful and thoroughly delightful young woman? Kit was such a bonus, such a treasure, that Cara wasn't sure what she'd done to deserve such luck.

Nothing would ever stand between the two of them again, he vowed. Nothing.

A moment later, as she walked inside the empty office building, Cara tried to keep that thought alive. No matter what, she'd always have Kit. If Tye didn't want her in *his* life, then there was nothing she could do about it. She'd learn to live without him. She'd accept whatever he said. She'd grow old by herself.

Bull.

Before Kit had wanted the truth from Cara, and nothing else would do. As Cara stepped down the darkened hallway to Tye's office, she realized it was time she faced the same. She loved Tye. Desperately. And now she had to tell him so.

The minute she turned the corner, she saw that the light was off in his office. Her heart plummeted, then bounced once and came back up. Tye's office was dark, but a dim crack of light showed under the conference room door. She could tell from the angle that the beam came from Monty's office. Maybe Tye was there. Watching the sunset. Just as he had been the first time she'd come in.

Her footsteps slowed, then stopped as she entered the conference room. She'd been right. Whoever was still here was in Monty's office, and since she hadn't seen the older man's Cadillac in the parking lot, it had to be Tye. She closed her eyes for a moment and willed herself to be calm. Was she doing the right thing? What would she do if he didn't want her back? How would she explain it all to Kit? She took a deep breath, raised her hand and pushed open the door.

He stood in the shadows staring out the window, a lonely figure with an air of melancholy about him. When he heard the door swing open, he turned slowly and looked in her direction.

She couldn't see his face; the shadows kept it for themselves. She could feel the tension vibrate across the room, though, and she didn't need light to feel the sudden, wild anxiety that gripped her. *What was she doing, for God's sake? He'd never love her again. Never want to share Kit*

with her. She was absolutely crazy to think it could have
worked.

Without a word, she swirled and began to walk away, but
his voice reached out and stopped her as surely and as
quickly as a bar across the door.

"Cara?"

Her name had never been spoken with such exquisite
anxiety. Slowly, ever so slowly, she turned back to face him.

He stepped out of the darkness and into a single beam of
light coming from an overhead spot. His expression was so
full of love, so full of pain, that suddenly nothing else
seemed to matter. "Don't go," he said, his voice cracking.
"Please, please, don't go."

"Oh, Tye." Her own voice broke, and she found herself
flying across the distance that separated them. In another
instant, she was in his arms.

His hands tucked her head against his chest, and he
sounded soothing murmurs. She lifted her face and stared
into his eyes. "Oh, Tye," she repeated. "I'm so sorry. I've
managed to mess this all up so thoroughly. Can you ever
forgive me?"

"Forgive you?" She didn't know which was more in
credulous, his voice or his expression. "My God," he cried.
"I'm the one that should be on my knees begging *your* for
giveness."

She shook her head. "No, darling. No. I was so wrong
so confused—"

He stopped her words with a single shake of his head.
"Just tell me you'll stay. That's all I want to hear."

"I couldn't possibly do anything else," she said. "How
did I ever think I could leave you in the first place? Where
was my mind?"

His blue eyes glistened in the dim light. "I wouldn't have
let you go, Cara," he said fiercely. "I'd already made up my
mind that no matter what it took, I was going to track you
down and bring you back."

She laughed through the tears that had sprung into her
eyes. "Caveman-style?"

"Whatever style it took."

e brought his hands to her face and cradled it. "You are
most important thing in my life. I would *never* have let
 leave me. I did that once, and once was definitely
ugh."

Then you'll take me back?"

You never left." He slowly lifted his right hand from her
k and put it on the left side of his chest. "Since the day
t you, Cara Howard, you've always been right here. In
heart."

he reached up and traced her own fingers over his face,
heart bursting with love. "And that's where I intend to
 from now on."

e crushed her to him with a cry that tore at her heart,
 as his lips claimed hers she had no more thought for the
ness that had passed between them. His hungry mouth
anded all her attention, all her concentration.

e finally lifted his head, but the stare in his blue eyes
tured her as surely as his mouth had a moment before.
'e'll deal with Kit together, Cara. I don't know how, but
will because we belong together—all three of us. And no
ter what else happens, *that* is the one thing that isn't
g to change. I won't let it."

Varmth like she had never known flooded Cara, and the
le she wore gave testimony to it. "Kit and I have already
ed. We...we worked out everything, Tye, and it was so
derful. She wants me here. She wants the same thing we
t."

is eyes rounded in amazement and utter delight. "She
e to you?"

Yes. I couldn't believe it, but we had a long, long talk,
everything's okay. In fact, she's the one that told me to
e to you."

e laughed and kissed her on the forehead. "Damn, I
w that kid was smart! I'm going to have to raise her al-
ance."

ara laughed with him, then frowned with mock disap-
tment. "Yeah, but when I tell you how she got to the
l..."

He shook his head. "I don't want to know. At least, right now. I'm just thankful she convinced you to come me."

"Me, too. I wasn't sure how you'd feel after eve thing."

"And are you sure now?"

Cara tightened her arms around his waist and let her l shine from her eyes. "I've never been more sure of a thing in my entire life, Tye Benedict. I love you, and the o place I belong is here. Here in Angelton with you and I We'll be a *real* family once and for all."

*   *   *   *   *

Hot on the heels of **American Heroes** comes Silhouette Intimate Moments' latest and greatest lineup of men: **Heartbreakers.** They know who they are—and *who* they want. And they're out to steal your heart.

RITA award-winning author Emilie Richards kicks off the series in March 1995 with *Duncan's Lady,* IM #625. Duncan Sinclair believed in hard facts, cold reality and his daughter's love. Then sprightly Mara MacTavish challenged his beliefs—and hardened heart—with her magical allure.

In April *New York Times* bestseller Nora Roberts sends hell-raiser Rafe MacKade home in *The Return of Rafe MacKade,* IM #631. Rafe had always gotten what he wanted—until Regan Bishop came to town. She resisted his rugged charm and seething sensuality, but it was only a matter of time....

Don't miss these first two **Heartbreakers,** from two stellar authors, found only in—

Southern Knights

Join Marilyn Pappano in March 1995 as her **Southern Knights** series draws to a dramatic close with *A Man Like Smith*, IM #626.

Federal prosecutor Smith Kendricks was on a manhunt. His prey: crime boss Jimmy Falcone. But when his quest for justice led to ace reporter Jolie Wade, he found himself desiring both her privileged information—and the woman herself....

Don't miss the explosive conclusion to the **Southern Knights** miniseries, only in—

INTIMATE MOMENTS®
Silhouette®

KNIGHT3

EXTRA! EXTRA! READ ALL ABOUT...
MORE ROMANCE
MORE SUSPENSE
MORE INTIMATE MOMENTS

Join us in February 1995 when Silhouette Intimate Moments introduces the first title in a whole new program: INTIMATE MOMENTS EXTRA. These break-through, innovative novels by your favorite category writers will come out every few months, beginning with Karen Leabo's *Into Thin Air*, IM #619.

Pregnant teenagers had been disappearing without a trace, and Detectives Caroline Triece and Austin Lomax were called in for heavy-duty damage control...because now the missing girls were turning up dead.

In May, Merline Lovelace offers *Night of the Jaguar*, and other INTIMATE MOMENTS EXTRA novels will follow throughout 1995, only in—

RITA award-winning author Emilie Richards launches her new miniseries, **The Men of Midnight,** in March 1995 with *Duncan's Lady*, IM #625.

Single father Duncan Sinclair believed in hard facts and cold reality, not mist and magic. But sprightly Mara MacTavish challenged his staid beliefs— and hardened heart—with her spellbinding allure, charming both Duncan and his young daughter.

Don't miss **The Men of Midnight,** tracing the friendship of Duncan, Iain and Andrew—*three men born at the stroke of twelve and destined for love beyond their wildest dreams,* only in—

Men and women hungering for passion to soothe their lonely souls. Watch for the new Intimate Moments miniseries by

Beverly Bird

It begins in March 1995 with

A MAN WITHOUT LOVE (Intimate Moments #630)
Catherine Landano was running scared—and straight into the arms of enigmatic Navaho Jericho Bedonie. Would he be her savior...or her destruction?

Continues in May...

A MAN WITHOUT A HAVEN (Intimate Moments #641)
The word *forever* was not in Mac Tshongely's vocabulary. Nevertheless, he found himself drawn to headstrong Shadow Bedonie and the promise of tomorrow that this sultry woman offered. Could home really be where the heart is?

And concludes in July 1995 with

A MAN WITHOUT A WIFE (Intimate Moments #652)
Seven years ago Ellen Lonetree had made a decision that haunted her days and nights. Now she had the chance to be reunited with the child she'd lost—if she could resist the attraction she felt for the little boy's adoptive father...and keep both of them from discovering her secret.

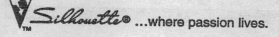